PRAISE FOR
WAKING THE MERROW

"A prickly and memorable protagonist fights to protect her family from wily merfolk in this promising debut contemporary fantasy."

— *PUBLISHERS WEEKLY*

"You know what's great about Rigney's horror-ific (that's horror-filled and terrific), hysterical debut novel? Besides the bloodthirsty merfolk, our antihero protagonist is an overweight, drunk, subpar mother, who also happens to be a funeral director. I can't even describe the premise of this book without getting giddy, because how many times does a plot involve both vicious mermaids and Rhode Island colonists?"

—*Nicole Hill, Barnes & Noble Book Blog*

"Rigney has struck gold with her first novel. It's humorous — hysterical at times — descriptive and has a nice flow to it."

—*Bobby Forrand, Motif Magazine*

"*WAKING THE MERROW* is a horrifying, addictive, and intriguing twist on the mermaid legend, and takes the reader on a bone-chilling ride through colonial and current times in Rhode Island. This is a fabulous debut novel by Heather Rigney.

Read it if you dare."

— *Penny Watson, Bestselling Author of APPLES SHOULD BE RED*

"In the essence of Stephen King and Clive Barker who are Ms. Rigney's inspiration she manages to thrill and scare with the best of them … I was hooked from the very first page and while I was scared at times I also couldn't wait to turn the page and find out what happened next. Written as a historical thriller the book does not disappoint at all."

—*John Brownstone, reviewer, MasqueradeCrew.com*

"This book contains several of my favorite things: monster lit, the ocean, a choice of monster that's not like every other book or movie out there, mythology, Gaelic/Celtic stuff, and New England."

—*Bella, Boombabyreviews.com*

"WOW... I mean, seriously WOW. I could not put this book down ... I usually try and find something critical to say about the writing or the story itself, but I can honestly say there is not a single negative thing I can offer about Waking the Merrow. It's an absolutely brilliant novel and I can't wait for the next book by this truly amazing author."

—*Suzy Turner, author of THE RAVEN SAGA*

"*WAKING THE MERROW* by Heather Rigney is a thrilling debut! Razor-sharp wit, sparkling prose, and a quirky, hard-luck anti-heroine make this fun, frightening, and completely unique twist on mermaid lore. A must-read."

—*Carolyn Crane, author of THE DISILLUSIONISTS*

"I absolutely loved *WAKING THE MERROW* ... Heather's writing is very descriptive. Her female heroine, Evie, is someone I could be friends with. I laughed so hard at some of her quips my husband asked if I was all right. I am looking forward to more in this series."

—*JKROWYN, book reviewer for BittenByBooks.com*

"*WAKING THE MERROW* is a delightfully dark fantasy that stirs in colonial history and some eerily fun mythology. Heather Rigney is doing what she's meant to do, and her story will have you laughing all along the way even as the scariest of creatures stalk this plot. I cannot recommend this sassy, dark, intelligent book enough. It's not every day you find your-self rooting for a cantankerous heroine with a hangover, but I think Evie McFagan can and will win you over."

—*Emm Cole, author of MERMINIA*

"Heather Rigney is a wonderfully expressive writer who manages to address an incredibly cliche subject and leave said chiches in her wake. The world she paints with words would not be beautiful if not for her striking and highly original prose but she truly creates a setting that is both dark yet colourful and exciting. If you're a fan of Dean Koontz then steer your amazon trolley this way because you're in for a lot of evil snick-ering and plenty of dramatic tension backed up with creative articulation. Honestly it was just so good- it's revived my love of reading after a pretty serious book hangover."

—*S.K. Munt, author of THE FAIRYTAIL SAGA*

WAKING

THE

MERROW

BOOK 1

WAKING THE MERROW

BOOK 1: THE MERROW TRILOGY

HEATHER RIGNEY

For the man who did listen each and every time I said, "I'm going to read this out loud to you. You don't have to listen, but I'm reading it out loud whether you're listening or not."

Thanks for listening, my love.

The Merrow, of [sic] if you write it in the Irish,
Moruadh or Murúghach, from muir, sea, and
oigh, a maid, is not uncommon, they say, on
the wilder coasts. The fishermen do not like to
see them, for it always means coming gales.

Fairy and Folk Tales of the Irish Peasantry
edited and selected by W. B. Yeats [1888]

Connor beheld a number of strange and, in the
dim light, mysterious-looking figures emerge
from the sea, and surround the coffin, which
they prepared to launch into the water.

"This comes of marrying with the
creatures of earth," said one of the
figures, in a clear, yet hollow tone.

Flory Cantillon's Funeral, by T. Crofton Croker

1

O n the first day of my undoing (and I say this as if I wasn't already circling the drain), the sun struggled to bleed through the fog, and the air was steeped in the bitter stench of brackish waters.

In other words, it was a typical shitty day in New England. The late fall sky seemed bruised and tired. The trees wore a post-prom look of shame. Their color and glitter lay littered and forgotten on the ground like soiled, discarded taffeta.

I sat on a park bench in the Village Playground nursing a hangover. You know the kind. The kind where you stay up late at night drinking bourbon and bidding on random crap on eBay because you don't actually believe you'll win anything, and then you do? Well, maybe hangovers are foreign to you. Maybe, days later, vintage TV dinner trays featuring colonial farm scenes don't show up on your doorstep.

Lucky you. Lucky me.

Children launched and hammered their bodies into the ground at thunderous decibels as the seesaw slammed into the earth over and over and over again. The thrust and pull of rusty swings rattled my teeth while five *(hundred?)* children screamed and hollered some chant about pinecone ice cream. I checked my ears and then my nose for blood. Nope, nothing. It only *felt* like my brains were leaking out of my head.

The noxious smell of the nearby Pawtuxet River surging into Narragansett Bay was not helping the thin grasp I held on reality.

My eighteen-month-old daughter, Savannah, played at my feet. Slack-jawed, I glanced down at her and noticed the dirt-brown smear around her mouth and the wood chips in her grubby little hands. Warm brown ringlets curled over her eyes, which crinkled as she smiled up at me.

A good mother would wipe her mouth.

A good mother would have brought something to wipe her mouth and perhaps would have given her child a snack, a *healthy* snack, instead of relying on the kindness of truly good mothers and the fallback of wood chips.

Evie (rhymes with heavy) McFagan, the unpleasant, local funeral director. That's me.

When you're young, you think you'll grow up and know everything. At thirty-eight, I didn't know shit. I had a drinking problem with no solution and a bleak social life. Compounding my already attractive profile was my complete lack of attractiveness. Short and overweight with dishwater blonde hair, frequently bloodshot eyes, and a roll-out-of-bed sense of style. A ripe, blistering stew of repulsion.

This is why I came undone. There wasn't far for me to go.

The creaking of the old gate jerked my train of thought from the possibility of actually doing something about my daughter who was now examining rocks the way a foodie examines *foie gras*.

Someone was entering the playground. Everyone over the age of thirty snapped to attention, all eyes fixed on the one and only entrance to the park.

Someone was entering the playground. Someone new to regard, someone new against which to judge the worth of one's life. Someone *new*.

I chuckled to myself and then winced at the pain it caused in my left temple. This was better than the Nature Channel. I'm not sure when I first discovered the fascinating quirks in the microcosm of playground society, but once I did, I found my mind-numbing visits there to be much more palatable.

If a woman entered the gate, I smugly watched the other females size up the newcomer's clothes, her children, her stroller, her purse, and even her travel mug. You could almost smell the calculating evaluations oozing out of these mothers who then reexamined their own goods in comparison.

Now if a man entered, things got really juicy. I would snuggle into my bench, maybe pull out some Cheerios (if I remembered to bring them), and enjoy the show.

I placed bets with myself on who would reach up and touch her hair first, who might sneak lipgloss out of her diaper bag, and who would visibly suck in her baby weight. All of these women who had raced out of their houses, wondering if they brushed their hair, their teeth, the dog hair from their asses. Suddenly they had these glossy, or not so glossy, plastic smiles on their faces for this poor man who had probably been told to get the hell out of the house by a woman who needed to breathe alone for twenty minutes.

This guy was probably happy to go—happy, until he arrived at the playground.

Here he was, thinking he would get some quality time with his kids—and, at the same time, get some quality time away from the female who used to be hot—only to have to deal with a whole gaggle of females who used to be hot and were all now trying to gain some sort of foothold on his already frazzled attention span.

Poor guy. Elated to have all this drama playing out right in front of me, his loss was always my gain.

Let's face it. I deal with the dead and the grieving. It's dreary and it's not pretty. I accept not pretty. I make money on not pretty.

So to watch humanity at its most awkward, at its most bizarre, was a wonderful thrill for me. It took my mind off what I really was there to do—spend time with a small person who does not talk well, walk well, feed herself (edible things) well, or wipe her own ass.

It sounds harsh. It's also the ugly truth. As I said, I accept not pretty.

But on this particular day, this bland New England day, the gate creaked, all heads perked up, and something truly pretty walked on through.

Pretty was an understatement. What walked through the gate was beyond words. I'm not even using the right verb. She did not *walk* through the gate. She *flowed* through the gate. She was like mercury. Her movements were precise, fluid, liquid. This extraordinary being floated through the air, and as she did, she seemed to suck in all the beauty around her, leaving everything else drained and mundane.

She was tall and lithe, like a dancer, yet strong and athletic in build. Her hair was a warm, inviting shade of brown, reminiscent of an expensive, exotic piece of wood that had been polished by an obsessive compulsive. Ridiculously long, that hair drifted around her as if it moved to its own rhythm.

Her skin was the color of milk, so pale it was almost blue, while her eyes were the lightest shade of gray I had ever seen. Those irises were so large I could see them from where I sat, all the way across the twenty feet that separated us.

I watched as she scanned the area like a lighthouse beacon searching for sinking ships. She nodded and waved to the other mothers who, like sinking ships, looked to her as though she was their savior. They smiled and waved back.

In the five months I had been dragging my daughter through those gates, not a single one of those women had given me even the smallest hint of recognition. Not that I cared. I was used to people shirking me. I reeked of death. But in walks this saucy new chick, and they all acted as if she was the second coming.

Whatever.

Something strange was happening, so I kept my eyes on Miss Fancy Pants. I'm not sure if she was aware of me, but as

I watched her, a wry smile crossed her full lips, and it struck me as wrong. Like a Christmas wreath on a July door, her smile hung with discord.

The playground mothers all rushed over to meet her and her angelic offspring, a small child, perhaps around the age of three, with chubby arms, warm, russet skin, and golden ringlets.

This tiny being was a complete contrast to her mother in almost every way. Chubby to her slim, light curls to her dark locks, innocent to whatever sketchy vibe this new chick gave off in foul waves.

Mother and child differed in almost every way, except for one—the eyes. That child had the same over-sized, light gray eyes as her mother. If not for this one similarity, I might have believed this ethereal creature had rented the child for the afternoon.

The new chick stood almost a foot taller than the other mothers, and as she greeted her audience, I felt a sudden change in the air. Before I could see it, I could feel it—a ghostly kiss on my cold cheek.

Fog was rolling in, and it was heavy. The horde of gathered mothers noticed it. As if waking from a spell, they collected their respective families, baggies of snacks, strollers, and travel mugs and started a caravan exodus through the rusty gate.

The new woman paid no attention to the thick air. If I was a betting woman, and you can bet your ass I am, I would have bet she enjoyed the fog. She scooped up her young child and wriggled her elegant, aquiline nose against the girl's small button of a nose. Then she strode past the wood-chip-and-goldfish-cracker-filled boat donated by the local marina and deposited the silent, grinning girl into one of the four vacant swings.

Something told me to leave—to leave immediately. For once, I listened to my instincts. I grabbed my own daughter and headed towards the gate. As I followed the sidewalk leading to the exit, I had the strangest urge to vomit. I brushed off the notion and managed to ignore it, edging closer to the gate.

But here's the thing. This was not my first hangover. Trust me. I can give you the guided tour of Hangoverville. This urge to vomit did not come from the inside. It came from the outside, if that makes any sense at all. The urge worsened the closer I came to that woman.

And then it was gone. In its place was an overwhelming calm—a calm I have sought each and every single time I've cracked open another bottle of bourbon. But I wasn't drinking. I was in a playground with a strange woman.

So what was it?

I glanced up. She looked right at me. In the millisecond it took until she broke the gaze, I heard these words in my head, *I know you, and you are beneath me, but come closer, closer, and I will tell you all my secrets. You will never be you again. You will be better than you, because you will be with me.*

Then she looked away. I stood there feeling naked and exposed, as if all of my clothes were now at the bottom of the Bay. I felt fear, then shame, and then something along the lines of curious elation.

She never looked at me again.

As if in a trance, I found myself on my way home. When I arrived, I had no memory of passing through the playground gate nor of walking the ten blocks separating our home from the park.

I put a lot of bourbon between me and that event. It did not make what happened any clearer or more believable.

By the next morning, I was beyond my usual haze. Savannah, thank God, slept until mid-morning. Putting her to bed mid-evening had something to do with it. I say this like *I* put her to bed. After hearing another woman's voice in my own sober head, I decided *not* to be sober for as long as I remained conscious.

Did that make me irresponsible? Damn right, it did. You try having some leggy bitch speak to you through your frontal lobe and see how *you* handle it.

So, what about my daughter—who put her to bed?

Patrick McFagan stared at me over his newspaper with his teeth, yellowed from years of smoking, set slightly apart, and his eyes, one larger than the other, narrowed.

"Decided to join the living?"

I stole his coffee and thought about ruffling his thinning, gray hair but then decided against it. My large, Irish love has awful dandruff, and my stomach just couldn't bear the sight of a follicle snowstorm.

I sipped his coffee and grunted into the mug instead. Paddy inhaled through the gap in his teeth and then coughed the cough of the damned. It always lasted forever. He shook his newspaper at me and returned to reading the sports section. I noticed bits of toast and jam on his over-sized chin.

Not a chin, or a neck, but rather a *chinneck*—a continuation of one's head into one's torso. Loose and flabby, it wobbled when he spoke.

Sometimes, when he would yell at me for doing something stupid, I would gobble at him. This always produced a torrent of Gaelic curses from his thin lips. The skin around his heart-shaped hairline would turn a lovely shade of cherry pink, and his twinkling blue eyes would appear even bluer.

I loved it when he cursed in Gaelic.

"You say the hottest things to me when you're spitting mad," I would tease.

His large, ruddy face would soften, and from his immense height and girth, he would look down at me and say, *"Múchadh is bá ort, mo rún,"* which roughly translates to, "Smothering and drowning on you, my secret love."

He said the sweetest things to me. God, I love that big man.

"So where's our offspring?" I asked and reached over to snatch his last piece of toast.

"She went to work with my aunt."

Paddy's aunt ran an Irish step dance school not far from our home.

Wonderful. I could look forward to a joyful, judgment-filled showdown with Catherine, the not-so great, when I went to collect Savannah. Catherine, as in Catherine McFagan O'Connor, hates me. It had been a long, slow marathon of hatred ever since her one-and-only-nephew brought my sorry ass home to meet her.

Sometime during the late '60s, the Irish-born Catherine visited her American McFagan cousins—the original owners of the funeral home Paddy and I now own—and she fell in love with a misguided, love-struck, local boy named Aiden O'Connor. There must have been some sort of magic in the summer air. Either that or a lot of booze. Well, he married her, for whatever reason, and she became a U.S. citizen.

Not too long after, across the big old pond in Ireland, a massive baby—fifteen-plus pounds, if you can believe it, was born. My large love. He grew up in the green lands until his poor, dear parents died in some freak boating accident.

Their will sent Paddy to Catherine and Aiden.

Young Patrick crossed the ocean alone, grieving, forever leaving behind everything he had ever known, to come and live with his distant, icy aunt and her whipping boy. Sadly, Aiden and Catherine never had children. God works in mysterious ways. In his wisdom, he sent the childless pair a large, quiet, stunned teenager.

Everything was sort of fine, for a while. Then Uncle Aiden died in his sleep sometime in the mid '80s. So much death. This might explain why Paddy chose to study the macabre arts, or perhaps it was inevitable.

For centuries, the McFagans dominated the funeral industry

in southwestern Ireland. Around the mid-1800s, they left for America and set up shop in our quaint Rhode Island village. I'm sure their migration had something to do with the Potato Famine, but why did they leave when the death business was booming? Who knows? The McFagans are a tight-lipped bunch.

"You look like shit," said Paddy.

I let toast crumbs trickle from my mouth as I replied, "Thank you. Does your face hurt? Cause, babe, it's killing me."

He sneered in my direction as he went to fetch another mug. Paddy poured himself more coffee and sat down across from me. He did not resume reading the newspaper.

"So I noticed ya had double your usual number of cocktails last night." He paused and took a sip of his coffee. "Anything … amiss?"

The spotlight was on me.

"Amiss?" I stalled. "Nope. All's right as rain here. Anyone interesting dead today?"

My husband was the city coroner. Weren't we adorable?

"Ah, avoidance. Nice try. All right. I'll play along, my lovely lush. By interesting, do you mean, did anyone die in a horrific crash, and can I tell you all the gory details? Naw. Nobody interesting died while you were in your cups. You did get a call from the Rileys that you should answer promptly. It seems old Seamus won't be down for breakfast ever again. Bless his ancient soul. That man hung on till ninety-three. Promise me that you will drug me in my sleep when I start to need assistance in the toilet."

I nodded and kept my head down, focusing on the nourishing effects of dry toast and crappy coffee.

"No comeback, Evie?" Paddy leaned across the table. His giant hands were folded on his giant arms. The table creaked under his weight. "That's it, woman. Spill it."

I looked up at him, my shoulders slumped, and twice I opened my mouth and then closed it.

"Out with it!"

"Alright, alright. Don't push me," I said. I thought about how stupid it would sound. *So Paddy, a woman at the playground spoke to me through my thoughts. How do you like that? Pass the butter.*

"So Paddy, a woman at the playground spoke to me through my thoughts. How do you like that? Pass the butter."

Honesty is the best policy in a marriage.

"Ah, Evie, you were drunk? And at the playground? I thought we talked about that. You promised not to drink around the wee one. You know what? You're going to that rehab center. Where's my phone?"

He started searching under the scattered pages of the *Providence Journal* for his missing cell phone.

"Paddy," I said. "Look at me. I swear. I swear on all that is Catholic including your namesake, His Holy Greenness St. Patrick, that I did not have one single drop before I went to the playground. When I got back, well, yeah."

I thought about the woman's voice, how clear it had sounded in my mind, how encouraging and comforting it had felt. I shuddered and looked at my husband.

I tried to make my eyes as pleading as possible, but I felt all the same shame I always felt when we discussed my little "problem." I hated the way he looked at me. Paddy's face contorted into a mask of disappointment, fatigue, and—what killed me the most—sadness.

I sighed and said, "I'm telling the truth."

Frowning, he continued looking at me, but he stopped searching for the phone.

"Please," I said quietly. "Believe me."

Something in his face yielded. His shoulders relaxed, and he turned his head to look out the window.

"Evie," he said without looking at me. "Promise me you will try to be more aware of your actions."

I knew he didn't believe some woman had spoken through my head in the playground, but he did believe I wasn't drunk—that time. So I took the olive branch.

"Okay," I said. "I promise."

Although if that bitch tries to mumbo jumbo me again, I'll flatten her. Okay, maybe not.

Actions, Evie. Be aware of your crappy, poorly chosen, impulsive actions.

So I wouldn't flatten her. I'd tell her to stay the hell out of my head. Yeah, that would sound sane.

Maybe Paddy was right. I needed to lay off the sauce. I probably imagined the whole thing.

Maybe.

One week later, I returned to the playground armed with my own, newly purchased travel mug, filled to the brim with the strongest coffee known to man, and the darkest sunglasses I owned slapped on my doughy face.

I had been sober for five days. I felt like shit. I looked like shit.

I stared at the closed gate. How the hell are you supposed to open a goddamn gate with a stroller and a travel mug? In the past, I had always walked to the park with Savannah on my hip, opened the gate, and plopped her down somewhere. It had never occurred to me to use the stroller.

But I was trying to be a good mom.

With his immense arms crossed like stacked wood, Paddy had come and watched as I dragged the stroller out from behind the hearse. He had this stupid grin on his meaty-looking face.

"What the fuck are you smiling at?" I barked.

"I just adore you, my darling," he chuckled and walked away.

"Yeah, yeah, yeah," I mumbled and went inside to find Savannah.

There I was at the gate. Savannah gurgled and cooed to her feet as she sat strapped in the jogging stroller that someone with a sense of humor had bought me when I found out I was pregnant. Hilarious. I couldn't remember who it had been, but my money was on Aunt Catherine, cheeky bitch.

The stroller faced me while the handle pointed towards the street. With my left hand holding my coffee and my right hand now free, I turned and struggled with the latch on the gate, then spun around to grab the stroller.

Savannah's gurgles sounded like they were retreating. As I turned, I watched in horror as she rolled into the street. The stroller upended backwards as it bounced off the curb, leaving my little girl staring at the sky, exposed to oncoming traffic.

"Motherfucker!" I screamed and ran out into the quiet street, spilling hot coffee all over my pants. The scalding beverage on my legs elicited more curse words. They flew from my mouth like startled birds fleeing into the safety of the sky.

The street was barren of vehicles. Savannah was laughing. I got off easy. I breathed out slowly through my nose and thought about turning a new leaf, putting my best foot forward, blah, blah, blah.

Bullshit. All of it.

I righted the stroller, brushed the excess coffee off my pant legs, and walked through the gate. Everyone was staring at me. Mothers covered their children's ears and stared me down.

"Yeah," I addressed the judgmental crowd. "I know. I suck at this. Carry on."

It took an eternity of thirty seconds, but the children went back to playing, and the mothers went back to gossiping or mothering, or whatever else it is that mothers do. I unbuckled my unscathed daughter, gave her a kiss on the cheek, and dropped her into the mulch-beached boat. I settled myself into the prow, slumped forward, and exhaled.

I played bail-the-mulch-from-the-boat with Savannah as penance for my negligence. Boring as hell, but I was trying. Somewhere around the fifty-third time I had helped her climb in and out of the boat, and then back in, and then back out, I heard the telltale sound of the creaky gate.

Like deer in an open field, we all jerked our heads towards the entryway.

It was *her*. My stomach lurched and my fingers, toes, and head went numb.

I can handle this. It never happened. You're a fool and a drunk.

The nimble minx walked in, and the world slowed down. The cool autumn wind picked up, sending her luscious hair swirling around her perfect features. From behind this vision, her tiny, golden offspring appeared and skipped over to the spring-loaded metal horses, then climbed aboard. Her mother smiled, exuded a warm, rich throaty laugh that made me forget where I was as she scanned the playground with her sparkling gray eyes.

For the second time, I marveled at those large eyes and found myself staring at this woman as if I were the village idiot. But she never glanced my way. For a split second, there was a hint of mischief—verging on malice—in her smile, and then it was gone. She found what she was looking for.

"Marla!" she cried. Her voice was even more honeyed than her laughter.

Marla, that snooty bitch. I would have paid money to see someone clean that woman's clock. I had lived up the street from Marla for a few years, before Paddy and I bought the funeral home from the McFagans, who are no longer on this earth.

Sometimes in the evenings, I would be sitting on my porch enjoying an adult beverage, and Marla would drive up in her ridiculous, oversized, prissy-ass, white SUV. Just like all the other traffic on our street, she would have to stop at the stop sign that is eye-level with my porch. At first, I attempted to be neighborly and offer a friendly wave. In response, that bitch would look straight ahead and then roll up the window.

At first, I thought it was a coincidence, but then I caught on. I would see her coming up the street, and I got ready. I raised my glass to her, "Here's to you, you snot-nosed skank!" And every time—she never disappointed—she would roll up her damn window.

Her stuck-up daughters were the same way. They looked away whenever I saw them with their more amicable father. He had the decency to stop and chat if he was walking by, but if Crude 1 or Crude 2 were with him, they would physically drag him away from me.

Nice. Real nice.

"Nomia!" Marla answered back, her voice like seagulls fighting over French fries. "Come sit with me!"

So the gorgeous, mind-speaker's name was Nomia. It sounded exotic. If I had been motivated, I might have looked it up when I returned home. That's one too many 'ifs' for me. Maybe the name was Greek or something. Whatever. I'm no expert in the root origins of names.

Nomia. It flowed off the tongue like a song.

The two women settled on a bench at the perimeter of the playground and started an animated discussion. Marla looked like a bag of sticks in her expensive, designer coat. Her over-done makeup (probably applied to look as if she wasn't wearing makeup) looked cheap and thick compared to the ethereal glow that seemed to emanate from Nomia's pores.

Nomia was dressed lightly in an emerald green jacket covered in ornate embroidery. Patterns of gold, red, blue, and green swirled and eddied around her thin arms and full chest. The jacket appeared almost alive, as though the designs could slither away and cause their own mischief. I found it mesmerizing, and if Savannah had not pulled my hair, I might have stared at her jacket all day long.

Savannah had tired of her first mate duties in the mulch boat. She was pointing her chunky fingers towards the baby swing. The swings were right in front of Nomia and Marla.

I steeled myself, took a nice big swig of what was left of my coffee, and hoisted my chubby bundle. Without making eye contact with the chatting women who didn't seem to notice me at all, I deposited Savannah in one of the black, bucket-like baby swings and gave her a good shove. My daughter squealed with delight, squishing her diaper around in her purple overalls that oozed out of the leg holes of the swing.

I set to my monotonous task of pushing, waiting, pushing, waiting, and then pushing once again. The ebb and flow of my little chunky monkey's giggles, along with the two-toned groan of the swing, filled my ears.

But that wasn't all I could hear. I was in range of Nomia and Marla's conversation. It's not like I was eavesdropping. Okay, I was eavesdropping. Call me Evie the Eavesdropper. Then sue me.

I hadn't had a drink in five days. I had coffee burns on my

legs. I had almost killed my own child. And I was at the play-ground—again. I deserved a little adult conversation, even if I wasn't an active participant.

"He just doesn't understand me!" Nomia lamented.

"They never do," Marla sighed.

"No, I mean, he will never *get* me. Never. He doesn't under-stand where I come from, my family, my upbringing. He just doesn't get me! We're so different! But I am so in love with him. Not just the idea of him, but *him.*" Nomia crossed her arms and leaned forward on her knees. She cocked her head to the side and swung her long hair behind her, edging closer to Marla, who hung on her every word. "We're always fighting. Always. But that's just us, you know?"

Marla nodded. "I know just what you mean."

Bullshit. I thought. *Your husband does whatever the hell you tell him to. That poor excuse for a man lost his 'y' chromosome the day he met you.*

Nomia continued, "We fight, I take off for a few days, I come back. We make up ..." Here she giggled, uttering a soothing sound, like thick wind chimes on a warm summer night. "And then it starts all over again."

"You take off for a few days?"

"Of course! How else would I calm down? I would hate to do something rash in the heat of an argument, so I just leave. When I feel ... better, I return."

"What about your daughter?" Marla asked.

"Pearl? She's fine with David. He's a wonderful father. Those two are as thick as thieves."

Marla leaned away from Nomia and was quiet with her thoughts. After a few moments, she said, "I could never leave my girls alone with Steven. He wouldn't know what to do."

"Your girls are like, what, six and ten?" asked Nomia.

"Yes. Piper is six and Blaire will be ten next month. But Steven, he ..." Marla's voice trailed off.

Nomia reached out a slender arm and, with her abnormally long fingers, touched Marla's hand. From the corner of my eye, I watched Marla's body relax and slump against the back of the bench.

"You need to take some time for yourself every now and then," Nomia said with a rich, gurgling laugh.

Marla nodded and murmured in a dreamy voice, "I do need to take care of myself."

Something was wrong. I turned and faced the seated women. Marla looked like she was in a trance, and Nomia now held Marla's limp hand in her own. I didn't know what to do.

The whole scene was so weird. I looked around the playground at the other mothers. No one else saw this strange girl/girl experience—Marla Bitch-Face melting into oblivion while the freakishly beautiful new girl caressed her hand.

When I looked back, both women had their eyes riveted to me. I grew nauseous again and almost doubled over with cramps. With no one to push her, Savannah swayed to a stop. The air grew thick and damp, and everything went silent.

And then it happened again. The familiar sound of someone else, someone unfriendly and foreign, resonated in my mind. Only this time, there were two voices speaking in unison.

Back off. This is none of your concern.

Then nothing. No comforting bliss like last time, no happy suspension of reality. Nothing. I blinked, and Marla and Nomia were no longer holding hands. Their expressions were both blank and unreadable. Just two mothers at the playground, observing another mother, who had coffee stains on her pants, not pushing her crying daughter in the swing.

Did I just imagine that? What the hell just happened?

"Your daughter is trying to get out of her swing," Marla said and pointed to Savannah.

I turned and grabbed her just before she almost fell, again. I held my bawling daughter close to me and noticed a change in the weather. A dense fog had filled the playground.

What's with this fog?

Somewhere in the distance, I heard the mournful call of the foghorn at the end of Pawtuxet Point. It was time to leave. I headed towards my stroller and felt the twin gazes of the weird sisters burning into my back. Other mothers were gathering their children, remarking about how the fog had been so persistent lately.

Before I went through the gate, I glanced back at the bench. The two women were still staring at me. I shuddered and left. It was the last time I—or anyone else—saw Marla again.

The HMS *Gaspee*
Narragansett Bay, Rhode Island
April 16, 1772
12:54 AM

The dark, cramped cabin reeked of mold. The smell oozed from the damp wooden walls like an infected wound. Clothing and bedding were strewn about the small interior, ruined by the salt air, mildew, and discarded tankards of ale.

Lieutenant William Dudingston could not stand to his full height in his small chamber. Instead, the tall man was forced to stoop. As he bent his neck at an odd angle, his shaggy hair fell forward and obscured his eyes.

William attempted to stretch his back. The noise of his movements filled the cabin with loud pops and cracks. He crouched, towering over what passed as his bed, and folded his long arms over his head.

He looks like a vulture, thought the girl.

Searching through the pile of clothing tossed beside the uneven platform bed, William retrieved his stockings from beneath the girl's threadbare shift. Once fully clothed, he sat down next to her and pulled her dress from the floor. Holding it up to the lantern, he could see the candlelight flickering through the thin, flimsy fabric.

"You're in need of a new frock," he said. His voice was a deep baritone. Gravel coursed through each syllable, and his Scottish accent made the 'r' in 'frock' rattle off his tongue.

She didn't respond. Turning from him, she faced the wall and searched the knots and whorls of the dark wood, seeking familiar images haphazardly created by the growth of a tree in a forest far, far away. In the dim light, she could make out the elongated semblance of a seahorse. Its tail curled into a concentric circle, and its head was in danger of being devoured by a bearded man.

Something landed next to her with a clinking *thud*. She turned to see a small leather purse on the soiled bed linens.

"For your frock," William said and then smiled, grinning devilishly.

She noticed his teeth were long and straight. She smiled back at him. Thinking he had pleased her, William continued to grin, but her smile stemmed from somewhere else.

She laughed and thought about breaking off every one of his teeth, then pushing their jagged points into the soft flesh of his stomach.

"It pleases me to delight you," he said.

The girl fought off a scowl. She narrowed her eyes and crawled towards him. The musty blanket fell, exposing her naked form. She watched his eyes crawl all over her body and did her best to keep the fake lust affixed to her face.

Never letting her eyes leave his, her hands moving on their own, she unlaced the breeches he had tied only moments before. William looked down and smiled at her, then placed his fingers deep into the web of her dark hair.

"So lovely," he breathed.

The girl smiled back, then continued with the task she had started.

When she was sure that he had dozed off, the girl crept from under William's sleep-heavy embrace. Never making a sound, she grabbed her thin dress off the cabin floor and pulled the loose garment over her head.

The girl wore no shoes, no undergarments, and no jewelry. She did not shiver in the cold night air or disturb the sleeping deck hands as she passed close by them. As if under a spell, all the men aboard the ship slept deeply, dreaming of water and lullabies, faint smiles gracing their weather-hardened faces.

No one saw her standing on the deck of the ship. No one saw her remove her dress and ball it up in the palm of her long hand. No one saw the moonlight reflect off her bare skin that glowed like phosphorescence, green one moment, white the next.

And no one saw the naked girl move with unnatural speed to the prow, where she stood tall, searching the darkened horizon for something known only to her.

Once she found what she sought, the girl raised her arms high above her head, inhaled deeply, and from the deck-rail of the HMS *Gaspee*, dove forward. Her body arced like a drawn bow and made no splash, no sound, as it entered the frigid waters of Narragansett Bay.

The great schooner with its sleeping British sailors rocked in the ebb and flow of the tide. Water lapped and licked her massive girth while somewhere amongst her mighty sails, now wrapped and dormant, metal pulleys chimed softly against the two masts. The anchor chain creaked and groaned.

The girl never surfaced.

At dawn, the lieutenant awoke. Light seeped in through the grimy glass windows criss-crossed with thick, black leading. Sitting up, he pushed his unbound hair from his eyes. It was a familiar gesture, but something was different.

A lock of his hair was missing. So was the coin purse.

So was the girl.

Lieutenant Dudingston had met the mysterious girl while strolling through the fish market, listening to gossip, passing stall after stall of fishmongers and other sundry merchants.

Dudingston's duty had brought him to the docks. He was His Majesty's man, first and foremost. He sought news for his king, to better serve him, to better eliminate the filth that sought to profit at the expense of the one true king. The lieutenant's spies were few, but they were reliable.

They disgusted him, these empty-hearted urchins who

would give up their fellow mariners and merchants for a few measly coins and, perhaps, the opportunity to smuggle their own goods, unencumbered by Dudingston's vigilance.

Since his arrival in March, the lieutenant had wielded his fist and flattened much of the illegal activity occurring in the colonial Rhode Island waters. Those who sought to defy him were punished. He took their goods and fed their provisions to his own crew. He sent their seized ships to Boston, stalemating their abilities to petition local courts for the safe return of their merchandise and vessels.

The lieutenant was indiscriminate with his search and seizure tactics. No one was safe. No smuggler, no merchant, no mariner, no fisherman was exempt from his watchful eye and stern condemnation. The people of Rhode Island hated him.

He loved their hatred. Their hatred was wrapped in fear, and fear was a good thing. It kept men in line. It also bode well for his career. Word of his tyranny and iron fist was already on its way back to London.

"Lieutenant Dudingston, sir," said his midshipman.

"Speak," he replied.

"There is news of rum-runners near Prudence Island. They intend to use the cover of the new moon in two weeks time to make their way out of the Bay."

"Very good," said the lieutenant. "We will be waiting for them."

His midshipman nodded, then hurried back towards the *Gaspee*, his work in the taverns completed. Dudingston continued his stroll. He endured the scent of night soil that wafted along the streets, then continued its unpleasant journey downhill to the sea. The smell of old fish mingled with the stench of human excrement. The fetid scents hung heavy in the spring air, burning his nostrils and contorting his face into a scowl of disgust.

Pausing at a tavern doorway, Dudingston debated the merits of entering. His gaze lingered on the sign above the door. The paint was peeling off in sheets leaving behind the faint outline of a horse. While his head was raised, an arm found its way around his waist, reaching into the depths of his breeches.

Dudingston grabbed the attacker by the arm with his left hand, intending to bring the scoundrel around to face him. He pulled back his right hand to strike, but did not.

His attacker was a woman—a beautiful woman whose strength and size rivaled his own. As much as he tried, he could not move her or remove the hand exploring the contents of his breeches. He looked down at his crotch, and a look of sheer horror crawled across his chiseled, weather-beaten face.

She laughed at his embarrassment and then licked his ear. The gesture aroused him, piqued his interest when it should have repulsed him.

The brazen woman spun in front of him, unabashed, her long, dark hair flowing free. It moved about her, the way seaweed drifts and ebbs in the tide. Her bodice was too loose for the brisk air, and even though her breasts beckoned his gaze, he found himself staring at the most unusual gray eyes he had ever seen.

They mesmerized him, and he found himself drifting, lost

in those strange, overly large irises.

"Who *are* you?" he whispered.

She leaned into his ear and answered with a voice like silk, "Who would you like me to be?"

A large smile spilled across his face. He felt like a schoolboy on the precipice of a first kiss. Without concern for her dignity or proper courtesy, William now allowed his eyes to roam all over her body.

They were almost the same height, which impressed William as he stood at just above six feet tall. Her hips appeared narrow, while her muscular legs, visible beneath her too-thin frock, reminded him of Greek marble statues he had once viewed in London. She was barefoot. This detail both disgusted and intrigued him, another nod to her wild, free spirit.

A spirit, he thought, *which might prove most generous in certain situations should they present themselves.*

He could not deny that she was, indeed, presenting *something.* Finishing his inspection of her person, he said, "Name your price."

She winked and leaned in close. Before he could protest, one of her hands was in his hair, pulling his head backwards. The girl held a firm grip on his bound *queue,* and he found himself staring at the sky, his back aching from the strain of his position.

"Your quarters, midnight," she whispered.

Her other hand slid across his chest, wandering through the inner contents of his white waistcoat, then returned once more to the front of his breeches. A low moan escaped her lips.

William's face turned a dark shade of red, and his brow

furrowed as both anger and shame fought for position. Before he could rebuke her proposal, she had disappeared. He spun around, his eyes searching the fish stalls, the alleys, and doorways.

She was gone.

For a moment, he thought he had imagined her, but the open-mouthed stares of the market-goers and the sudden disappearance of his coin purse were valid proof. His encounter with the strange, elusive woman had happened indeed. He hoped he would never see her again.

Most of him hoped he would never see her again.

The rational, pragmatic side of Lieutenant William Dudingston dismissed the experience as a temporary lack of discipline on his part—he had allowed some street urchin to bewitch him out of his coin purse. It was unacceptable.

Actions such as these did not further his rank. In the future, he would not allow something like this to deter him from his career. He felt foolish. Thank heavens his midshipman had not been there to witness the event. The results could have been disastrous.

Dudingston went on with his day, a nagging burning in his gut fueling his ire. The woman had embarrassed him. Her actions demanded punishment. No one laid a hand on an officer of the Royal Navy—not without paying a heavy price. No one. A woman had violated him, taken his money, and laid her long, slender fingers on his manhood. The thought of her touch brought a rush of blood to his cheeks.

No, he thought.

Dudingston shook the thought from his mind, straightened his blue officer's coat, and fixed his gaze high. He had work to do. The burning in his belly carried him through the remainder of the day. Close to dusk, he found an opportunity to release his boiling fury.

An ale merchant crossed his path on the docks. A few weeks past, the merchant had been seen consulting with smugglers in a Providence tavern. It now brought Dudingston both incredible joy and release to beat the man and, as further punishment, to seize the merchant's goods, an entire hold filled with casks of ale. His crew needed ale.

That night, he allowed his crew to celebrate. As an officer, he celebrated alone in his own quarters, relishing the dark liquid as well as the light-headed feeling it produced. It helped him forget the morning's distasteful encounter.

Ever vigilant and dedicated to his post, even as he drank, Dudingston set to the task of examining nautical maps of Narragansett Bay. He studied the endless coves, inlets, and islands, pushing himself to memorize each nook and cranny, anything suitable to conceal a vessel. His eyes blurred in the low light as the clock on his small writing desk chimed the midnight hour. Dudingston held his breath.

What did he expect?

That she would *magic* herself to the *Gaspee*? Or perhaps, at midnight, she would commandeer a small craft, row herself alone to his ship, climb aboard unnoticed by his drunken crew, then present herself in his quarters? He thought of her strong physique and wild nature. If any woman could accomplish something so seemingly impossible, she could.

Pinching the top of his nose with his fingers, he closed his eyes and dismissed the thoughts as ridiculous and distracting. He listened to the sound of the Bay lapping against the hull, the distant singing of male voices somewhere in the common crew quarters, the slow tick of his clock, a gift from his mother far across the sea in Edinburg. A floorboard creaked, and he opened his eyes.

His heart stopped.

She stood in the doorway, soaking wet. Her gray eyes, feral and ferocious, fixed on his. Her chest heaved up and down, as though she had overexerted herself. She was naked.

He never called out to anyone. He never sounded an alarm. He couldn't move or speak. He could only stare. This woman, this goddess stood before him, tempting him with her gaze, offering herself to him.

Rational thoughts be damned. He took her. He punished her for the embarrassment she caused that morning. He punished her for her strength and her wildness. He punished her for eluding his crew—a crew bound to protect their officer, but who had somehow allowed a naked woman to move unnoticed among them. And he punished her because it felt good.

She accepted all of his aggressions, welcomed them, encouraged him, and urged him on. Her appetite was boundless, as if he were a meal that could not fill her hunger. She devoured him and came back for more.

It was an hour before dawn when he fell to the comfort of his most uncomfortable bed, exhausted, dehydrated, dizzy with elation. She crawled up his legs and laid her head to rest just above his navel. Her dark locks splayed across his midsection tangling him in their dark web.

"I don't know your name," he said, speaking to the crown of her head.

"Does it matter?"

"I suppose it doesn't," he replied. "Does it?"

Dudingston drifted into a brief but deep sleep, and when he awoke, a few moments before dawn, she was gone. He dressed and went about his duties with a crisp spring in his step. The sunlight seemed a little brighter to him. The air seemed a little cleaner, a little fresher. He gave his commands with the slightest of smiles, something so unlike his gruff character. The crew took notice and remarked to one another when they were sure he was out of earshot.

The events of the evening and the resulting effect on his demeanor germinated like a seed deep inside his being. He craved her, and his need for her became all-consuming. It rivaled air, water, nourishment. It grew within him, day after day, caressing his insides like feathers, and then it grew hungry, like a fetus demanding to be fed, clawing at him from the inside out.

Was it love?

Certainly not. It was pure lust, and he was willing to do whatever it took to keep her in his bed. He wanted her. He needed her. The need drove him to seek her out, to try and find her time and time again. Although he never did find her.

She found him.

It was not clear how she came aboard. She always appeared in his doorway, naked, dripping seawater onto his floorboards. He assumed she swam to the *Gaspee*. The idea seemed preposterous, but he had no other explanation. He found he didn't care enough to ask how she arrived. He cared only that she had arrived. When she did, he welcomed her with open, willing arms.

They would spend the entire night doing things he never even dreamed possible, and when he awoke, several hours later, she was gone. He slept a deep, dreamless sleep during those brief hours, leaving him refreshed and rejuvenated upon awakening.

Two months passed from when her nocturnal visits had first begun. In those months, his searches and seizures of Rhode Island vessels had increased ten-fold.

The girl knew things. Not only was she skilled in the carnal ways of the bedroom, she was resourceful. She knew when and where certain smugglers would be making their runs. She knew which merchants were in league with the smugglers and which fishermen were taking on extra work under the guise of fishing trips.

Lieutenant William Dudingston had never been happier. Or more successful.

One night, he managed to not fall asleep after their delicious routine. She was coiled around him like a snake on a tree, her hands in his hair, massaging his scalp.

Contentment gleamed across his skin. William glanced down at the girl and said, "With all the success I am having here in the colonies, Vice Admiral Montagu in Boston has taken notice. He's sent word to the British Colonial Secretary, Lord Hillsborough, in London."

She lifted her large gray eyes to his, then slid her leg further up his inner thigh.

"Tell me what that means." Her voice was like honey to his ears, soothing, comforting.

He could feel his desire for her renew itself.

"It could mean a promotion," he said as he ran his hands over her smooth skin. "It could mean a transfer back to London."

"Would you want to leave this place?" she asked as she pressed herself, her hips closer to his legs, moving her body up and down against his thighs.

"I have had my fill of this filthy, savage land," he said as he slid his hand between her legs. "I prefer England with its cleanliness and order."

She let her own hand find its way to his inner thigh. Within seconds, William gasped and tightened the muscles in his face.

"Would you take *me* with you to London?" she purred, her voice rising at the end of her question.

He let her hand continue what it had started, while his breathing became more and more irregular.

"Would that please you?" he asked, his voice barely above a whisper.

"Does this please you?" she asked.

"Oh, yes," he said. "Yes, indeed."

3

The police found Marla's SUV in the small parking lot near Gaspee Point Beach. Her abandoned vehicle contained her purse, an overnight bag with some clothes, and all her jewelry. But it was her phone that had everyone in a titter.

The phone revealed messages from an untraceable number labeled *M*. Marla had received numerous racy texts from *M*, and her responses made many of the seasoned members of the local P.D. blush. The last message instructed Marla to meet her mysterious suitor at Gaspee Point Beach for a midnight rendez-vous. There was nothing else.

Marla had completely disappeared. Foul play was suspected, but without a body, there wasn't anything anyone could do.

The next night, Paddy—wearing his coroner hat—had been called to the site of an unfortunate midnight-lawn-mow-er-drag-racing accident. Someone fell, and someone erroneously had their blades on, so someone ended up in pieces. Paddy had the pleasure of picking them all up.

While bagging up bits and pieces, Paddy caught up with his good friend Detective Oliver Lyons. When Paddy first came to America to live with Aunt Catherine and Uncle Aiden, Oliver lived three houses down and one street over. Easy-going and friendly, Oliver had befriended the new, overly large kid wandering aimlessly around Pawtuxet Village. The two were soon inseparable, and as time moved on, as it always does, one became a coroner/mortician, the other a cop. Oliver and Paddy didn't stay as close as they once were, but they still played poker once a month, and then there's the odd meeting over severed limbs.

At least one of us has friends.

Oliver gave Paddy the inside scoop concerning Marla's mysterious disappearance. Since the horrible experience with Marla and Nomia, I had not gone back to the Village Playground. Instead, I started driving Savannah to the playground in Roger Williams Park. No one knew me there, and that was the way I liked it.

"What could Steve have done to make his wife take off like that? What'd he do? Forget to take out the trash?" Paddy said to my back as I stood at the sink after dinner. I had enjoyed the lawnmower story, but this was a topic I did not wish to discuss.

"They questioned the new woman in the Village—Nivea? Noriega?"

"*Nomia?*" I croaked.

"Yeah, that's it. Nomia was quite upset. Turns out she was the last person to speak with Marla. She *claims* she knows nothing about Marla's boyfriend, but the boys believe Nomia is holding back something."

"Interesting," I murmured into the sink. "Nomia seems so ... nice." *I knew there was something fishy about that leggy bitch.*

"Well, you know how girls are," said Paddy.

I paused in my cleaning. "No, Paddy," I said. "How *are* girls?"

"You all cover for one another," he said. "It's in your DNA."

I turned and looked at him.

"Well, if you *had* any girlfriends, they could cover for you when you run off with another man." He winked at me.

I returned to my dishes.

"Anyhoo, Marla told Nomia she needed to take a break. Take a break from what? Pedicures? Poor Steve. He's got to handle those girls by himself now. Maybe he should just move to Boston and be near his parents. He wouldn't have any trouble joining another dental practice up there. That's what I would do."

"If some psycho put a spell on your wife and dumped her in the Bay?"

"*What?* Evie, do you think Marla's dead?"

"What does it matter what I think?" I said and slammed down my sponge.

"I know you didn't particularly care for Marla, but I do suppose you have a point. All her valuables were left in the car. It is a bit strange. Think she met some psycho on the interweb or something?"

"Umm," I stammered. I wiped my hands on a dishtowel, then tossed it on the counter. "You know what? I think I need some air. Yeah, some air is just the thing." I grabbed my scarf, a heavy-duty flashlight, my coat, and then headed out the back door.

"God, I need a drink," I muttered.

We were approaching the holidays, and the ground was covered in alternating layers of virgin snow and bits of dirty ice. My boots made faint crunching sounds as I walked down the driveway. It was raw and cold, and I was glad to find my mittens stuffed into one of the pockets of my over-sized parka. Fighting back a shiver, I stuffed my hands into the warm wool, then looked around.

The funeral home was on the corner of two main streets, Park and Broad. I had two choices. Turn right and make my way to the river, or don't turn and make my way to the Village.

Be good, Evie. Walk towards the river and the wildlife preserve. Don't go to the Village. Avoid the bars. Be good, Evie.

I inhaled deeply. The air was damp and thick with the smell of the sea. All the other smells were just as dead as the vegetation. The absence of greenery left plenty of room for the moist salty air to overpower all it encountered.

I inhaled again, relishing the relief in my sinuses. After being cooped up with forced hot air for almost a month, the moisture was greedily absorbed. I weighed my options and looked longingly down Broad Street, imagining the lively scene at any one of the three pubs.

Be good, Evie.

I turned right on Park and pulled the hood of my parka up over my ears.

"Bah!" I yelled out. But no one was around to care.

With the exception of the amber street lights, the sidewalk was full of shadows. The sky before dinner had been purple and pink, like cotton candy at a low-budget carnival, but all that was over. It was a world for dog-walkers and people who walked with a purpose, like perhaps they didn't have a car or a whole lot of sense. It was too cold to stroll. But there I was, heading towards the dark woods, without a dog—out for a stroll.

I tried to put Marla and Nomia far from my thoughts. I tried to put the calming effects of alcohol even farther from my thoughts. I also tried to ignore the numbness in my goddamn toes. Instead I kept fixating on all three issues.

So much for clearing my head. I mean, really, who actually clears their head when they're overloaded with stress? I turned left and picked my way over the slippery patches of ice blanketing Milton Street.

Almost there.

Illuminated by the streetlight's anemic glow, the frozen ball fields sprawled in front of the darkened woods like a deserted wasteland. I could barely make out the entrance to the Pawtuxet River Trail, but because I was in a foul mood, I chose not to turn on my flashlight. It's not like I'm well-known for making smart decisions.

Why start now?

I made my way across the dead grass of the ball field, my boots crunching the frozen blades with each step. At the far edge of the field, the forest stood pensive and silent, like an animal waiting to pounce. I paused at the first makeshift bridge, a collection of boards nailed together to allow pedestrians a cleaner walk over the muddy path. The woods around the river were a lot darker than I thought they would be. It was quiet, too, as if all the sounds in the world had been absorbed until spring.

Resolved in my decision to stroll, I pressed on. Before too long, I noticed a light and heard the tell-tale tinkling of a dog collar. It was to be expected. This was a popular dog-walking spot. I would have an opportunity to try and be 'friendly.'

It didn't happen. Within seconds, a furry beast was staring me down.

"Hi, there," I tried in my 'friendly' voice.

The medium-sized dog planted its front paws and leaned backwards. Then it growled.

"Really, dog? I used the *friendly* voice."

More growling. No, it was more of a snarl at that point. Not good.

"Biscuit!" came a shrill call from what I hoped to God was Biscuit's owner. "Biscuit?"

"She's right here, and she looks hungry," I said as loudly as I dared.

The owner made her way towards me. Biscuit lunged. I didn't even have time to scream. In seconds, I was on my back while my face was filled with dog teeth, dog breath, and—worst of all—dog slime. There was a sound like an enormous jacket being zipped and then a yelp as Biscuit was jerked backwards on her leash. In the darkness, I never saw the thing. It must have been one of those clothesline leashes that whoosh back into the handle.

"What the hell just happened?" I shouted, attempting to get to my feet.

"Oh my. I am so sorry! That's the second time this evening she's done that."

"The *second* time? Really, lady? I can recommend a real nice solution for your problem. How about you give that dog about twenty Valium when you get home and call it a night—for good?"

So much for *friendly* Evie.

The woman inhaled sharply, emitting a high-pitched whine. "Well, I never," she mumbled and hurried along the path, heading back the way I had just come. Her dog kept looking back at me, snarling the whole time.

"Biscuit is a stupid fucking name, by the way!" I yelled at the retreating duo. "Stupid bitches," I added while swiping Biscuit drool from my face.

I needed something besides my sleeve to wipe away the incident. I needed a napkin. The kind of napkin that comes with a nice, fancy highball glass.

At a pub.

"Screw it. I'm heading to the pub," I said aloud, now steadfast in my new decision.

I kept walking towards the river. The Pawtuxet River Trail eventually made its way to Rhodes on the Pawtuxet, a large turn-of-the-century ballroom. Back in the day, it was a huge casino and pavilion. The mucky-mucks of Providence had summered in the area, and Rhodes was their playground. I've seen a few antique postcards of the place. It was quite the scene. The casino is now gone and the ballroom is mostly used for proms and such. It was off-season now, so Rhodes would be deserted. I knew I could make my way past the silent ballroom, cut up to Broad, and voilà! I'd be in the Village, dog-slime-free, and well on my way to oblivion.

It had been a glorious plan. Nothing in my life goes according to plan. If I had just turned on the goddamn flashlight, maybe everything would have been different. But no, I failed. I failed epically to alter my fate.

Cursing Biscuit and his stupid-ass owner under my breath, I resumed my stroll. Within minutes, I could see the security lights surrounding Rhodes.

Almost there.

I could smell the rich, smoky scent of bourbon. I could taste it as it burned my throat and traveled through my system, making my insides boil.

I smiled. Then I heard them. The smile slid off my face, and thoughts of bourbon evaporated like moisture in a winter-dry house. A man and a woman were arguing on the small footbridge. Their words were heated and loud.

The pair stood above the rushing tributary that fed into the mighty Pawtuxet River. Autumn rains had made the river swell, and as I walked closer to Rhodes, I could hear the roar of the falls that marked the end of the river and the beginning of the Bay. The falls were farther downriver, but not much.

Not wanting to disturb the pair, I stopped, frozen in my tracks, deciding what to do. I could smell the brackish result of fresh river water meeting the more brine-inclined sea, and my digits, in their respective socks and mittens, were starting to crack from the cold.

These two individuals stood in the way of my drink. My brain screamed at the intrusion. If I turned around, I could just go home. If I interrupted the couple, it would be awkward.

Fuck it.

I was used to awkward. I was just about to turn on my flashlight when my finger froze, hovering over the switch. I knew that voice. It was her—*Nomia.*

"No, David. I do not want to move again!" she shouted.

"Then keep it in check, you selfish bitch!"

That had to be David.

"Why? No one knows what happened to her. No one ever will. I needed a distraction, for Christ's sake."

"A distraction? From what?"

"From you! From my controlling family! What do you care, anyway? Oh!" She started laughing. "You're jealous, aren't you? You're jealous!" She laughed and laughed.

"No! I'm not jealous! I'm sick of moving, Nomia. I'm sick of your freakish family obligations. It's a small state. Sooner or later the shit's gonna to hit the fan. There are lives involved. Are you laughing about this?"

"Just shut up, David." She laughed. "No one's going to give a shit about the disappearance of one stuck-up bitch. It's not my first time at the rodeo, you know. Besides, you knew what you were getting into when you married me. Awww, poor you. Poor Pearl. I can't wait until she's older. It'll be twice the fun!"

"Keep her out of this!"

"Oh, I don't think so. She's just a much a part of this as I am. Oh, the fun we'll have!" Nomia laughed again. Her warm, rich laughter lifted into the crisp air like mist rising on a lake.

"No!" he screamed, and I heard a splash.

A large one. The kind of double splash you hear when a person jumps into a pool. There is the initial splash, then the vacuum created as the body displaces the water, followed by a second splash as the water smashes together, covering over the now submerged person.

Oh God, one of them is in the icy water.

I ran to the footbridge. A figure—I couldn't make out who—was already off and running. The person ran up the hill towards Broad Street, beyond the giant ballroom parking lot high above Rhodes. The river was secluded, downhill from street level. The fast-moving figure bobbed up and down and then disappeared over the hill.

The person was gone. I looked over the railing. Nothing. Then I heard splashing downriver.

Oh my God. The falls!

I turned on my flashlight and ran along the river's edge. The beam danced along the swift, frothy river as I ran. Rocks, waves, and reeds alternated in the light. From beyond my line of vision, farther ahead came the sound of another splash. I trained my light towards the sound and watched as something disappeared beneath the bubbling current.

I couldn't tell what it was. It was gone in seconds. I pressed on, tripping over roots and rocks along the river's edge. Branches scratched at my face, and I felt dampness on my cheek. One of the sharp twigs had drawn blood, but I kept going. The roar of the falls grew louder.

They're going to go right over! They'll be smashed to pieces!

I could swim but not all that well, and besides, I was running out of time. The path rose high above the river, creating a steep embankment that separated me from the water. I looked down. It was a fifteen-foot drop.

Shit. I was already at the bridge.

The bridge was a crucial landmark in the Village. The street crossing it started as Broad Street in Cranston, where I lived farther north, and then it changed to Narragansett Parkway as it passed over the river into the city of Warwick. The bridge also marked the end of the Pawtuxet River and the beginning of Pawtuxet Cove, an inlet of Narragansett Bay.

It was also right beside a gorgeous rocky-ass waterfall.

The crashing water bellowed and filled my ears, obliterating any sounds of splashing that may have alerted me to the person's condition. I stopped and scanned the water far below with my flashlight. In the inky blackness, I saw nothing but gray rocks, white water, and ...

What the hell was that?

It couldn't have been. My eyes must have been playing tricks on me, or that dog, Biscuit, had knocked something loose in my brain, because I had not just seen a giant fin.

No fucking way.

I moved the beam of light backwards, back to where the river crested, just before it plummeted over the rocks and found salvation in the immensity of the cove, then the Bay, and then the great blue sea.

Nothing. Whatever the hell it was—*a tuna? a shark?*—it had now become the property of Pawtuxet Cove.

I stopped and listened. No shouts or cries, male or female. The person in the river, if they lived, was now on their way to the Bay. Maybe not in one piece. Maybe part of the food chain, if whatever I saw was the hungry, scavenging type.

What a strange and grim situation ...

I scrambled up the rocks to the bridge above the river, above the cove, above whatever else was lurking beneath me. The street was dead, devoid of foot traffic and vehicles. I dusted myself off and ran to the cove side of the bridge.

Holding my breath, I looked over the edge, and braced myself for the carnage, the blood, the floating body. Rushing waters splashed against the narrow causeway. The water eddied and swirled below the amber lights of the homes and businesses lining the banks. On and on the black water flowed, making a beeline to the east and then, after a few hundred feet, making a sharp right turn to the south.

Looking up and facing east, I could see the dim lights of the expensive homes on the peninsula. I scanned the shores, the docks, the seawalls looking for any sign of life or death. The body had to be somewhere.

But what would I do when I found it?

Awkward indeed. Call the police?

Hey, I was not on my way to the bar and decided to cut through the woods. I was almost attacked by a dog, heard a crazy broad

*and her husband fighting, and, oh yeah, one of them chucked the
other into the Pawtuxet.*

*What did I do after that, Officer? Well, I followed the possible
splashing of a person who—now that I think of it—may or may
not have fallen into the river. And, might I add, I may or may not
have witnessed some sort of aquatic predator or maybe even a sea
monster in the river.*

No, Officer, this was before the copious drinking.

All these thoughts ran through my mind as I stood, out of
breath, freezing my ass off and scanning the river with my
flashlight, while trying not to shine the beam into anyone's
home. Then I saw something caught on a rock, just below the
bridge.

I grumbled to myself and crossed the bridge towards Warwick, climbed gracelessly over the wall, and made my way down
the steep embankment to the inlet.

Using a stick, I pulled a brightly colored object out of the
water. An emerald green woman's jacket covered in gold, red,
green, and blue embroidery. Nomia's jacket.

Nomia was in those waters. Here was my proof.

I stood up quickly and scanned the cove again. A sound carried itself over the waves to my ears. It was subtle at first, lilting
and soft like a baby's gurgle, and then it grew cruel and shrill.

A woman's laughter.

I looked across the cove, and I saw her. I didn't need the
flashlight. In the dim light, she glowed like a thousand-watt
bulb. She stood there, naked, her body as white and perfect as
any marble statue. Her head was cocked to one side, and she

was wringing water out of her hair as if this was an ordinary summer day and she had just gone for a nice refreshing swim.

But it wasn't summer. It was freezing out. I could not feel my goddamn fingers, and this bitch was standing over there, bare-assed, wringing out her hair!

What the ...?

My jaw was hanging like an open door. I must have looked like a moron, gaping at my first real, live, naked girl.

Now what?

As I was deciding what my next move should be, she turned around—and she stared right at me. I froze, and then *I* felt naked. The familiar feeling of nausea crept over me, forcing my hands to my abdomen as if I could push the pain out of my gut.

I had seen a bobcat once, at my grandparents' home in upstate New York. I remember the moment when the beast saw me, and I saw it. Our eyes locked, and time fell away. I'm sure the encounter lasted only a few milliseconds, but it felt like an eternity. I remember the metallic taste of fear in my mouth that lingered long after the animal had retreated into the brush just as silently as it had appeared.

On that frigid bank, it was *deja vu* all over again, except this time I had the added agonizing discomfort of nausea. Somehow I knew the bobcat and Nomia were one and the same. Predators. I knew something else, something crucial. I was the prey.

Chubby, naive me was lower on the food chain, and I was trespassing where I didn't belong. I had interfered twice now. Once in the playground when she was with Marla, probably toying with her, and now here, by these icy waters.

No sane person runs in front of a lion or an alligator, and you bet your ass, they don't do it twice. But I had.

The nausea increased, bringing me to my knees.

You again. I see you, and if I see you again—you'll join Marla.

Our eyes met across the expansive darkness of the cove. Then it was over. With a swish of her long, wet hair, she turned and ran up the dock towards the large house looming behind her. The darkness embraced her, then swallowed her whole.

She was gone.

Of course my husband thought I was insane. I don't know what I was thinking when I told him what happened. Paddy had gone to bed early and was asleep when I got home, and I just didn't have the energy to wake him.

Instead, I went into the kitchen and made myself a strong pot of coffee with a shot of whiskey. I sat at the table all night, until Paddy came down with Savannah sometime in the early morning.

"Where the hell were you last night?" he asked as he plopped our smiling child down in her high chair. "Did you sleep in your study?"

"No," I said, then mumbled, "I was out chasing homicidal bitches who may or may not have supernatural powers." *And who may or may not be stalking my stupid ass right now.*

"Hmm. Supernatural bitches now," he said. "That's colorful."

"But before that, this dog attacked me, so I started towards the Village for a drink."

"Evie! You said you were just going out for a walk!" he bellowed, his jowls shaking the whole time.

"I know, I know." I ran both of my hands through my hair, creating a rooster crown on my head. "But then he pushed her into the water, and then I saw a shark or, uh, a river monster, or I don't know, and then she went over the falls, and I found her jacket. And then she was naked! And unharmed! Not a scratch on her, walking around, wringing out her hair. Naked! In twenty-degree weather! Who the hell does that?"

"I don't know, Evie. Maybe this mythical 'she' rode the magical sea monster and derived warmth from its magical hide." He covered his face with his sausage-like hands and rubbed vigorously. "Evie, my darling, I think it's time to call the rehab center. Maybe just for outpatient services. You wouldn't have to live there, mind you. Just go, talk to people about your drinking … and sea monsters …"

"Stop right there," I said and glared at him. "Get this, Paddy. I. Am. Not. Going. To. Rehab. End. Of. Fucking. Conversation."

I stormed upstairs to my study and slammed the door. My favorite leather chair smiled at me. Okay, it didn't really smile at me, but it felt like it did. At least someone or something wasn't judging me.

"I'll be right there, chair," I said.

Now, I'm talking to a chair. Maybe I am crazy.

I walked over to my bookshelf and scanned the spines.

"Ah, *Atlas Shrugged,*" I muttered and pulled the heavy book from the shelf. Settling into the comfort of my chair, I inhaled the warmth of leather and felt my muscles relax. With the book on my lap, I looked out the large eyebrow window.

My study was on the third floor of the funeral home. The second and third floors were our living quarters, and the first served as the official funeral home. The basement housed the *meat lockers.* Paddy hated it when I referred to his realm as the *meat lockers.*

Fuck Paddy.

As I looked out at the view, I saw the Bay far beyond the other homes in the Village. As Villagers, we were on the fringe. I was on the fringe. I thought about the icy waters and the events of the previous evening.

And fuck that bitch, Nomia.

She was messing me up. I could do that just fine all on my own.

Somewhere in the house, Savannah started crying, and I sighed. Looking down at my lap, I flipped open the book.

"Thank you, Ayn Rand," I said.

I reached into page forty-four and took out the bottle of crème de menthe that fit so neatly into the crème-de-menthe-shaped hole I had painstakingly carved out in high school many moons before. Taking a deep tug, I let the minty-fresh beverage warm my insides while I thought about my situation.

I can't let this go on any longer.

Nomia was up to no good. She had killed Marla and would

kill again. I was going to get to the bottom of it, even if it killed me, which—if I believed that skank's voice in my head—was a very real possibility.

Well, bring it on, bitch. This is my Village, my people—even if they think I'm a drunken looney. We have a history of eliminating psychotic bullies around these parts. If no one was going to believe me, well then, I sure as shit would handle it myself.

I drank to that.

A short rap sounded upon the door of Lieutenant William Dudingston's chamber.

"Enter," he called.

The door opened with a creak, and his midshipman, a short youth from the South of Wales named Roberts, stood there, pensive, his face drained of color, unable to make eye contact with his superior.

The young man was not alone. Dudingston could make out the faint outline of another individual lurking in the small, dark passage.

The midshipman stepped forward, his eyes fixed on the floorboards.

Roberts' companion also entered the cabin.

Dudingston closed his ledger and laid his quill to rest on a small ceramic figurine of a mother and child. His ink-stained fingers flipped closed the lid of a treasure chest that sat between the ceramic mother and son, serving as a hidden ink well. Another gift from Dudingston's mother.

He kept his gaze on the individual but addressed Midshipman Roberts who looked as if he was close to fainting.

"What is the meaning of this?" he asked.

The youth cleared his throat.

"We was about our morning duties, sir, when we hears this call from below ship. When we looked, we saw a small craft moored just beside us. Master Talbot called down and asked the occupants of the dingy to state their business."

Roberts paused and stole a quick glance up at the person by his side.

Beside him, stooping under the low ceiling, stood a lady of means, tall and regal, dressed for travel. Her dress was a pale, ice blue, interspersed with lace-work that frothed about the hems making her neck and wrists appear as if they had burst forth from the foam of the sea. The woman's hair, which grazed the wooden planks above her, was coiffed high on top of her head in the latest style, elegant with a French influence, one small tendril of warm brown coiling its way around her neck. Beside her was a large satchel.

"We were hailed to throw a ladder down, and we refused, sir. Truly we did. But m'lady said she knows you, sir." Roberts paused once more, fidgeting with the hem of his waistcoat.

"Go on," urged Dudingston.

"Sir," the young man continued, "we never would have allowed her to board, but she, uh ..."

"For goodness' sake, spit it out, young man."

"She knew things about you, sir, and she knew things about the Brown seizure from a fortnight ago. Intimate things, sir."

The tension in Rhode Island had grown dense, like the humid air thickening the spring days. Locals all around Narragansett Bay claimed that they were being unjustly insulted, their trade interrupted by Dudingston's actions.

The rumor of a warrant for Dudingston's arrest was circulating the colony. He had angered the wrong merchants. The Browns and the Greenes, to name a few, had not been amused when Dudingston had seized their ships and then had both their goods and their vessels sent to Boston. Not an easy task to undo, once done.

But the letters sent to London made Dudingston's career shine. He could have cared less whether a few, bloated merchants had their britches up in knots. He was doing his job, and he was doing it well. It was all thanks to a certain informant.

Dudingston raised his gaze to the stooped woman, then looked back down at his desk. He straightened the ledger, his ink well, then his quill. When he looked up again, his face was composed, placid like still waters.

"You may leave us, Midshipman Roberts."

"Sir?"

"I will not repeat myself. Close the door behind you, and return to the deck. In ten minutes time, you are to return with Master Talbot and two other crew members. Have I made myself clear?"

"Indeed, sir," said Roberts as he hurried out the door.

William rose from his chair and placed both hands on his

desk. He leaned forward towards the woman and took in her finery, her elegantly arranged hair, then her satchel, which sat beside her. His inspection stopped at her feet, which were covered in fine satin. She was wearing shoes.

Keeping his hands on his desk, he looked into her gray eyes and asked, "What is it you think you're doing?"

"You said you would take me to London. I'm ready. The sooner we leave, the better."

The silence hung between them for several long moments. It spiraled in the air above the pair like a storm gathering strength, pulling into itself, seeking violent release.

He broke the quiet first. He laughed. It echoed—a loud, raucous guffaw—in the sparse cabin. Tears appeared in his eyes as the laughter flowed and flowed, pushing William back into his chair.

"London, is it?" He managed the words in between breaths, still laughing, clutching his sides. "You mean to sail with us to London, as my lady, I suppose?"

The young woman squared her shoulders as best as she could, then raised her chin slightly upwards. Keeping her gloved hands folded in front of her, she observed the lieutenant.

"I don't even know your name, and you think I will be taking you to London? I've never seen you wear shoes until this moment, and you think you have what it takes to be a proper wife of a Royal Navy officer. Oh, this is too rich. Too rich, indeed!"

A new fit of laughter bubbled from his lips, and he leaned back in his chair to release it towards the cabin ceiling. "Do you even know how to serve tea? Do you even know what tea is?"

The hilarity of the last question doubled the lieutenant over and brought tears to his eyes. He wheezed with mirth.

She waited for him to compose himself, never moving. Her jaw grew tighter and tighter with each moment that passed.

When he was through with his folly, the silence fell once more.

She broke the quiet with one word, "Nomia."

"Beg your pardon?"

"Nomia," she said. "It's my name."

"How unusual."

"Yes," she said. "It is."

They regarded one another for a moment longer. William didn't like the way she was looking at him. A chill crawled over his back, settling somewhere near the base of his skull.

"You will come to regret your decision, Lieutenant William Dudingston."

Much like the first time he had encountered her, he felt wrath boiling in his gut, a mixture of shame, embarrassment, and pure lust.

"Are you threatening me?"

She repulsed him, yet he wanted her. The familiar polar magnetism flared anew. He stood and slammed his fists down on the desk. He had meant to grab her, to take her one last time and prove to her who was in control. She was nothing more to him than something to be used and discarded, but before he moved, she was on him.

Her left hand grabbed him by the scalp and pulled his face

backwards while her right hand closed around his neck, pushing the flesh upwards into his jaw. He struggled to breathe and felt the nails of her fingers draw blood. His hands flew to her arms as he attempted to pull them away. She was so strong. It was as if all the times they had been together in the past she had been an actor in a play, hiding her true self, her true strength from him.

"You *will* regret your decision," she said placing her face close to his, so close he could see into her mouth. "Your life, your career, all your expectations, your dreams are all mine now, and I *will* do with them as I please."

He barely registered what she was saying. His head swam, and his fading conscious could only register the lack of oxygen and her teeth—her *teeth!* Sharp canines, each and every one of them. As she squeezed tighter and the world dimmed, he heard the familiar creak of his chamber door.

"Lieutenant, sir!"

His crew members burst into the room. It took the four of them to release the girl's grip on their commanding officer's throat. She screamed, and the sound was as unnatural as her teeth—a shrill screech that pierced their ears and shook the leaded glass in the small cabin window.

William was on his hands and knees, panting, trying to return air to his lungs as fast as he could. Nomia kicked and struck out at the sailors, tossing them like rag dolls against the walls of the cabin, smashing the lieutenant's desk, and sending white ceramic shards flying like shrapnel. She was vicious and wild, regardless of her fine clothing. The pale fabric disintegrated into shreds and tatters with each blow she landed.

In the end, the four sailors wound ropes around her frame, preventing her from striking out and inflicting any more damage to the cabin or crew. In the process, they had bloodied her lip and almost broken her left arm.

The *Gaspee* sailors were not without their own wounds. Master Talbot sported a black eye, while Midshipman Roberts held his ribs tenderly with his right arm, fearing breakage. The other two deckhands watched as their own severe wounds bloomed like night flowers, blue and black petals marring their faces and arms.

"What shall we do with her, sir?" asked Talbot.

Dudingston was on his feet once more, rubbing his neck with his left hand and straightening the buttons on his waistcoat with his right. He, too, had bruises spreading across his whiter-than-white neck. He would wear her handprint on his throat for another week.

He looked at Nomia with nothing but contempt. His desire for her had withered. She had emasculated him for the last time.

"Throw her overboard."

"Aye, Lieutenant."

The sailors carried the kicking and screeching girl to the upper deck. Looks of alarm spread like wildfire across the faces of the other crew members. They took in the injuries of their fellow crew mates, noticed the handprint forming on their commanding officer's neck, stared open-mouthed at the feral girl who cursed and screamed in a language unknown to any of them.

Without ceremony, she was dumped overboard. They all watched as she fell from the height of the *Gaspee*. With a loud splash, she entered the water and was swallowed whole by the waters of Narragansett Bay.

Nomia never surfaced.

Late in the evening on June 8, 1772, Captain Benjamin Lindsey of the *Hannah*, a small short run ship, entered Sabin's Tavern at 124 South Main Street in Providence. Lindsey was accompanied by the well-known, wealthy merchant John Brown and Brown's devoted sea captain, Abraham Whipple.

The trio settled into a corner of the tavern and ordered ale and bread, then hunkered down, deep in conversation. Before long, they were joined by nearly sixty men. Ale flowed freely, and the tenor of the crowd escalated to a frenzy.

"We should kill him!" shouted a man.

"It's high treason!" cried another.

"His reign of terror needs to end!"

"We should sink the ship!"

"Aye!" came the cry from many voices in angered unison.

"Good gentleman, I ask for silence!" came a voice. It was the strong, booming baritone of John Brown. He was well known by all in attendance and not one to shy away from public speaking.

Brown was respected, and his request was heeded.

"Thank you, good sirs. This is what is known. The HMS *Gaspee* has been run aground on Namquid Point, thanks to the crafty navigation of our good friend, Captain Lindsey! Hear, hear!"

A great cheer rose from the men, and many tankards clanked together as the crowd acknowledged Captain Lindsey's fortuitous act. Brown again motioned for quiet, and when the crowd finished its back-slapping and good-natured jeers towards Lindsey, everyone complied and returned their attention to Brown.

"Lieutenant Dudingston and his crew will be unable to release themselves until the tide returns in nine hours. I say opportunity has presented itself, good friends. Opportunity is asking us to look deep into our hearts and decide—are we men of action or are we men of compliance? Do we seek to be beaten into submission, taking these illegal search and seizures as if we deserve them and ignoring our God-given rights to feed our families and prosper in these here waters? I ask you, good sirs, are we men or are we dogs?"

"We are men!" came the cry of the crowd.

"All right, then!" answered John Brown. "We have a plan, good sirs!"

The crowd settled down, and as the anticipation of action crackled in the air like an electrical storm, all eyes were fixed on John Brown, who stood on a chair, allowing the moment to build.

"We have need of eight captains ..."

Brown's words were interrupted by sobbing. From the back

of the tavern, a young woman came forward with an older man by her side. She towered over her companion as if he were a child and she his parent. The way he cooed and stroked her hair suggested the opposite. Her unkempt hair straggled around her shoulders, and her dress looked more like a collection of fancy rags. Tattered and shredded, the garment hung on her slender frame threatening to expose her delicate white skin.

Her face looked as if it had been badly beaten, but the bruises and cuts scattered across her face like cracked and peeling paint could not mar her innate beauty.

The man looked to be in his late forties and wore the clothes of a fisherman or dock-worker. He stood with a slight hunch in his shoulders, as if years of bending towards the sea had warped his small frame.

"What says you, friend?" asked John Brown addressing the newcomer.

"Mr. Brown, sir," said the man. "I don't mean to interrupt your fine speech, but I think you need to know what I have witnessed."

"Continue," replied Brown. "Please."

"Well, sir," said the man, removing his hat from his head and turning it over and over again in his gnarled hands as he searched for the right words. The girl next to him clung to his side, burying her face in his shoulder. Turning to her, the man put his arm around the beaten girl and murmured something reassuring in her ear. She nodded, and he continued.

"You see, good sirs, I am a fisherman. My name is Brian Durum, and I hail from Bristol. I was on my way home, traveling up the Bay like I always do. I happened to spy the *Gaspee* at anchor near Prudence Island, close to where I live. I kept my distance, not wanting any troubles from the lieutenant and his men."

There was much murmuring. Brown and several others nodded. They knew the type of "troubles" Durum had been avoiding.

"Well, I heard a noise, a horrible noise, sir. Like a woman in distress. So I takes a look and happens to see the form of a body being hoisted over the side and dumped into the Bay like a bag of moldy potatoes."

Here Durum paused because the girl by his side began to cry and sob into his shoulder. He shushed her and patted her arm.

"It was she that had been dumped into the Bay, good sirs. I saw it with my own eyes." The man's face told the truth of his story. His leathery skin was tight around his wide eyes. He glanced around the tavern, daring anyone to refute his claim. The quiet was palpable as everyone digested the words laid forth by the fisherman.

Then the crowd erupted with cries of outrage. Ripples of concern and anger flowed throughout the room as if a large rock had been tossed into a calm lake.

"Let him speak!" cried Brown, and the crowd grew silent once more.

"I ... I ... uh ... " stammered Durum.

"Go on," urged Brown.

"Well, sirs," said Durum. "I have a daughter about her age, and if he had done to her what he did to this young lady ..."

Durum paused and drew the girl into a close, protective hold by his side. "Well, I'd burn the bastard in his bed!"

The crowd leaned in, their eyes wide, their minds whirring with the awful possibilities of what could happen to a young girl among men known to disregard good will and fairness, given the opportunity for self-gain.

"He ravaged me!" the girl cried. "Dudingston ordered his men to bring me to his cabin where he had his way with me, and then when it was over, he had me thrown into the sea! I will never be suitable for proper marriage now. My life is over!"

Here she leaned into Durum. Her body heaved up and down with the violence of her sorrow.

The crowd ate her words, devoured them. Knowledge of this atrocity fueled their need to serve justice with a firm hand. They were crazed with thoughts of revenge. The colonies had swallowed the king's tyranny, ingesting each bitter meal. Now they had reached their capacity. They needed to purge the poison, rid themselves of the bile that climbed up their throats.

"We should burn him!"

"Dudingston is vermin and should be treated as such!"

"Aye! Let's shoot him!"

All reasonable doubt was eliminated. All thoughts of abiding by the law and leaving the *Gaspee* to the tides was gone forever. There would be vengeance. There would be blood.

As the men formed teams to man the longboats and discussed the specifics of navigating the Bay at night, the girl and Durum faded out into the darkness. They walked away from the noise of the tavern, then stopped a few yards down the cobbled street. She leaned over and kissed Durum on the forehead, then stroked his face. He asked her again to allow him to escort her to her family there in Providence. She shook her head and smiled.

"No," she said. "I will be fine. What more could possibly be taken from me?"

He didn't want to part from her. It seemed wrong to abandon her now. But she insisted, assuring him that her family's home was just up the hill on the newly named Benefit Street, a short walk from the tavern. He finally acquiesced, squeezed her arm gently, then headed back to the mouth of the Providence River where his small fishing vessel was moored, awaiting his return.

The girl watched him go, waving to him when he turned to see her still standing there. When he was gone, she strolled towards the splendor of Benefit, a large smile on her face as she listened to the angry mob pouring forth from Sabin's Tavern downhill from where she had stood.

Reaching into the confines of her bodice, she pulled out a small leather bag fastened to her person with a strong cord. Drawing the bag open with one hand, the girl reached inside with the other and produced a lock of a man's hair.

The girl stared at it for some time, then smiled. Heading towards the prestigious homes along Benefit, she tossed the hair into the gutter.

She whistled as she walked away.

As dawn split the horizon on the morning of June 9, 1772, Rhode Islanders surrounded the HMS *Gaspee* with torches. The ship sat, still handicapped by the tide, in the waters of Narragansett Bay, not far from Pawtuxet Village.

Its commanding officer, Lieutenant William Dudingston, dressed only in a shirt and blanket, was taken in by a local resident of the Village who was loyal to His Majesty King George III. In the safety of the loyalist's home, Dudingston received care for his wounds. A bullet had passed through his left arm, breaking it, and had then come to rest in the confines of his groin.

Dudingston's crew had been spared, and they huddled in groups on the shore, lamenting their losses, wondering what would become of them. Their leader, the lieutenant, pondered the same. He lay on a bed, bleeding, ashamed, near death. He watched as the morning sunlight glowed all the brighter as his ship—his king's ship—was devoured by the colonists' flames until it sank, defeated and charred, into the waters of the Bay.

As it disappeared beneath the surface with a loud hiss, a woman's laughter could be heard from somewhere across the crimson-orange waves. The sound chilled all who heard it. No one knew where it came from, but all hoped they would never hear it again. From within the walls of the guest room where he lay bleeding, William heard the laughter.

He wept at the sound.

5

When I awoke, my head was thicker than a bale of hay after a rainstorm. My neck was stuck in a right-facing position, and I was still in my chair in the study.

Sunlight streamed in from the nearby window, blinding me. I lifted my arm to my eyes like a vampire, blocking the burning effects of the obnoxiously bright rays. The sunlight was bouncing off the neighbors' windows and illuminating the back wall of my study, heralding mid-morning.

I had slept almost fifteen hours. After I had finished my crème de menthe the previous morning, I had dug around and found a few other hidden, liquid gems. I polished them off as well. I had myself a nice party-of-one. A pity party. I ignored everyone, including (and most especially) Paddy.

Several times he had come a knock, knock, knocking on my study door, but I had refused to let him in. I was going to stay in there and catch up on all my DVRed reality television while

I tried to forget him and all the wretchedness of the past few weeks.

Then I passed out.

As the sunlight tried to burn a hole in my retinas, I stood and kicked the leaking crème de menthe bottle with my right foot. My left foot landed in a squishy disgusting puddle. Looking down, I saw a semi-dry, green liquid smear on the carpet. My sock was sticky, and it sounded like Velcro when I lifted it from the ruined floor covering.

"Fucking great," I mumbled.

The smell of breakfast wafted up the stairs, beckoning me from below. The stomach rules the heart. My husband had been a dick the day before. Perhaps I could overlook it. That dick makes a mean breakfast sandwich.

I took another step, and the sonic boom of my sock hitting the carpet reverberated through my skull like a gong. I put my hand to my temple, hoping to stop the ringing. If I held two of my fingers to just the right spot, the pain subsided. But as soon as I took the fingers away—disaster.

I limped to the door with my sticky, minty foot, my fingers against my temple, and my dry tongue feeling like I'd licked a cat's ass. I have no idea why I punish myself the way I do.

Useless Irish blood. Nothing in there but whiskey, tobacco, and rational-thought-killing adrenaline. It certainly fueled my follies.

As my grandfather always said, *If it weren't for the whiskey, the Irish would have ruled the world.*

Yes, but we are fun people. *Most* of us.

Wait a second. Catherine and Paddy do *not* fall into the fun category. That's not fair. Why should I get all the crazy juice?

Maybe they were happier people before poor Uncle Aiden passed away. I wasn't really in the picture then. Maybe, just maybe, Paddy and Aunt Catherine were the life of the party back then. I laughed out loud. Then I howled from the pain.

As I descended the staircase to the kitchen, I could hear Mrs. Good Times herself, Aunt C, squawking to Paddy about something. As I moved closer, the words became clearer.

"Will Sleeping Beauty grace us with her presence this morning, Paddy?"

Bitch.

"I have no idea," answered Paddy. "Why don't you make up a nice tray and go gently wake her? She'd love that, especially after the night she had."

"Out painting the town red, I suppose?"

"No, not quite. She had a little pity party for herself last night. She thinks I don't know about her little biblio-stash of liquor. She saves it for especially rough events."

Damn him! Is a girl not allowed to have any secrets? Where has the mystique gone in our marriage?

"What happened now?"

"Oh, she claims she saw something in the river the night before last. Evie went out for a walk in the reservation. The next morning she went on and on about some girl arguing with her man and then swimming in Pawtuxet Cove. Then she started spinning some yarn about a mythical sea creature that almost ate the swimming girl."

"But it's been so cold. That can't be right."

"Evie was so frantic, I didn't get into the logistics of November swimming during a New England cold snap."

"Wait. What was Evie doing in the woods at night?" Then she added in a whisper that was not a whisper, "Was she drinking before she went out into the woods?"

"Not exactly," replied Paddy. "We had been discussing the disappearance of Marla, our old neighbor. You remember her, don't you?"

"Oh yes, lovely girl." It sounded like Catherine was sipping tea. A teacup hit a saucer, and she continued. "Such a tragedy. Her daughters attended my school."

"True enough. Her poor husband ..." said Paddy. "You know, it's odd. I didn't think Evie was all that fond of Marla, but when I mentioned how Nomia, that new woman in the Village, was questioned, Evie acted very strange, then ducked out for a walk."

"And a *sea creature*!" laughed Aunt Catherine. "Really, now. Well, go on, let's have us a good laugh. How did she describe it?"

"Oh, I don't know ..."

"Come on, man!" urged Catherine. "Did it have claws? Scales?"

Savannah started cooing. Paddy murmured something soothing and sweet in return.

"Patrick," said Catherine. "Seriously now, this is hilarious! Do tell me, did Evie mention if the sea-girl had a tail?"

There was a pause as the teakettle whistled, and then silence as one of them removed the kettle from the burner.

"Well, now that you mention it," replied Paddy, "I'm not quite sure if Evie mentioned that it was a 'she' or not, and I don't remember if a tail was brought to my attention, but really, a *sea monster*?"

Catherine emitted, a nervous hiccuping laugh, and then she said, "Oh forgive an old woman for her silly questions. Just looking for some fodder. I just love to tell my friends about Evie's latest shenanigans."

Paddy sighed and said, "I know my bride is less than perfect, but do you think, every now and then, you could cut her a little slack?"

I had heard enough. I stormed down the stairs and burst into the kitchen. Two of the McFagans were sitting, drinking tea while the third squealed with delight when she saw me in the doorway. I went to my baby girl and rubbed my nose against hers.

"At least someone is on my side, yes, you are!" I said in my baby-talk voice, and then I turned on *them*.

"You know what you need, Catherine?"

She never made eye contact. Never. She picked a spot somewhere to the left of my head on the wall behind me and focused on it. When she spoke, she spoke to the spot, not to me. It had been this way since day one.

"*Evie*," warned Paddy.

"Leave it, Paddy," I spat with as much ice as I could muster, and then I put on my best Irish accent and said, "Listen up, Catherine, you're in need of a right good buggerin'. But first, the poor bastard would need to remove the stick that is so firmly up your ..."

Paddy stood, knocking the chair over behind him, and grabbed my arm before I could finish. Catherine slammed her teacup down and stood as well. "I will not be spoken to in such a manner. You need to clean up your filthy habits and grow up, Evelyn. You are an absolute disgrace!"

Oh, the full name. I was in for it. Well, screw her. I was done with her bullshit.

Catherine made her way to the door and took her coat from the peg on the wall.

"Well, at least *my* husband didn't go to sleep and die just so he wouldn't have to spend another goddamn minute with me!" I yelled at her retreating back.

Catherine froze, and the world slowed down. My words hung there like rotting meat. There was nothing I could do to remove the newly formed foulness in the air.

She turned slowly, her bottom lip trembling. For the first time ever, she looked me directly in the eyes. Her own ice-blue eyes burned with fury and grief, and I wished she would go back to looking at the spot behind my head so I could avoid her stare.

She never said a word. She opened the door, and I listened to her descend the stairs to the first floor. I turned to Paddy. He shook his head and looked away from me, sadness hanging on him like an ill-fitting shirt.

The door to the outside world opened and then closed. I would have slammed it. It was worse that she didn't. A heaviness sat on my chest. It was familiar and unwanted. I had fucked up. Again.

"You went too far, Evie," was all Paddy said as he collected

Savannah and headed into the living room, leaving me in the kitchen alone.

"Yeah," I said to no one. "I did." I slumped into a chair and stuffed a breakfast sandwich into my mouth.

It didn't taste as good as it should have.

Paddy refused to speak to me. I didn't really blame him. I decided to leave with Savannah and allow him some time alone to work—something I hadn't done in a while. I had meant to call the Rileys two weeks ago about poor old Seamus, but it turned out that Paddy had done it for me. I had a nasty habit of avoiding things I didn't want to do and leaving Paddy to pick up the slack.

Go on—*judge away*. Everyone else does.

I decided to go to my happy place, The Pawtuxet Café and Charcuterie—or Heart Attack Heaven, as Paddy so fondly called it. All the right things, coffee and meat, in one convenient location. It was just what I needed—caffeine and salty, artery-hardening meats.

When the place opened, the locals scoffed at the ridiculous notion of fancy meats and fancy coffee. I think most of their reservations and scorn stemmed from the closing of a neighborhood standard. The previous coffee shop had been owned by a man who had never really wanted to own a coffee shop. He just wanted a place where he could talk to people. Now he's a real estate agent and, from what I've heard, a damned good one.

This new shop opened shortly after the failure of yet another Thai restaurant. There were three in the Village—how many frickin' Thai places could one half mile handle, for Christ's sake?

Heart Attack Heaven was always packed. It had late hours and open mic on Wednesday nights. I frequented its warm, inviting interior often. It was a place where I could go and center my chi over some delicious meats, cheeses, olives, and most importantly, expertly brewed coffee.

I opened the old, wooden door and found solace in the tinkle of the little bell hanging over the threshold. I needed some solace.

"Evie! Savannah!"

Our fan club was assembled, enjoying cappuccinos and *The Pursuit of Prosciutto* plate, one of my personal favorites. The men in our fan club are a jovial, elderly group, full of piss and vinegar. Tony, Giovanni, Joe, and Angelo had been greeting me almost every morning since Heart Attack Heaven had opened five years before.

Once Savannah arrived, she took center stage. They adored her. Paddy believed they were all trying to stay in my good graces so I would give their families a discount in a few years, but I know they're fans of my sterling charm and rapier wit.

"Good morning, old bags!"

I looked forward to a nice heated discussion, coffee, and possibly a *Salami Mommy* plate. Savannah loved to gnaw on salami. I motioned to the tattooed barista, who nodded and smiled. I felt better already.

"Evie!" Giovanni stood, quicker than his bad hip would allow, and he almost fell. He recovered with the help of Joe's shaky, but strong hand. "So good to see you and my little chic-ki-enella! Sit, sit, sit. Tony, move your dusty ass over. Let the girls sit down."

Tony put his arm around me, and I did my best to not cry into his corduroy jacket that smelled warmly of too much after-shave and cedar chips.

"There, there. Where's that iron bitch we know and love? What's wrong, dear?"

I choked, remembering all that had transpired in the previous few hours, days, weeks. It took a cup of water, a few olives, and a nibble of some salty prosciutto to calm my nerves.

What should I tell them? I couldn't tell them everything. I would sound crazy, and I didn't want them to think I was *totally* insane. So instead of telling them the strange and sordid tale that had become my life, I told them Paddy was leaving me for a younger woman.

You wanted me to tell them the truth? Come on.

There was no way I was going to tell them the truth. And besides, I was under pressure. It just kind of came out of my mouth. It's not like I could reel it back in once it had been released. The lie flopped around on the table, staring at me with its one dead eye. I felt nauseous, but hey, shit happens.

"What did Catherine say? She must be sick over all this." Tony had a sweet tooth for Aunt Catherine. He had asked her out a number of times, but she always turned him down. He was still determined.

That fiery minx can't resist this dusty ass forever!

I felt the blood boil in my veins at the very mention of her stupid name. I paused and imagined a large piano landing on her perfectly coiffed head. It made me feel a little better.

"You know she hates me. Of course she's taking her big fat nephew's side," I said, toying with an olive pit.

"She doesn't hate you," said Joe. "She just thinks you're an unfit mother. You know, like when you hit the sauce a little too hard. We understand, Evie. Dealing with us and the rest of the dead, old bags can be an enormous undertaking ..."

Angelo burst into fits of laughter.

"What? What are you laughing at, you old fart? You're gonna take a heart attack."

I smiled. I couldn't help it. That old Rhode Island saying always cracked me up.

"You said, *undertaking.*" Angelo giggled like a little girl.

"Yeah, so what? What's so funny, old man?" asked Giovanni.

"*Undertaking* ... to Evie," he gasped and then guffawed even louder. His outburst was followed by a long, phlegmy coughing fit. "She's an *undertaker*, for Pete's sake!" His laughter turned into a wheeze, and he turned red.

You had to laugh at him, or with him. It wasn't the pun that was so funny. It was the way he laughed. It was infectious. We all joined him, and for a moment, I felt a tiny bit better.

"Now seriously, Evie, why would Paddy ever want to leave you?" asked Joe.

Well, he didn't. His nut-job of an aunt hates me. I think this new neighborhood bitch killed another neighborhood bitch, and, oh yeah, I think I saw a sea monster in the Pawtuxet River the other night.

"I don't know," I sighed and stared at the table.

Feeling like something was missing, I looked up at the barista and pointed to my empty spot at the table. Being a regular, that meant, *I would like a large Americano in a generous mug with a biscotto on the side, please. Oh, and if you just so happen to accidentally put two biscotti there by accident, well, your tip just increased.*

"It's a shame that Aunt Catherine isn't being more supportive," said Tony. "After losing her husband so tragically, she should be more understanding."

"What are you talking about? Uncle Aiden died in his sleep. I thought he died peacefully."

"Aw, you've gone and said too much, Tony," said Giovanni.

"No, I didn't," said Tony. "Evie's husband is walking out on her. She has a right to know about her husband's shady family history."

"Oh jeez," said Angelo as he threw up his hands. "Now you've done it. You can kiss a date with Catherine good-bye, my friend. Loose lips sink ships, and you might as well be strapped to the anchor headed straight for the sandy bottom."

"Never mind them, Evie," said Tony as he edged closer to me. "So, you were told Aiden died in his sleep. That's a bunch of crap."

I nodded, wide-eyed, and grabbed another olive to stuff in

my face. This was getting good. Tony looked left, and then he looked right. He leaned in, real close, and whispered in a whisper that was not a whisper at all, "He was killed."

"What?" I almost choked on my olive.

Savannah cooed with delight and clapped her hands. Tony nodded smugly, like the cat that had just eaten the canary. He was full of secrets, and he was bursting to tell.

"Oh boy, here we go," said Giovanni. "You're really going to spin this tale, aren't you? He wasn't killed, you old fool."

"Yes. He. Was." Tony made a point to tap the table with every word. "He was killed, and his body was never found." He sat back and crossed his arms across his shrunken chest. His mouth was one straight line of self-righteousness.

"And next you'll start spouting old tales about the missing McFagan bodies, how they were never buried, how the crypt is empty. Yada, yada, yada." Giovanni threw both his hands and his eyes towards the ceiling in an over-exasperated gesture of drama. "Rumors, all of it. Useless rumors told by foolish old men to waste time."

Angelo took out a newspaper and shook it so loudly the neighboring table gave him an annoyed glare. He feigned reading while Joe preoccupied himself with some sharp cheese on his plate.

"Bah, I'm not getting into the crypt tale right now. We're talking about how Aiden was killed. That's right, I said *killed*." Tony nodded knowingly and then leaned in close, his voice a hoarse whisper. "He had been fishing in the Bay. It was the night of Catherine's big dance recital, and Aiden was noticeably *not* there. My sweet Lila, rest her dear soul, thought he might have had a missy on the side."

"Was she killed, too?" I asked with a sassy bend to my eyebrow.

He scowled at my proposal and waved my suggestion away with a gnarled, vein-bulging hand. "No, no, no. Stop interrupting."

Joe rolled his eyes and reached out for Savannah. She launched herself into his open arms.

"Continue," I said to Tony and handed a napkin to Joe. Savannah had snatched one of his biscotti and was drooling all over his arm. He didn't seem to mind.

"So, he had been out fishing. It was right around the time Catherine's aunt had died. He went out into the Bay ..." Here he paused for effect, leaned in again, and made eye contact with each and every one of us who was paying attention to his drama, "... and he never came back."

I looked at Tony, expectantly, waiting for him to continue. "That's it?"

Tony nodded a long time, dragging out the attention. "That's it."

All the old men looked at each other, unease crawling all over their wrinkled faces. I didn't get it. Something was missing from the equation. Why had Aunt Catherine and Paddy told me Uncle Aiden had died in his sleep? Wait. Did Paddy know about this malarkey? Or was he keeping secrets, too?

"Well," I said. "Okay then." My coffee was finished, and I really needed to get out of there. "I guess I need to, uh, go home and throw Paddy's clothes all over the lawn, or something like that."

"Are you sure he's messing around, Evie?" asked Joe. "I mean, really sure? It's just so … unexpected."

I considered his words as I glanced at the worn lines of his face. I thought of road maps and dead ends. I thought of journeys taken, journeys forced upon us, and journeys that did not end up back at home—with the ones you love. Marla had not made it home to her loved ones. Neither had Aiden.

My gaze fell into my lap, and I looked at the lines on my own folded hands. I thought of my own journey. "I'm not sure about anything anymore," I muttered.

That, at least, was the truth.

Rhodes on the Pawtuxet
Ballroom and Casino
Pawtuxet Village, Rhode Island
June 21, 1898
5:32 PM

The veil of anticipation, the promise of adventure, hung thick like humidity in the evening air, while the sun made its slow and steady descent, setting fire to the horizon, welcoming the onset of summer's first eve.

Poised by the parlor window, Sarah Potter filled her lungs with the sweetness of the gloaming. Her shoulders relaxed, and she exhaled slowly while dabbing at the relentless perspiration at her hairline. The entire weight of her unshorn hair, piled high on top of her head in the popular Gibson Girl style, bore down heavily on her pale, slender neck. Although her dress was silk, it did little to allow the heat radiating from her body to escape into the gathering night.

Sarah's gown was the very latest in high fashion, and it had come to her by way of Paris. Cream white, with just a hint of color in the foam-like lace layered over its rich, silk base, the gown was cut in such a way that delighted Sarah immensely. Her ivory-white chest was exposed, emphasizing the fullness of her youthful breasts. Sarah wiped her brow again and gave a silent thanks for the decline of high pouf sleeves. The newest sleeve style was shorter, with lace trim flowing just above the elbow. These were daring times, times in which a woman could expose more and more skin to her suitor.

This promise of exposure had sold the dress.

Sarah Potter, at age sixteen, had been introduced to society one year past. Since then, she had sifted through the lot of prospective suitors whose surnames were appropriate for the likes of a Potter. And find a suitor, she had.

Byron Greene.

Tall, lithe, handsome, Byron was an aggressive compilation of sharp angles in a well-tailored suit. He had everything her parents wanted—wealth, power, good breeding. And he was easy on the eyes. The moment Sarah saw Byron, she had felt a foreboding energy in places she dare not acknowledge.

She was a young woman, a ripe and beautiful one, ready to experience the world and its pleasures, as long as those experiences fell into the categories of good taste and decorum. It seemed ironic, this dichotomy of raw natural urges intermingled with what was expected of a woman of her age and respected stature.

She was a Potter. There were certain rules for Potters—rules written into her genetic code long before she graced the earth. Potters were meant to court and marry other families who shared their higher, wealthier status. The Hoxsies, the

Aldrichs, the Browns, and—most importantly—the Greenes fit this mold.

Byron Greene was a perfect fit. Their immediate attraction to one another was a force of nature. Whenever they were near each other, the air crackled. They kept their gazes straight ahead, sneaking glances only occasionally, as they attempted to deny the magnetism between them.

It was a heavy, palpable courtship, an inferno that gathered more and more heat as it all but devoured itself. Their respect for one another's decency, however, was a mirage. The two played a role for all who viewed their courtship, an act in which these two youths pretended to know nothing of the carnal ways of the world. Beyond offering the customary arm of a gentleman as they walked side-by-side, the pair had not moved past the slightest of accidental touches.

It had not escaped Sarah's notice when Byron's gaze had lingered on certain areas of her body. However, he had never once ventured to take her hand in his. She found his restraint intoxicating. He found her purity addictive and maddening. It was more fuel for the fire.

Both Sarah and Byron held secrets. Both Sarah and Byron believed their secrets to be their own. This was far from true.

The Potter family and the Greene family had been made aware of the indelicacies of their respective children and had plotted and schemed long before Sarah ever *discovered* Byron. Once the two were married and no longer the responsibility of their elders, this orchestrated union would solve a great many problems of decorum on behalf of both families.

Sarah, for all her properness and good manners, had a penchant for older working class men. She believed, like a young fool, that her indiscretions with the family's groomsman had gone unnoticed. She assumed that his sudden disappearance had everything to do with his sick grandmother in Boston and was in no way connected to her mother's newfound, icy demeanor.

Byron, on the other hand, as a man, was given more leeway when it came to certain unmentionable proclivities. But he, too, foolishly believed his visits to the local tavern had been seen only as *visits to the local tavern*, where one goes for a beverage and good conversation with other males.

Byron had no idea that his father had sent spies to follow him on these fortnightly visits. Byron also had no idea that these spies had returned to his father with explicit details of Byron's exploits, specifically those with a certain dark-haired beauty known to haunt the back alleyways near his favorite tavern.

This year, the summer solstice fell on a Saturday. To celebrate the longest day of the year and the opening of the summer season in historic Pawtuxet, Rhode Island, the Rhodes on the Pawtuxet Ballroom and Casino was holding a gala event in the brand new ballroom that overlooked the mighty waters of the Pawtuxet River. Featured events would include dancing, feasting, strolling, and even canoeing on the river, compliments of the extended daylight.

People from all over Rhode Island would make their way to the former seaport, now a booming textile town, to make merriment. Sarah and Byron would be in attendance.

Byron arrived at Sarah's home to find her composed and

ready. After exchanging the appropriate pleasantries with her mother, the two were on their way to the gala.

They strolled through the crowd, nodding to the members of society whom they recognized, receiving nods in return. They sipped on Pimm's Cup cocktails—a delicious blending of fruit and gin which had been chosen to pair with the raw, local oysters. Both the drinks and the aquatic delicacies slipped down the pair's throats in a most delightful, indecent manner.

The sunlight was due to linger until well past eight in the evening. The couple danced, laughed, and made the rounds of appropriate conversations with the expected individuals. The heat did not subside much, even after the sun had made its final descent. Earlier, several women had left the event after a few entertaining fainting spells. But once the sun set, many partygoers were hesitant to leave and so had sought privacy in the gazebo, under the nearby trees, or at the small tables and chairs designed to encourage polite conversation.

Some had wandered to the edge of the river where the air did indeed feel cooler, less stagnant. Fireflies began their dance in the rushes and weeds across the water giving the evening an aura of magic and enchantment. The crickets sang their violin songs, birds bid their farewells to loved ones, humidity bugs hummed their steady vibrations. In the fading light, tiny white bugs darted like fairies above the water's surface and were occasionally gobbled up by fish.

Lanterns were lit along the edge of the river, and several brave souls had ventured out into the semidarkness in canoes, eager to explore the banks of the Pawtuxet.

"Shall we go exploring, Ms. Potter?" asked Byron with a devilish smirk on his chiseled face.

Sarah glanced down at her feet, taking in the expanse of fine metal beadwork that encompassed her gown. She thought of what her mother would say if she found out her daughter had been in a canoe in such a gown, a gown that cost more than several months' wages for three of their servants. Sarah raised her blue eyes to Byron's, a coy smile spreading across her face.

"Yes, Mr. Greene," she replied. "I think I would rather enjoy seeing the inside of a canoe with you." She even risked a little wink at the end of her reply.

Byron received the wink and stood still, assessing his companion for motives certainly not present in such a fine young lady with such fine breeding.

"Is something amiss?" quipped Sarah as she made her way past Byron towards the dock. "I didn't think I was unclear with my intentions."

Byron let his exhale pass slowly through his lips and glanced around. No one seemed to be paying any attention to the two of them. Most of the partygoers were engaged in hushed conversation.

As he made his way down to the dock to join Sarah, Byron spied a fellow he recognized from school, engrossed in a close conversation with a fetching young woman. He thought the chap's name was Edward.

The long tendrils of a delicate willow tree obscured most of Edward's companion, but the slender branches did nothing to hide the placement of Edward's hands. One was on the tree above the girl's head, while the other disappeared into the confines of her silken gown.

Byron looked away with a smirk. He joined Sarah on the dock. After a quick set of instructions on the finer points of canoe mastery from the dock-boy, they headed off towards the mouth of the river where it joined Narragansett Bay.

The pair passed under a bridge after carefully navigating around the beginnings of a dam. The river would soon be slowed and allowed to swell, but there was still enough room to slip into the open waters of Pawtuxet Cove and, beyond that, Narragansett Bay.

As they left the river behind, the brackish mix of river water and seawater filled their nostrils with its sharp, tannic odor. The smell was clean, yet mischievous—a mingling of two entirely different fluids as they intertwined and dissolved into one another. Lanterns hung from suspended poles at both the rear and the front of their little craft, illuminating where they were headed and where they had been.

Sarah let her hand trail in the cool water, her face softly framed by the amber light. Several small fish, attracted by the light, followed them and nipped at her fingertips. As they made their way through the cove, she leaned back towards Byron and sighed. The pleasant, self-satisfied sound put her suitor at ease as he paddled.

Her fair head was close to his lap, a point of interest that he tried but failed to put from his mind. On he paddled into the ever-darkening night. The last vestiges of purples, pinks, and warm oranges crisscrossed low on the horizon, as the ink-black darkness pressed down from above.

"It really is a glorious evening, wouldn't you say?" asked Byron in an attempt to distract himself from just how close she was to him. He could feel the heat coming off her golden tresses, and he fought the urge to slide his hand down the front of her bodice.

"Hmmmm," she murmured as she nestled closer into his inner thigh.

Byron's eyes grew wide with alarm, and he struggled to remember how many Pimm's Cups they had each consumed.

The sun was completely gone now as the lantern-lit canoe floated along, a small craft with small lights in the wide, dark expanse of the Bay. Byron glanced around in the darkness. He could almost discern the lights from the houses far off on the banks to his right and his left. They seemed distant and removed from the little world he had right in front of him.

He looked down into his lap and observed Sarah. She had closed her eyes, and a delicious smile spread across her face, stretching her full, red lips. Byron removed the canoe paddle from the water and placed it in the small space behind him. His passenger stirred and stretched her arms over her head, allowing them to rest on Byron's thighs.

Perhaps she was sleeping, perhaps not.

Byron reached down, his hand hovering just above the edge of the bodice on her chest. He held his breath and let his fingers graze across the whiteness of her skin. She sighed. It encouraged his hand.

Before long they were beyond the stage of light, cautious touches. They were adrift, alone at sea with the stars as their only witnesses. Their passion blinded them to the outside world, and the darkness shielded them from the rules of propriety. They took no notice when the rocking of their small vessel increased, thinking their own actions had made it sway in such a violent manner.

They also attributed the loss of one of their lanterns to their own vigorous, amorous exploits. The pair paused to laugh at their folly, and then returned to one another's embrace.

Byron squealed like a young girl, causing fits of laughter to burst forth from a partially clothed Sarah.

"Why did you shriek?" she asked through her giggles. Sarah's hair had come undone and spilled over her shoulders as she lay in the bottom of the canoe. Byron grinned sheepishly, a false shyness that Sarah found delightful.

"It tickled when you touched the back of my thigh. It surprised me," he said and returned to nuzzling her neck.

Sarah laughed a small, nervous laugh.

"I didn't touch the back of your thigh," she said, pushing him away in an attempt to see his face.

"Yes, you did," he said with a laugh and then returned his chin to her neck.

Sarah gave in to the warmth of his kisses, but something about their encounter had changed, like a cooling in the night air, a subtle thing, different in a small but noticeable way. She closed her bodice around her exposed breasts, and Byron stopped his kisses and leaned back.

"What is it?" he asked.

She gazed up at him. His eyes were filled with concern, a

gesture that made him even more enticing. She let go of the warning that was crawling into her psyche and with one hand reached for him, drawing his lips to hers. He leaned in and returned her kiss with more fervor than before, sliding his hand up and under her dress near her warm thighs. She clutched his hair tight, her other hand tangled in her bodice.

Byron pulled back once more and looked at Sarah. She withdrew her hand from the back of his neck, pulling it to her chest alongside her other hand. His eyes grew large.

"What is it?" she whispered, her own eyes widening.

"Your hands," he said with a slight tremor in his voice. "I can see them both."

One of the corners of Sarah's mouth drew up into a mocking smile.

"Yes," she murmured and reached up to play with his hair with one hand, while pulling her bodice open with the other. "You can see more than my hands."

But he didn't move, and the look of alarm didn't subside.

"Stop your foolery, Byron." Her voice rose an octave higher.

Byron shifted to his left and when he did, Sarah stopped breathing. Her gaze fixed behind Byron.

They were not alone in the canoe. Byron knew without turning his head. There was someone behind him. He could tell from Sarah's gaze, and he could now feel another presence leaning on him from behind.

He could feel bare breasts pressing into his back, and hands, like cautious snakes, were winding their way around his torso, caressing his bare chest.

It was a lot for a man to swallow—the intensity of a woman beneath him and an unknown woman behind him. The erotic intrigue combined with sheer terror froze Byron in place.

Sarah was breathing heavily. Perhaps she, too, was intrigued and even repulsed somewhat by the realization of a third party on board, but her eyes never left the woman's face as she lay there with one of her hands still in Byron's hair, the other clutching the silken fabric below her own bare breasts.

Byron turned his head to see the face of this new entity. When his eyes met hers, recognition spread like blood from an open wound. He knew her.

"Hello, Byron," she purred.

She was naked and dripping with seawater. Her hair was wild and dark, her body long and lean. Sarah stared at her, open-mouthed, with both fear and wonder. The new woman's skin almost glowed, as if it had a light source of its own just beneath the pearly white surface.

"You know this woman?" Sarah squeaked as she gathered the bodice of her dress tighter over her nakedness, drawing away from Byron.

"What are you doing here? How did you get here? We are ... we're in the middle of the Bay," Byron stammered.

The woman slid her hand around Byron's legs and squeezed his inner thigh. He jumped at her touch.

"I was out for my nightly swim, and I heard a disturbance in the water. It sounded like little fishes struggling before being devoured by a hungry, larger fish," she said. The woman leaned back, toyed with a lock of her dark, wet hair, and then smiled.

Byron shivered. Sarah could not move nor could she stop herself from staring at the woman's breasts. She had never viewed another female naked before, had never seen another woman's bare chest.

The newcomer leaned forward again, into Byron. With one hand still buried between his thighs, her other arm reached forward, seeking and finding Sarah's leg. Sarah drew herself away from the strange woman's touch. But the woman was persistent as her fingers twined around Sarah's ankle. As Sarah looked on in horror, the woman began to caress her leg, her ministrations moving steadily upwards.

Byron was trapped between one naked and one partially naked woman. Part of him wanted, *willed* the events to play out to his advantage. Another part of him knew something was wrong.

"Calm yourself, Sarah," he said, deciding to explore *what if.* "She knows what she's doing. Don't you, Nomia?"

Byron turned his head and smiled at Nomia. She returned his grin and leaned closer, pressing her naked form tighter against Byron's bare back.

"Byron, what is the meaning of this? Get her out!" Sarah shrieked. She kicked, striking Byron in the chest with her bare foot, sending him crashing backwards onto Nomia.

The canoe rocked back and forth, splashing seawater into the air around them. The remaining lantern swayed from side to side, illuminating and then not illuminating Sarah, who was scrambling to her own end of the boat, as far away from the two other occupants as possible.

Nomia threw Byron off her, volleying him back towards

Sarah as if he were a seal being tossed by a shark. Once free of Byron, Nomia stood in the small craft, towering over the pair below her. She hissed down at them.

Sarah started screaming, but it wasn't a hysterical scream, more of a frightened warning of a scream, one born from confusion. Confusion makes one see strange things.

Nomia's hissing gave way to growling. Her pale, phosphorescent skin took on a dark green hue.

Was it the light?

Her veins bulged and pulsed as blood was pumped in a rapid succession down to her legs.

It must be the light …

The flesh on her body and face rippled, fluttered, and re-formed itself.

We drank too much. This isn't real.

The lantern had stopped swaying, and it fully illuminated Sarah as a white point of light in a dark craft. She stopped screaming and watched, riveted to the spectacle before her. Byron glanced at Sarah's face, then returned his gaze to the standing intruder.

Nomia's legs grew closer together, and the flesh on them merged and absorbed itself, transforming into a long, single appendage. Nomia's skin pulsed with her heart, each beat signifying a new change. Scales appeared, pushing their way out of the ever-darkening skin, overlapping one another, and shimmering in the dim light.

Her feet rippled and expanded into something new, strange, and singular. Like a flower petal unfolding, rolling outward from its center, a flat appendage of thick skin pushed out from the surface of Nomia's now conjoined feet.

Nomia threw her head back and laughed, emitting a deep, rich peal that changed in timber, grew even deeper, and finished as a growl. She flexed her hands, and webs appeared between her fingers. Each nail lengthened and formed into a talon.

Slits appeared, dividing the skin on her neck. There were eight of them in total, four on either side. As they flexed and opened, tiny hairs feathered each opening. A gasping noise emanated each and every time a slit unfurled.

Nomia's face grew tighter, more drawn. Deep hollows appeared beneath her cheekbones until they looked sharp enough to draw blood. As her facial skin contracted, her already overly large eyes widened and expanded, the pupils doubling in size, dwarfing the light gray irises.

And her teeth. Her lips had all but vanished, drawing away from her mouth, exposing the sharp, pointed canines of a skilled predator.

She rose up on what were once her legs, now ending in a large, flat fin on which she balanced before arching herself forward, slamming into Byron. Sarah screamed in terror, a shriek of mortality. As Nomia hit the side of the canoe, she rolled like an alligator turning with its prey. Byron was her prey. His cry cut short the moment he and Nomia hit the water with a resounding splash.

The black waters swallowed them both. The Bay folded over them, concealing them in its depths, and Sarah was left alone, screaming in the semi-darkness in the small canoe.

Before dawn, a fisherman left Pawtuxet Cove, something he had done every day for the previous fifteen years. He didn't think much of the canoe floating, drifting near Salter Grove until the craft shifted and twitched in the still waters. Thinking it was probably a drunken reveler from the Rhodes party the night before, he almost passed by it.

Let the rich sort out their own kind.

But he heard a mewling, a pathetic whimpering. Curiosity won him over. The fisherman pulled alongside the canoe and looked down into it.

Inside sat Sarah, her dress from Paris in tatters around her exposed body.

"He's gone. He's gone. He's gone. She was a beast, and she took him. He's gone," she muttered.

The fisherman could get nothing more from the girl, but he recognized her from the Village and saw her safely home.

The Potters kept the event from reaching the papers. Grateful to have their daughter back in one piece, despite her altered mental and emotional state, they paid the fisherman a handsome sum to keep his silence. He kept his word. The amount of money from the Potters was enough for him to relocate his small family to Baltimore, where the weather was better and the crabbing industry was burgeoning.

As for the Greenes, they suspected Sarah was somehow to blame for Byron's disappearance. They arrived on the Potters' doorstep, their metaphorical pitchforks and torches blazing. In a matter of moments, they knew something horrific had transpired in the waters of Narragansett Bay.

Sarah smelled terrible, refused to bathe, had gone so far as to throw things at her maid when the notion of a bath was suggested. Small, bloody, bald patches were scattered over Sarah's scalp, a manifestation of her new altered state. As the Greenes watched in horror, she pulled at her hair, tugging and jerking until it came out in thick, ragged clumps.

"She was a beast, and she took him. Down, down, down, down ..." Sarah mumbled.

"Who took him, Sarah dear? Who is this *she?*" pressed Mrs. Greene, tears forming in the corners of her eyes.

Sarah stared at Mrs. Greene, no sign of recognition on the unkempt girl's face. She stared at nothing until drool rolled from the corner of her mouth and dripped onto her white shift. Sarah looked down and watched the saliva darken on her lap.

"The girl's gone mad," said Mr. Greene.

Sarah stood and gazed around the room, her eyes vacant and distant. She looked at her parents, she looked at Byron's parents, then she looked out the front window and watched a seagull land on the porch rail. It sat there a moment and opened its wings wide, flapping them with a loud *whoosh, whoosh, whoosh!*

Sarah started screaming.

A search party was formed. The constable and every willing mariner scoured the Bay, but no signs of Byron Greene were ever found.

In the weeks and months that followed, Sarah became less coherent and more and more violent. She screamed in the middle of the night. When her maid or her parents burst into her room, sleep still clinging to their addled minds, they would find Sarah huddled in her closet, yammering about a dark-haired woman who had appeared in her room. But each time, after a careful inspection of the house and surrounding grounds, nothing was ever discovered. As time passed, they would awake to find Sarah squirreled away in a closet, rocking and muttering to herself as she pulled and tugged at what was left of her hair.

The Potters knew their once vibrant and vivacious daughter was gone forever. The fate of the girl left in their care was debated for weeks. A decision was made. Sarah would be sent to an institution in upstate Vermont.

She never did recover. She spent the rest of her days in a quiet, peaceful place far, far away from the sea.

Years passed, and the Potters left Pawtuxet Village. Their house was sold time and time again. Many decades later, a family moved into the Potter home, and a young girl explored the same closet where Sarah Potter had sought shelter so many years past. Sitting on the floor, the small girl ran her fingers along the back of the door.

A word was scratched along the bottom of the dark wood. It was a word she did not know.

It read, *NOMIA*.

7

McFagan & McFagan Funeral Home, Inc.
Pawtuxet Village, Rhode Island
December 21
6:46 PM

Thanksgiving had been icy, and I don't mean the weather. There was a crisp, frigid temperature in the room as Aunt Catherine served her perfect turkey. Paddy, Savannah, and I did our part. We looked on approvingly and pretended everything was peachy keen.

It was not.

Paddy and I had come to an agreement. I would avoid the subject of his aunt and long-gone uncle, and he would ignore my binge drinking. Catherine, meanwhile, acted like nothing had happened. She returned to *not* speaking to me when she spoke to me and was increasingly taking Savannah on little outings. She had even offered to take her overnight a few times. Fine with me.

I didn't want to hold up the lie of Paddy leaving me, so I avoided the coffee shop and my boys. Instead, I had been doing my homework, studying (*okay, snooping around*) Nomia and her husband, David.

After some well-placed inquiries at the post office (the women who work there are a limitless wealth of local gossip), I discovered the location of Nomia and David's home. Turns out, they had lived in the Village once before but on the Warwick side. It must have been their pre-Pearl years. That would explain why I had never seen them before.

Aunt Catherine had wanted to take Savannah on another overnight. Her Irish American Ladies Club was headed to see the nativity lights at LaSalette Shrine in Massachusetts, and she wanted to show Savannah off to her girlfriends. That left Paddy and me kid-free for the evening.

"Are you sure you don't want to come with me, Evie?" Paddy called to me from the hallway.

The local police department was having their Christmas party in Providence, and Detective Lyons had asked both of us to attend.

Turning back and forth, Paddy admired himself in the full-length hall mirror.

"I am one handsome devil," he said and gave his sweater a good tug. He straightened up, sucked in his gut, then smoothed out his hideous knitted Christmas monstrosity.

Aunt Catherine had taken up knitting five years before. This was her latest masterpiece. It was green with a red reindeer dancing across a field of tiny, white cotton pom-poms. He looked ridiculous.

I smiled at him in spite of my dark mood.

"Oh yes, you in that sweater? You practically scream, 'Hottie, rich, and single, ladies. The line forms right in front of the reindeer!'" I winked at him from the couch. "I would only cramp your style. You go on and have a good time without me. I'll be fine."

He turned and faced me. "Evie, are you sure? It pains me to know you'll be sitting here all by your lonesome."

"No really, Paddy. I'll be okay," I said. "I desperately need to watch all the shitty television I've recorded. And besides, I'm safer if I'm here and not in a bar. Wouldn't you agree?"

He pinched his lips together, forming a straight line with his mouth. "All right then," he said, sounding resigned to the state of the evening. "I'm off to be the belle of the ball!"

"Do tell Oliver I said hello," I said and turned on the television.

He smashed an enormous red Santa hat on his gigantic head, bent to give me a kiss on the cheek, then left. I waited to hear his car pull out before I turned off the TV and hopped off the sofa, springing into action.

Dressed all in black, I drove into the Village towards Nomia and David's house. I didn't have far to go. Their home was a short two blocks from the playground. I crept past their small cottage home, my eyes on the windows. All the lights were on.

Two windows faced the street, one on either side of a red door. The left window was bright but devoid of anything worth noting, while the other window was filled with an enormous white Christmas tree sparkling with blue lights. On my second pass, I thought I saw David walking past the empty window. On my sixth pass, I saw what I needed to see.

She was home.

Nomia's presence made the window look ten times brighter than the Christmas tree on the other side of the house. The light illuminated her slight form, making her look like a religious postcard. Her large gray eyes were raised to the night sky, and her dark hair framed her pale face.

She was still at the window on my seventh pass, glancing out into the cold night, braiding and unbraiding her chocolate-colored hair.

I spun around the block for the eighth time and guided my car into a parking space on the opposite side of the street. I was about sixty feet from their cottage. I killed the lights and put on my black winter cap.

Then I waited. Stakeouts are so fucking boring.

Nothing much happened for the first hour. Their Christmas lights twinkled, and no one returned to the windows again. To break the boredom, I had brought a thermos of coffee with a little something extra to keep the edge off the cold night. I unscrewed the top and poured the steamy liquid into the lid that served as a handy cup.

Then I sipped. I watched. I waited.

Two hours later, something smashed into one of the windows from the inside. I almost choked on my last cup of coffee when it happened. The window rattled but didn't break.

Then it happened again. It was hard for me to tell what was smashing into the windows, but after the third object hit, I realized the missiles were stuffed animals. But no child was throwing them. No child I knew could generate that kind of fuzzy bunny velocity.

I eased my window down and listened. Yelling. Loud yelling, as in the familiar tones of David and Nomia arguing at high decibels. But this time, I could not make out the nature of the argument.

I weighed my options. I could exit my car and creep up to the window. Or I could pull my vehicle forward and blatantly spy, out in the open, hoping their argument was so all-consuming that my presence would go unnoticed.

My decision was made for me. Nomia stormed out of the house, slamming the door behind her. The door reopened and David stood there, silhouetted by the warmth and indoor lighting of the house. He scowled at her as she retreated down the street towards the Village center. Then he went back into the house, only to return and throw what looked like heaps of women's clothing out into the snow.

Then he, too, slammed the door.

I waited a few minutes, then opened my car door and took off after Nomia on foot. It didn't take long to find her. I turned the corner to see her disappearing into a fancy Italian restaurant in the center of the Village. It was past dinnertime, so she wasn't heading in to load up on carbs. The restaurant is well known for its fancy bar with fancy drinks at fancy prices.

Trust me. I knew it well.

I also knew the bar across the street had a perfect view of the one and only entrance to the Italian restaurant, and it had reasonably priced drinks. Who was I to deny myself another drink while on my little stakeout?

There was a band playing at the bar when I walked in, which meant zero chance for conversation. Perfect.

I nodded to Katie, the bartender, and she poured my usual. Being a lush has its privileges, like not having to order or talk to anyone when you don't feel like it.

I nestled into the corner seat facing the large picture window and fixed my gaze on the restaurant across the street. Time passed. The band was horrible, but the drinks were not.

Somewhere around third-drink-o-clock, Nomia emerged from the restaurant. She was not alone.

A mid-twenties-looking guy had his arm around her waist. He was handsome in an I-work-in-a-coffee-shop-but-really-I'm-waiting-to-be-discovered-as-a-model kind of way. I watched as she threw her head back and laughed, throwing her arms around the young man who was staring at her as if she were the only female left on the planet and it was his job to repopulate. He had that goofy grin guys get when they've had too much to drink and the world is their playground.

He whispered something in her ear, and she laughed again. I couldn't hear it over the awkward wail of the ill-tuned singer ten feet away from me, but I shivered as I remembered the night I had heard her laugh by the bridge.

I watched as she whispered something in his ear. He stopped walking, and the dopiest smile spread across his face as he nodded vigorously. They crossed the street towards me and then turned and disappeared down a side street.

I threw two twenties on the bar and caught Katie's attention, pointing to the money. She gave me a wave and continued pulling a beer from the tap. I grabbed my coat and walked out the door.

The world was frostier than when I had gone into the bar, so I fished my hat and gloves out of my pocket and quickly put them on. Rubbing and blowing on my hands didn't help, but I did it anyway.

I went left and, using my jedi skills of deduction, turned left again once I heard ominous laughter heading towards the water. The pair turned left again, then right, then left.

They were headed for the Rhode Island Yacht Club around the corner, nestled in one of the Village's many inlets along Narragansett Bay. I wondered what on earth would draw them there. Maybe they were going to break into one of the boats and fool around. I didn't know, but I couldn't stop myself from trying to find out.

Sure as shit, they made their way to the docks and headed towards the few winter boats still moored in the frigid waters. I kept my distance and hid behind a dumpster.

The sounds of a giddy, drunken hook-up were in progress, and I was soon questioning why I was out so late at night, freezing my ass off, trailing some woman, hiding behind a dumpster.

The noise changed. I heard a splash and the screams of a man. I jumped out from behind the dumpster and started to run towards the docks. I heard her laughter and his screaming, and as I moved closer, the gurgling, splashing sounds of someone being held underwater.

I ran faster, my footsteps pounding on the wooden dock.

One lone, yellow streetlight near the boathouse guided my way. The rest of the light was ambient from the streetlights across Stillhouse Cove, some three hundred yards away from the isolated docks. Everything looked amber and sickly, mirroring the way my insides felt as the adrenaline in my body sloshed against the alcohol in my gut.

I turned left towards the struggle and stopped short. I was drunk. I had to be. This was not real.

In an empty boat slip, sandwiched between two large vessels, I saw the struggling pair. The guy's eyes bulged as he looked at me, pleading, his mouth open in a large "O." A wheeze whistled from the back of his esophagus.

I could not see Nomia, but I knew that another figure was in the water behind the young man. An arm was across his throat, and as I watched, another hand came out of the water, into the light, heading towards the guy's forehead.

That hand. It was human, and yet it was not. The fingers were long and slender, ending in sharp, curved fingernails. Skin filled the gaps between the fingers. Webs. I was seeing webbed fingers.

The hand crept up the man's face, caressing it. As it moved towards the hairline, it paused, then stroked the man's skin. He stopped squirming and his eyes, locked on mine, relaxed for just a second. A smile crossed his lips.

Everything's fine. I thought. *Well, everything except that webbed hand, but yeah, everything's fine.*

And then it wasn't. The webbed hand dug its nasty fingernails into the flesh of the man's forehead and spun his head in a counter-clockwise direction. I heard a gut-curdling crack, and he went limp.

As I watched in horror, his body slipped into the icy, dark

waters and disappeared. I stumbled backwards, and I saw the attacker.

It looked like Nomia, but it couldn't have been. She was naked and her hair fanned out behind her, coiling in the water like snakes. Her mouth looked different, menacing and dangerous. Then she smiled at me, and I saw that her teeth were filed into sharp points like shark teeth.

I recoiled at the sight and tripped over one of the many metal cleats protruding from the decking. My left leg splashed into the frigid waters, while the rest of my body lay awkwardly on the dock like an upended crab. My limbs flailed uselessly.

I screamed. She lunged at me, and I saw more of her frightening form. A giant tail, flat and paddle-shaped like a manatee's, rose out of the sea behind her and slapped down, propelling the Nomia-thing towards me. The collision of tail and water made a splash, soaking me with freezing water. The shock of it made me suck in a sharp breath, preventing me from screaming at the sight before me.

Her open maw, all teeth and tongue, raced towards my face. Frozen with fear, there was nothing I could do.

She latched onto my neck with her mouth and dragged me off the dock into the dark depths. She embraced me, and for a moment I felt calm, peaceful.

The calm ended the second she ripped the flesh from my neck with her teeth. I opened my mouth to scream and heard my bubbly cry echo in the water. The muted gurgle mixed with underwater laughter.

The dark liquid filled my nostrils, my ears, my eyes, and my open, screaming mouth. I was going down, and she was pulling me.

In the milliseconds before the heavy, liquid darkness encompassed me, I thought of my daughter and how wretched I've been at motherhood. I pictured my husband and, despite our strange relationship, realized how much I did truly love his freaky ass. And I suddenly regretted how poorly I had taken care of myself over the years. But mostly, I thought about how much I hated the bitch who was ending my life.

All these thoughts entered the encroaching dimness of my poor, oxygen-starved brain.

A bang like a gong ripped through the darkness, and the death grip on my body relaxed. Something else had a hold on me from above. I saw the surface getting closer.

Through half-lidded eyes, I looked up through the inky waters and could make out the diluted image of someone large and familiar pulling me from the depths and back up onto the dock.

And just like that, I vomited water and gasped for air, all at the same time.

Christ on toast, I was colder than a pile of penguin shit. But I was alive. I was alive!

"Paddy!" I gurgled and spat. "You saved me!"

He smiled at me with that big doughboy face of his.

And then I was back in the water. That fucking bitch pulled me back into the drink. Her sharp claws pierced through my mom jeans, drawing blood from my chunky thighs.

I looked to my savior, and he was ready. In his giant arms

he held an anchor high above his enormous head, and with a strong, steady motion, he brought the anchor down on the slippery, aqua skank.

Clank!

Right in the head. Her scaly arms and webby fingers released me, and I watched both her and the anchor slip down into the darkness.

For the second time, Paddy pulled me up onto the docks and cradled me like a tiny child. He moved me back away from the water and took off his ugly sweater. The warmth from his body and the hideous knit perversion felt divine.

"There now, snuggle into me," he said, and he wrapped his giant limbs around me. "I knew you were up to something. Not like you to turn down a night of free drinks. I followed you, and a right, good thing I did." He brushed a damp lock of hair away from my eyes and then looked out into Stillhouse Cove. "I'll be damned," he said. "A *merrow.* But no cap on this one."

"Paddy, I have to tell you," I said as the world began to swim from my consciousness. "I love you and Savannah so much. I'm sorry I've been so shitty. I'll be better now. I promise."

"There now, it's all right," he said and made a shushing sound. "*Múchadh is bá ort, mo rún,*" he said and stroked my cheek.

I tried to laugh at the irony of his pet phrase, but my mirth was weak and lame.

"Paddy," I whispered.

"Yes, my love?"

"I'm bleeding," I wheezed.

"Oh my! You're bleeding!" he shouted. "Don't you worry now! We'll get you help! Stay right there!"

Where am I going to go?

As my eyes threatened to close, I heard him struggle to his feet and run down the docks, yelling for help the whole way. I tried to turn my body and watch him go, but I ended up facing the water instead. My neck burned from where that bitch had bitten me, and seawater stung the open wounds on my legs. Man, I was going to have some crazy-ass scars.

I stared out at the water. It was calm, and a fine mist was beginning to rise from the smooth glassy surface. Farther off, towards the center of the cove, I saw something break the flat plane.

It was *her*. The familiar nausea came over me like a plague, and her voice filled my head as clear as day.

This isn't over.

She bobbed there for a moment and then dove back under. Her tail followed her trajectory.

It was the last thing I saw as my world faded to black.

The dark sky was as crisp and clear as fresh pressed linen, and the sea, as it always did, roared at no one in particular. Waves broke along the shoreline, smashing, shaping, smoothing the thousands upon thousands of stones. Far above the froth of the waves, the moon lazily made her way to her zenith. She floated there, round and lovely in her fullness, as brazen as a pregnant whore in a church pew, flaunting her sins for all the world to see.

Mary nodded to the fertile moon as her own hand slowly drifted towards her midsection, rubbing the place where another life swam within.

Screaming and howling, the wind raced along the waves, whipping everything it encountered. Mary squinted into the wind, making her plain, ruddy face appear even fouler than normal. Stray, nut-brown hairs escaped her coarse woolen scarf and licked her shrewd, narrow eyes. She exhaled, and as she inhaled deeply, she savored the rich brine that entered her weary sinuses. The long days of mourning spent indoors amidst the caustic, drying nature of peat fires had taken their toll, and the sea air left Mary feeling renewed and refreshed.

The unforgiving rocks forced Mary to continually shift her weight from foot to foot as she stood her vigil. Next to her feet lay a wooden box, a narrow house of death, the only other object on the dark, empty beach. The box was a small, constant reminder of the task at hand.

Mary's mother lay in the wooden box. She, Mary Fiona Cantillon Riley, had passed in the wee hours of the morning on November the twenty-fourth. With the traditional wake now at its end, there was only one thing left to do.

The eldest and only child of the Cantillon lineage, Mary Fiona Riley, betrothed to Seamus James McFagan, stared at the open ocean. She drew in another deep breath and let it out slowly as she waited. Warm air from her lungs plumed and swirled, forming tiny ice crystals. They collected on her woolen scarf and sparkled brilliantly in the pale moonlight.

"I mean to see this through," she mumbled under her frozen breath and inhaled deeply once again, wincing as the frozen air squeezed her lungs with its icy talons.

Mary's hands shook violently, and she found herself grasping and releasing the rough fabric of her skirt over and over again. Despite the chill, sweat pooled under her armpits. She eased her shoulders back and forth attempting to eliminate the discomfort of the cool moisture beneath her shirtsleeves.

Mary glanced at what was left of her mother.

There's something you need to know before I leave this earth and go on to find your father. That bloody bastard best be waiting for me and not fooling around with that twit, Coleen O'Shannon. He thought I didn't notice the way he'd size up her backside, but I most certainly did notice, and when I see his rumpled face again, I mean to let him know just how much I noticed. What was it we was discussing, Younger Mary? My mind keeps wandering.

Older Mary had broken out in a thick fit of coughing, then spat into a bloody handkerchief. Younger Mary bit her lower lip and watched her mother, the soon-to-be-dead Older Mary, recover from her fit.

The smell of decay and impending death had been overwhelming, and Younger Mary fought the urge to cover her nose with her arm. Nausea washed over her in waves, but she held her discomfort at bay. It would have been rude. And telling. No need for the failing Older Mary to know about the illegitimate life surging within Younger Mary's womb.

In the coming spring, Younger Mary and her sweet Seamus were set to board a steamer bound for the setting sun. They would seek a new beginning beyond the waves of the Atlantic, far from the sin they had committed on their native soil. Seamus James McFagan had been trained in the funerary profession as had all McFagans since the land had turned emerald green.

Folk all need to die, Mary, Seamus had told her when she had discovered the life-changing result of their weak but blissful moment. *Folk will die wherever we go.*

She had looked at him with a mixture of queerness and disgust.

What I mean is, Mary, I'm in the business of folk dying. We can go anywhere, and there'll always be work for me. You will want for nothing, my fair one.

And so they had booked passage out of the Port of Cork in late April.

Father Cafferty had already heard Older Mary's last confession, which he had done elegantly enough with very few pulls from the flask he kept in his vestments. It wouldn't be too much longer now.

Younger Mary? Older Mary had wailed. *Are you still there?*

I'm here, Mother. Younger Mary had reached for her mother's hand. It felt like seaweed that had been left to dry in the sun.

You need to know, Mary, that we came from the sea. A long time gone, saltwater fed the roots of our family tree. The richness of the ocean nourished one of us and, from that union, made us who we are today. A pledge was made—the water-born honor the grounded Cantillon. It is what is done. It is what has always been done. Now it's your turn, Mary, my only child, to continue the tradition. Honor the Cantillon roots, as your ancestors have done before you, and when my breath no longer flows, return me to the sea, my darling girl.

Younger Mary wiped at the tears rolling down her frozen cheek and stared out at the black waters.

My darling girl.

Her mother had never before been as tender as she had been towards the end. Perhaps Mary had agreed to the ghoulish task in response to such rare tenderness. There she was on the banks of Ballyheige Bay at an ungodly hour, standing like a fool in the gelid wind, next to a dark casket.

The night before, her loving future husband had humored both Marys and filled a twin casket with rocks. Older Mary had specified that—supposedly, like so many other Cantillon caskets—this empty vessel, void of human remains, would enter the hallowed ground in place of Older Mary.

"Really, my love," said Seamus. "What do you truly think will happen on a beach in the middle of the night? Perhaps magical underwater men will arrive and whisk your mother to the bottom of the sea. *Hmm?*"

"Please, Seamus," said Mary. "I'm all she ever had. 'Tis a small thing to honor this one last request."

"Standing on a frozen shore till the wee hours of the morning in your condition, *alone?*" said Seamus. "'Tis *not* a small thing."

"I'm curious," Mary had said as she picked up one of the rocks and placed it carefully in the red herring of a coffin. "Aren't you?"

"No."

"Come now, Seamus," said Mary. "You and I have both heard the village tales of the twin merrow."

Everyone had heard the tales. Whispers, passed down through generations, all pointed back to the ocean. If the tales were true, it would mean that another village existed somewhere off the coast. Only this village was beneath the sea, populated by another race of people, who sometimes intermixed with the local land-dwellers. There was even an outlandish fairy tale concerning twins who had sprung forth from the union of both peoples. It was rumored that the twins were Cantillons.

"Nonsense, ridiculous nonsense, told by drunken fisherman to their half-wit wives, who then pass these bits of fancy on to the local children. It's all just a means of passing the time, an attempt to make a bleak existence a little more fanciful. 'Tis all it is, my darling."

Seamus had stood from his work and put his hand on Mary's arm. He had squeezed gently and smiled in his soft, shy way. "But I will do this for you, for your mother, because I love you."

Alone now on the beach, Mary stared up at the clear night sky. It would soon be dawn. The Great Bear Mother overtook the inky blackness, looking for her cub. As more time passed, doubts about her mother's sanity crawled up Mary's back and rested on her shoulders like an unwanted cat. Asleep on her sore feet, she was ready to head home and face the Seamus I-told-you-so look.

Honestly, what *did* she think would happen? Who was going to come and claim her mother's tiny remains? It *was* nonsense.

Another hour passed. Finally, Mary turned from the sea and sighed. She would go home. She and Seamus would return for her mother later in the day. But as she drew her shawl closer to her body, a distant and distinct splashing erupted from the waves.

Mary spun around in alarm. The wind howled, and the waves smashed the shore at Mary's feet. Her gaze raced along the rolling horizon of the black sea until she found the source of the splashing. It was the first time she saw them, emerging from the waves like mythical beasts.

Her long-lost cousins from the sea.

McFagan & McFagan Funeral Home, Inc.
Pawtuxet Village, Rhode Island
March 9
3:08 AM

Teeth. A sea of teeth. Everywhere I looked, my vision was filled with sharp, pointed teeth, filed to precision by years of eating flesh. There was no sound. There was only seawater, and it filled every cavity I owned.

God, I hate seawater. What the hell do we need the ocean for anyway? It's not like we can drink the damn stuff. Fucking useless liquid. Oh, I know, where would the cute, little dolphins live?

Who gives a shit?

And screw those damn dolphins—they sure as hell weren't saving my drowning ass. There were teeth everywhere and enormous rubber duckies. They were coming for me.

Large, looming, and yellow, bobbing around, leering at me while something else, something far more sinister, darted about, sliding in and out between the rubber duckies, flashing those vicious, unforgiving teeth at me.

But I am wearing an apron, and I left a cake somewhere ...

And then the duckies parted. Long claws crushed the rubber, and the duckies started to deflate as if they were melting, all the bright yellow colors dissolving into the water leaving only *her* with her wretched dark scales.

I saw her, and she wasn't alone. All their mouths opened in unison, and I knew they would devour me—all of me—including my soul.

I told you. This isn't over, and you have something we want—your daughter.

All the air escaped my lungs in a giant *whoosh!* Panic-fueled adrenaline jolted through my body like shit through a goose, and I sat upright.

The clock ticked a steady cadence, slicing through the silence. Each movement of the second hand sounded thick and deliberate, almost menacing in its regularity. The only other noise was the foul-sounding, flatulent boom of Paddy's snores.

That mountain of a man, he's so sexy.

I wiped the sweat from my brow and sighed a deep, thick sigh. It was just a dream, and I was back in my bedroom. My left hand flew to my neck, caressing the scar I would wear like a cheap accessory for the rest of my life.

It was proof. Proof she had been real. Proof I was not a complete nut.

I gazed at my hulking mass of a husband and sighed. For the past few months, he had been secretive, withdrawn, hesitant to discuss the events on the dock.

"Why can't we talk about what happened, Paddy?" I had whined. "I know you saw her, saw what she was—I mean—is. And you called her something—a *merrow with no cap*. What exactly is that? What do you know about them?"

Paddy had been ducking my questions. He was good at it.

"I thought we could get that soaking tub put in," he said. "You know, the one you've always wanted?"

"A soaking tub? For *me*? Really? When?" I was squealing like a teenager.

Damn him! He threw something shiny at me every time I brought up the incident at Stillhouse Cove.

I was now the owner of a new soaking tub, a meat smoker, and my very own game system—I'm fond of dance games. Sue me. And a brand new Land Rover—black, just like the buyer's soul.

I frowned at my snoring, generous avoider.

What are you hiding, Patrick McFagan?

The streetlight filtered through the curtains as they blew about in the breeze flowing over our bed.

It's March. Why is the damn window open?

Paddy and his fresh air.

I threw back the coverlet and got out of bed. The floor was freezing beneath my bare feet, and the air was just as frigid. Cursing under my breath, I rubbed my hands up and down my arms and padded towards the open window.

I never made it to the window. Without warning, I found myself staring at the ceiling as pain exploded from the back of my skull and traveled all the way down my spine to the backs of my ankles.

"What the hell?" Paddy roared from the bed above me.

"I slipped," I muttered.

I slipped?

My feet were wet.

Why were my feet wet?

With a groan I rolled onto my stomach and glanced at the floor below the open window.

Wet footprints gleamed in the streetlight.

A stiffening chill replaced the pain in my spine. My pulse, which had calmed itself only seconds before, quickened as my gaze darted from the floor beneath the open window to the baby monitor on the bureau nearby.

The white speaker-like object was on its side and the cord looked frayed, as if someone had been chewing on it. It swung useless in the gentle breeze that flowed into the arctic room.

Oh God, no.

I grabbed a fistful of the comforter from the bed above me in an attempt to haul myself to my feet. I felt the blood reversing in my veins.

Hold on, Evie.

"Bloody hell, woman! Evie, darling, why am I awake at this ungodly hour, and why are you on the floor? And why is the window open? It's March, love. I know you like fresh air from time to ..."

"Paddy," I whispered as my vision drifted in and out of focus. "Shut the fuck up."

"That's not very lady-like. It's 3 a.m., and I have …"

"The baby monitor is trashed," I said with all the strength I could muster. I couldn't hold on any longer. The blood surged in the wrong direction.

I was losing consciousness.

The last words I uttered before the hardwood floor raced up towards my sleep-swollen face were, "Our baby's gone. She took Savannah."

When I rejoined the land of the conscious, I found Paddy down the hall in Savannah's room, phone in hand. Nothing made sense. The room was a mess. Her clothes, her toys, diapers and talcum powder, lotions and wet wipes were everywhere, scattered all over the place as if the room itself had vomited its own contents.

A struggle had taken place, and somehow I, *her mother*, had slept through the entire event.

Her stuffed animals looked like roadkill, trampled underfoot. Some had been torn, and a bear lay on its side, stuffing flowing freely from an open wound. Furniture was broken and chipped.

I've been to my share of crime scenes for body retrieval, but nothing, I mean *nothing*, prepares you for the horror of entering your own child's bedroom, her nursery, for Christ's sake, to find a scene like this one.

And there were things missing. I glanced around her room and realized that some of her clothes, some of her favorite toys, and a box of diapers I know I had placed in the corner of the room the night before last were gone.

Someone had taken my child along with some of her things.

"Where did she *go*?" Paddy shrieked.

"She's gone. Not 'out for cigarettes' gone, more like 'a dingo stole my baby' gone. But it wasn't a dingo, Paddy—it was a fucking mermaid! You should have hit that bitch harder!"

"Oh Evie, don't start with the mermaid business again ..." His voice trailed off when he saw the look on my face.

"Really?" My voice rose to the annoying shrill of a hysterical woman.

There was nothing I hated more. Being in the funerary business, we encountered all sorts of grief, all sorts of ways of dealing with shit I'd prefer not to deal with. Most people did it gracefully. There was no grace in this moment.

I looked at my husband and tried to picture the man who had heaved a boat anchor over his head and then mercilessly smashed it down on the vicious she-beast from the deep, a vicious she-beast who had attempted to end my life and who had now stolen our child.

When I looked at him, all I saw was a tired, frumpy man. A man who desperately needed to start passing on the bacon. A man who was beyond being in dire need of some sort of exercise regimen.

I wanted to slap his fat face.

"Fuck you, Paddy! I cannot believe you're turning Judas on me now."

He stared at me for an uncomfortably long time, so long that I felt as if an eternity had passed. Then he said in a calm, quiet voice, "Our child has been kidnapped. We need to call the police. If you so much as say one word about a mermaid's involvement, I swear I will insist you be taken into custody."

He never allowed me to respond. He turned down the hall while dialing the phone. I was left there alone with the mess, the silence, and the hole in my life. I missed my beloved little girl.

God, I'm such a shitty mom!

The worst sight to behold was her vacant crib. I stared at it. Then the world turned fuzzy at the edges. I was going down all over again.

I leaned on Savannah's dresser for support and swallowed hard. I could not lose consciousness again. I had to stay awake at all costs. I dug my fingernails into my palms and bit the inside of my cheek until the warm, metallic tang of blood filled my mouth. It hurt like hell but it helped, and I held it together.

I felt the sobs coming and tried to choke them down. It was akin to stopping oneself from vomiting. Fruitless.

I crumpled to the floor, racked with grief, and let the tide of sadness wash over me. I wailed and wailed and wailed until there was nothing left.

I was exhausted, lost, empty, all those crappy things that wrap themselves around the indescribable horror of losing one's child. I lay on the soft pink carpet and pressed my face into the thick, comforting pile.

I stared at the dust bunnies hiding under Savannah's crib, far away from the obliterating path of the vacuum. They were keeping company with something dark, something green, something shiny and bulbous.

I crawled over to the crib and stretched a trembling hand towards the strange object. My fingers reached out and recoiled at first contact.

It was still wet. I drew it out into the light and confirmed what I thought it might be. Kelp.

The bubbly kind, reminiscent of dark, mossy-colored bubble wrap. I rolled it around my hand, squishing the tiny orbs against my palm with my thumb.

Standing, I rubbed my swollen eyes and wiped my runny nose on the sleeve of my nightshirt, staring at the seaweed glimmering in my hand. Then I crushed it with all the strength I had.

Paddy was right. Telling the police a mermaid stole my baby would only end with me in the looney bin. This shit was personal.

I needed to get my daughter back, and if *anything* got in my way, I had every intention of taking it off this great, green earth—for good.

I paced in the driveway, attempting to wear a hole in the pavement. Without alcohol, this whole ordeal was completely unbearable. After the incident on the docks, the incident Paddy had now summed up as *the incident where Evie was so drunk she fell off the docks*, I had sworn off drinking. I was trying to be a better Evie.

So I had taken up smoking. Unfortunately, this new vice left me as calm as a squirrel on a nut-filled highway.

The police hated me. It was all over their stupid, square faces. Clearly, I was suspect number one. Once they had left, I could not go back into the house. There was bad juju everywhere, and I was doing my best to avoid it. Paddy was barely speaking to me, and Aunt Catherine refused to come to the house.

Without actually saying the exact words, she said that I must have had something to do with the disappearance because I was a bad mother and more or less despicable.

I needed to talk to someone or something. But how could I explain this to my fan club? They adored Savannah. She was their mascot, their surrogate grandchild. Besides, they thought Paddy had left me. How could I explain I had lost Savannah, too?

Oh, my baby girl! I hiccuped and cried all over again. I pulled it together after a few good drags of nicotine and then resumed my pacing.

Maybe I could call Rachael, our part-time bookkeeper. She's from Staten Island and has a heavy drinking problem. We're great friends—when we're drunk. Yeah, that meant she was out.

My parents are both dead. I have no siblings, aside from my brother who does not speak to me. There was no one to call, no one to offer words of comfort.

Most of the people I worked with were transient, as in *dead*, as in moving between this world and the next.

There was my cousin Bridget, but we didn't have a chummy, chummy relationship. Mostly because I had slept with her boyfriend. Don't judge me. It was in high school, for Christ's sake. How long can one person hold a grudge? Apparently, until hell freezes over or pigs fly out of my ass or both. These were the suggestions made to me by cousin Bridget. Was she the type of person I could call up and say, "Hey, my child has been kidnapped by an insane, vindictive mermaid. Do you think you could stop by with a casserole while we figure this shit out?"

No, probably not. So she was out, too.

Alone again. I looked back at the house. I couldn't go in there. It was so quiet. No gurgles of joy, no screeching at nothing in particular, no giggles, no Savannah. My heart was breaking. With shaking fingers, I raised the coffin-nail to my parched lips and inhaled deeply.

"Think, think, think," I muttered.

Where would I keep a small child if I were a mermaid?

What a ridiculous statement. Yes, yes, it was. Move on, Evie.

Okay, the ocean would be your home if you were a mermaid. The whole ocean.

Then where would you start?

Something clicked, and then it hit me. Go ask the person who knows her best.

I stood outside David and Nomia's home for a long time, smoking, thinking, procrastinating. The ground at my feet looked as if white worms had partaken in a mass suicide. As I dragged my toes through the discarded cigarette butts and coughed into the crook of my arm, I mentally practiced my opener.

Hey there. You don't know me, but my husband dropped an anchor on your wife's head while she was a mermaid a few months back, and yeah, now my child is missing. Well, she's not missing. She's more like stolen. But you seem like a nice guy. Want to do a fellow human a solid and tell me where the hell your nasty saltwater bride has taken my offspring?

Yeah, that sounded good enough. I stomped out my cigarette, straightened my jacket, and marched up the steps to the small cottage.

"Here we go," I muttered and then rapped the seashell-shaped door knocker.

After a few minutes, I heard the pounding of little feet approaching. There was a pause, then the door flew open and the same tiny, chubby girl with radiant blonde curls from the playground stared up at me. Pearl. My gaze was riveted to her light gray irises.

"Um, hello there," I stammered.

What the hell am I doing here?

"Hello," said Pearl.

Silence fell between us, thick and suffocating, like a wool blanket in summer. While seconds turned into what felt like hours, I peered into the house. There were moving boxes everywhere, and the room looked as if it had been systematically dismantled.

"Is your mother home?" I ventured.

Silence. Not even a blink.

Then, after another uncomfortably long time, she opened her full pouty lips and these six chilling words dropped out, "My mother doesn't have your daughter."

Huh. How about that?

"Pearl? Haven't I told you to *not* open the door?" David appeared in the doorway and moved his daughter behind his legs. He looked at me and said, "Can I help you?"

"I don't know—can you?"

"I'm sorry. Do I know you? What is this about?"

"It's about your wife, David. If that *is* your real name."

He looked as if I had just slapped him. I could see the gears in his mind turning, thinking, checking facts, names, places, anything to put me where I belonged and expedite my departure from his stoop.

His eyes narrowed as he said, "Look, I don't have any idea who you are or what you want with my family, but I strongly suggest you get off my property before I call the police."

"No, *you* look. I know what happens to your wife when she hits water, and I know what she's capable of. I just want my daughter back. Parent to parent, could you at least give me a clue as to where she is or how I can get in touch with her? Please?"

"Daddy, Mommy's not coming back for a long time. You know that, right?"

"Pearl! Go to the playroom, *now.*" David opened the door wider and came out onto the landing. He shut the door behind him.

He was only slightly taller than me. I could see that he had been handsome when he was younger. *Or maybe before he met that slippery wife of his.* Dark pools of sleeplessness had made hammocks beneath his fierce blue eyes, and his forehead looked as if it had a ladder carved into it. If I climbed that ladder, I would find myself in a nest of receding, thinning hair. His clothes looked rumpled, and his feet were bare on the icy cement.

I almost felt bad for him. Almost.

"My wife is no longer involved in this family. I want no part of her dealings. I don't know you or your child. I have Pearl and myself to look out for now. So I'll say it again, real slow, *leave or I'm calling the police.*"

"Go ahead," I said and then laughed. "They've already been to my place—looking for my missing child!" I screamed and stormed down the stairs.

As I fumbled for another cigarette, I heard the door re-open and David's voice, "Hello? Yes, I would like to report a deranged woman who just threatened my daughter ..."

I didn't hear the rest because when I spun around to look, David backed into his house. He slammed the door so hard the stupid seashell knocker reverberated with a loud *clack,* then swung sideways as one of the screws flew off.

I wandered down the street, scowling, smoking, and wondering how things had gone so wrong.

How would I ever find my daughter?

The poor-me syndrome crept onto my shoulders and nestled
there like an annoying monkey. I hoped she was safe. I hoped
she was warm. I hoped that bitch at least smiled at her once in
a while.

My sweet baby girl. Oh shit.

The tears flowed freely down my cheeks as I walked. I wiped
at them with the back of my wrist and cursed under my breath.
I am not the crying type.

I mean, come on. In my field, with my training, any emo-
tions beyond the *I understand* nod or the calm, gentle *let me
take care of things for you* smile (which I have perfected) are not
acceptable to those in need of comfort during a difficult time.

What?

I can hear your judgmental thoughts from here. You don't
think I'm capable of professionalism, do you? Well, it's not like
I've really shown you.

I *am* capable of comforting the grieving. Our funeral home is
well respected. (Okay, so my neighbors think I'm crap, but screw
them. They can have somebody else bury their sorry asses.)

I'll have you know that I am well esteemed in my field. I
have volunteered—on more than one occasion—to work with
the state disaster relief task force. When disasters such as plane
crashes have occurred, I have spent many, many hours sorting
through body parts to make sure the right parts end up where
they belong. I've done this so that the living may have some

closure. It is what I do. I provide comfort, strength, and, most importantly, resolution to those in need.

So I'm not the most together person in my private life.

Are you judging me, again?

Let's make *you* a target of a vindictive, cruel mermaid, merrow—*whatever*—and see how you handle it.

Screw you, reader.

Anyway, while I walked, smoked, and wondered why my life was crap, all while trying—and failing—not to cry, I found myself wandering towards the center of the Village. With squealing tires, a car I recognized pulled up onto the sidewalk in front of me.

Real subtle.

The window buzzed down with a dull, mechanical *whirr.*

"Hello, Catherine," I all but spat at the open window.

"Evie," was all she said in response.

A long silence ensued. She looked at me. I looked at her. No love passed between us.

"So." I trailed my foot in the sand on the sidewalk making lame figure eights. "Seen my daughter, by any chance?"

She glared at me so hard, I thought my face would crack in half, and then she said something so surprising I almost fell over, right there in the middle of the street.

"She's at my house at the moment." Her voice was clipped and curt, like her hair, her manicure, her disposition.

"*What?*" I screamed. Startled starlings tore off a telephone wire and screeched into the sky.

"You heard me. She is at my house right now watching her

favorite show, cozy on the couch with a dear friend of mine."

"Well, do you think, maybe, I could have my daughter back? Or are you still practicing your lunatic kidnapper skills?" I was trying not to punch her snide, smug face.

"No."

"What do you mean, 'no'?"

"I said, 'No.' You're an unfit mother, and you're in over your head. That sweet child will remain with me. You're not to contact the police. You are not to tell anyone she is with me. Consider it a kindness I even bothered to inform you of your child's whereabouts."

And then she whizzed her car window up and tore off the sidewalk.

"And I'm the crazy one!" I screamed at her receding vehicle.

I whipped out my cell phone and called Paddy. When he answered, I never gave him an opportunity to speak. "Are you aware that our Savannah is not missing, but is with your batshit crazy aunt?"

There was a painfully long silence.

"Paddy?" I yelled into the phone. "Are you there? Hello?"

"Yes," he said quietly. "I'm here."

"And you heard me, right?"

More silence.

"Oh," I said. "I see. It's all coming into focus now. I get it. I'm the only one in the dark." My voice was close to cracking. This was too much. I mean, my child is stolen, turns out *not*, then I find out that a relative has stolen her and won't give her back, and then my husband, the person who is supposed to have my back, for Christ's sake, knew all this before I did.

"Yes," he said. "I know. I'm sorry, *mo rún*. She told me. I had hoped to tell you before she did, but I'm gathering she already found you."

"Yeah," I muttered. "You gathered correctly. But she never said why or when we would be getting her back. What gives, Paddy?"

"It's complicated, Evie." I could hear the static in the line, echoing into oblivion, numbing my mind. "We'll talk more when you get home."

And then he hung up on me.

I pulled the phone away from my ear and stared at it. It felt as if I had a coiled snake in my hand, so I threw it as hard as I could right into the bushes.

Cars whizzed by, birds chirped, the air was still frozen. My chest wheezed as I stifled hyperventilation. I stood there, stewing.

Oh, did I stew. My child was with Aunt Catherine, my husband knew about it, and the police thought I was a deranged mother who had done something unspeakable to her child. The only thing stopping them from arresting me was my snake of a husband, Paddy. His buddy Oliver had probably pulled some strings.

It was next to impossible for me to accept that Paddy was okay with all of this. I mean, how long had he known that Savannah was with Aunt Catherine? Why hadn't he told me the second he found out? In other news, was I going to be arrested?

After a time, I felt my heart slow down. I started to feel

somewhat in control, although I'm not really sure I ever was. Scratch that. I know I was never in control. Aunt Catherine had just pushed that issue out into the open. She was good like that.

I stood there for a few moments, collecting myself, watching the cars whizz by. When I felt calm*ish*, I hung my head in shame, then crawled under the bushes of the neighborhood law office to retrieve my phone. My fat ass was pointing towards the street and not one, but *three* cars offered me cheerful, yet lewd beeps.

I dusted myself off and lit up again—inhaling as much as I possibly could. Before long, I found that my feet had taken over and had decided to walk me towards my favorite coffee shop.

I needed meat. And coffee. Three months had been too long.

The bell chimed, and I inhaled the sweet smell of cured meats interspersed with the warm, bitter scent of good coffee. The knot in my shoulder relaxed a little. Just a little.

It was a small comfort to know that my daughter was with family and not somewhere in (or, God forgive me for thinking it, *under*) the Atlantic Ocean. But what the hell? Why was I being treated like a child? Being left in a need-to-know limbo until—when?

I felt powerless, useless, annoyed beyond all belief. I scowled at my situation. *I need a drink.*

Tony and Joe waved me over.

"Evie!" said Tony. "We've missed you! Where have you been?"

"Look at her face, Tony," said Joe. "She's still not with Paddy. A Sicilian knows these things. Am I right?"

Tony leaned in, studied my face, then yelled, "Gina, she needs a double espresso and a *Salami Mommy,* on the double!"

I slumped into a chair and managed a wan smile.

"Oh," said Joe. "There's some sunshine."

He smiled back at me, and I felt a little more of the ice slide from my shoulders.

My bottom lip quivered a little, but I held strong and thought of a quick lie. "It's just so hard being a single mom. Catherine took her, bless her heart, so I could have some time to myself."

I hated lying to them, so I quickly changed the subject. "Where's Angelo and Giovanni?"

Tony's facial expression changed from concern to all business. "Oh, Giovanni had an appointment with his plumbing doctor, so Angelo drove him. I guess the receptionist there is quite the looker." Tony wriggled his eyebrows at me.

I smiled again, then had a thought. "Hey Tony," I said. "You mentioned something about the McFagan crypt last time I saw you. What was it you wanted to tell me?"

"You mean to tell me you've never heard the rumors?" asked Joe.

"What rumors?" I really had no idea what he was talking about, but something was going on in the family. I had been kept in the dark for too long.

"Jeez! You being in the business and all. Can't believe you've heard nothing about this," said Tony.

My double espresso arrived with a nice twist of lemon, along with my meat plate. Food always made me feel better. I mean, why wouldn't it? Food is love.

The tattooed barista winked at me and said, "I put it on Joe's tab, sweetie. Looks like you need a pick-me-up." She ruffled Joe's non-existent hair on her way back to the counter.

He frowned at her but then smiled at me. See? Not everyone hates me.

"Thanks," I called her way.

Tony cleared his throat, then continued when he was sure no one else was listening. His voice was a half-whisper, hoarse and raspy. "It's kind of a funny rumor, with you McFagans being in the death business. It doesn't make any sense. What I mean is ... how do I say this?"

"The crypt is empty," interrupted Joe.

Tony looked at Joe with annoyance, opened his mouth to speak, then closed it. He looked at me, sat back, and nodded.

"It's true. My sister's husband's brother told me his cousin saw it with his own eyes."

"Oh well, then," I said. "It must be true if an obscure relative, four times removed, confirmed it."

Tony and Joe gave me a blank stare, as if I was the one who had just said something so outrageous it was beyond belief.

I broke the silence first. "Come on," I said. "You mean to tell me it's really empty?"

"When was the last time you checked the crypt, Evie?"

"Hmmm," was all I could manage. Now that I thought about it, I don't ever remember being in the crypt. Ever.

Wait a second, I couldn't remember the last time I was around for a McFagan funeral either. Wasn't that odd?

Cue the pivotal music. Something was amiss.

"You know what, boys?" I stood and put on my coat, then said, "I need to go and get my baby girl."

I left the coffee shop, marched home, and had a nuclear blowout with Paddy.

"What do you mean you're okay with our daughter staying with Aunt Catherine while the cops think I'm some sort of psycho? On what planet is that okay? Get your fat ass off that couch and call your pinched-faced hemorrhoid of an aunt and tell her to give our child back right now."

Paddy had looked at me over his reading glasses. A few toast crumbs were lodged in the wrinkles of his neck, and he had butter smeared on the corner of his mouth. I wanted to hit him hard enough to send both the crumbs and the butter flying. But I restrained myself.

He cleared his throat and returned his gaze to his paper. Then he said, "No."

Those two little letters flew at me, sending me into a head-cracking rage.

"*What?*"

He cleared his throat once again, then repeated himself, "I said, 'No.'"

"What is wrong with you? I cannot believe you are taking her side on this! She's a lunatic! She probably killed your Uncle Aiden out in the Bay, too!"

That got his attention. He slammed the newspaper down, took off his glasses, and stared at me.

"Yeah, you heard me. I found out that he didn't die in his sleep. He died in the Bay, under very strange circumstances. So whatcha got now? Huh?"

"I don't wish to discuss Uncle Aiden's passing at this time. It's irrelevant."

"*Irrelevant?*"

This time I echoed my disbelief with a butter knife poorly aimed at the back wall. I planned for it to stick in the wall right above Paddy's head. You know, like a circus knife thrower? It didn't work out so well. It thudded against the wall, leaving a smear of butter on the wallpaper, then landed on the floor with a dull *thunk*.

Paddy turned and looked first at the wall and then down his nose at me. His mouth was turned up at one corner in a bit of a scowl. "Classy," he muttered.

"Irrelevant?" I asked again. "What is that supposed to mean?"

"Google it."

"You're not funny, Paddy. I'm starting to really wonder about your family. Why is it that when one of your relatives dies, I'm suddenly not needed around here? Yeah, I like a day off every now and then, but it's starting to add up to more than a coincidence."

"You're starting to sound like a conspiracy theorist. Next up, the mermaid talk."

This time I grabbed a fork. This time it stuck in the wall. Then I left. And I slammed the door as hard as I possibly could.

Frustrated, I went and sat in the hearse and smoked half a pack of Camels until I felt better—if you could call lightheaded better, well, then yes, I felt better.

I sat and thought about all the McFagans who had passed through the wrong door of the funeral home. There was quite a list.

And they all had one thing in common—me, or the lack of me. I had been sent away for each and every one of those services. It had never occurred to me before. I had seen the dismissal as an opportunity to indulge in selfish laziness.

We own a house on Prudence Island in Narragansett Bay. More often than not, if Paddy didn't need me (or *said* he didn't need me), I would head to the island, especially during the summer months. But now, looking back, maybe I had missed the pattern.

Maybe I *had* been drinking too much.

You see, I was what is commonly referred to as a "functioning alcoholic." I was capable of doing all of life's normal tasks. I could hold a job, talk to people, grocery shop, raise a child, et cetera, et cetera, but I did all these things while just a teensy, weensy bit tipsy.

It's a talent, really. Or it's sort of sad and pathetic, if you want to think about it that way. I don't like thinking about it, so why should you?

But now that I'm more on the ball, *look out world!*

I glanced at my reflection in the rearview mirror. Through a cloud of cigarette smoke, I saw the eyes of someone who was not under the influence of alcohol. Instead, I saw a sharp-witted, clear-thinking individual, someone who was capable of getting to the bottom of a secret, not the bottom of a bottle of bourbon.

Something had been going on without my knowledge. My

daughter was no longer under my care, and I was being kept in the dark about it. Enough was enough. I stubbed out my cigarette and entered the empty office.

Twenty minutes later, I emerged with a graveyard manifest, an envelope marked, "Family Mausoleum Key," a flashlight, and more questions than ever.

Evie, super sober sleuth, was on the case.

I wandered through the New Pawtuxet Graveyard feeling like the biggest moron on the planet, dreading what I might come across. I mean, who the hell wanders around graveyards? You're thinking, well, Evie, isn't that your job? Well, yes and no. My work normally ended in the large, ceremonial building in the center of the graveyard. We say a few words, shoot the guns for our brave service personnel, and that about wraps it up.

People are always stunned when they realize they do not get to stand next to the hole in the ground, like in the movies. That's not how we roll. Too many things can go wrong next to a deep grave. Old people, more often than not, are the ones next to the grave. Old people are clumsy and fall into holes. Hey, more work for me. But that's not really how we want to get our business.

Then there are the people who recreationally visit grave-yards—yeah, that's a whole other ball of wax. Goth kids looking for kicks. Winos looking for solace. Grieving widows. And me. A fool looking for answers.

The wind picked up, and the temperature started to drop. I shivered under my thick coat and grabbed my lapels in a lame attempt to return some warmth to my neck.

The sun was making its descent, thanks to stupid daylight savings nonsense. I mean, are we still farmers? No, we are not. We are snoopers of graves, and we need our daylight, damn it.

I felt naked without my usual hat, gloves, and airline-stewardess-of-the-1950s dark blue skirt and jacket, my uniform for the grieving, if you will. On this day, I was a woman with a notebook, sporting mom jeans and a really ugly down coat. You know the type. It's long, puffy, obnoxious, and frequently mistaken for a comforter.

But damn, was it warm.

The graveyard manifest showed the family tomb to be in the northwest corner of the graveyard, the old section, inaccessible by vehicle. I had a new appreciation for the gravediggers.

I stumbled up the rutted road in my pink polka-dot wellies. Gnarled, ugly trees scowled at me with their wrinkled-bark faces as they lurked among the tombstones. I felt like scowling back.

I had no idea what I was doing. It was like having a piece of food stuck in your teeth. Your tongue just can't manage to dig it out. You could reach in there and yank it out, but you would risk looking like an uncivilized ape. The piece of food in this case was something that Tony had said at the coffee shop—the empty crypt.

Something in my head would not let it go.

I pulled out my flashlight and switched it on. Then I stopped dead in my tracks. The last time I had been out in the dark, in the cold, with a flashlight, things had not gone very well for me. And yet, there I was, out in the ever-encroaching darkness, with a flashlight, in the cold, wandering around.

Yes, I really am a half-wit.

It was fully dark by the time I found the McFagan mausoleum. It was as pristine as Aunt Catherine's hair. Tall and majestic, it towered over all the other tombs. All four walls and the high vaulted roof were made entirely of pale green marble. It was impressive, out of place among the other common tombs of colonial sea captains and townsfolk, long dead and gone. On either side of the entryway, two large columns stood, each covered with intricate knot-work of strange symbols resembling seals, fish, and beautiful women with long, flowing hair. The sea creatures swam round and round the pillars, endlessly chasing one another as they dove through the knots.

A large iron gate surrounded the main tomb. I placed my hands on the metal bars and pushed. Nothing. I grabbed the bars again and shook like a mad woman.

Nothing.

Placing the flashlight in my mouth, I fumbled in my pocket for the envelope I had stolen from the office. As saliva from my open mouth slid down the handle of the flashlight, I dug in my pocket until I found what I was looking for. I scowled and wiped my wet lips on the back of my sleeve. Placing the flashlight back in my mouth, I ripped open the envelope carefully marked with Paddy's obnoxiously perfect penmanship.

I dumped the contents into my open waiting palm, and out tumbled one freaky key. It was beyond old, heavily rusted, and it was shaped like a fish or, rather, a fish's fleshless tail. The bones of the tail stuck out straight, like the tines of a fork.

"Huh," I said. "How about that?"

I turned my flashlight on the lock, fit the fish key into the keyhole, and turned the key.

It worked!

With a cranky *click*, the lock popped, and the gate opened. The rusted hinges groaned as I pushed through the opening and approached the second door.

The door was immense, made from a single large piece of smooth stone. Intricately carved waves and several nautiluses adorned the frame. I ran my hands over the cool surface and gave a little whistle.

I searched for a handle, another keyhole, a latch, any means at all to open the tomb door, but I could not find any way to enter the tomb. I scanned the massive door with the flashlight a second time but again found nothing. I had reached a dead end. Damn it.

The wind howled and leaves rustled behind me, beyond the open gate.

What the hell was I doing? This was so stupid.

Frustrated, I leaned against the door, but when my weight hit the heavy marble, the slab of stone swung open like a screen door in a summer breeze.

Yeah, just like that, I was in.

"Well, all right," I said, smiling.

Leaving the world outside, I stepped inside and had a look around. I was stunned at what I discovered. I discovered—nothing.

Not a single thing was in the tomb. The four walls I faced were as smooth as the back of the door, and there wasn't a damn thing to see. *Where was a body supposed to go?* I moved closer to the walls for a better look. Maybe I was missing something. But all I found was more and more nothing.

Where the hell were the caskets, the urns, the damn skeletons of the McFagan family?

Paddy had some serious explaining to do. I was pissed and full of questions, and man, oh man, did I want a drink more than ever.

Something stirred behind me in the open doorway. I froze. I was not alone. I willed myself to turn around. All the synapses in my brain were telling my body to just turn around.

Just turn around and see who or what is behind you!

Something was behind me. I could hear it breathing. But I could not turn around.

Then the room went black. Whatever, whoever it was had closed the door. I cried out and stumbled towards the memory of the faint outdoor light. With my hands out in front of me, like some deranged blind woman, I fumbled for the door. My hands scratched against the slippery surface, but I couldn't find a handle on the inside.

When I had entered the tomb, I had pushed the door open. The door had been designed to open from the outside—not the inside.

I sat down in the darkness. The floor was cold, so cold. I drew my knees to my chest. Hot tears burned down my face as claustrophobia set in.

I was trapped in the tomb.

10

*R*ed sky in morning, sailor's warning.

Dawn streaked along the horizon, a thin, blood-red smear slashing water from sky. The waves pounded the shore, and the creatures from the sea busied themselves with preparations for Older Mary's final journey.

They spoke with hand gestures and nods, and from what Mary observed, it did not appear as if they needed to communicate verbally at all. Their movements and actions were symbiotic, as if one creature moved with many limbs. Deftly crafted ropes made from seaweed and remnants of hempen lines were thrown and knotted about her mother's casket. Driftwood logs were laid with great care in a row under and in front of her long wooden box, forming a path to the water's edge.

Mary marveled at the duality she felt as she examined her cousins in stolen secretive glances. They were both beautiful and horrific, an orchestrated blending of repulsion and attraction.

It was whispered amongst the crones in her village that the males, if they still existed, did not share the alluring beauty of their female counterparts. Mary thought of this as she examined their talon-like hands, but she found herself, more than once, staring at their chiseled faces and well-muscled bodies. Each time, she blushed a deep crimson and forced her gaze back towards the waves.

These are my kin, she reminded herself, but her thoughts wandered, sifting through questions concerning the origins of their braided pasts.

Was it a man or a woman who joined our bloodlines?

The females were known to lure and then destroy the human men who caught their fancy. Wicked creatures they were and best left alone, and it was difficult to identify them if they chose to walk on land. If the rumors could be believed, more than one doomed man had met his end by mistaking an aquatic beauty for what he thought was merely a lost, country girl.

And what of the Cantillon twins? Which of them had remained on land? Which one returned to the sea? Who was their mother? Their father? And dear God above, if our bloodlines are crossed, could my child have fins?

Mary sighed and shuddered. Times were changing, and talk of modern wonders like machines that did the work of many, were replacing stories of the wee folk, the selkies, the banshies, the merrow.

I'm sure the merrow are grateful to the machines for their distractions, thought Mary as she watched the proof of fairy tales toil and labor over her mother's remains. She choked down the urge to blurt out her burning questions.

Rolling it along the driftwood logs, her strange kin pulled the coffin towards the waves. Before they entered the water, they paused, and the one she assumed was their leader made his way to Mary.

He was taller than the others with a leanness often found in hardworking farmhands. Towering above Mary, a diminutive woman, he gazed down at her with eyes impossibly large and wide. Mary inhaled sharply when she noticed the color of his irises—an almost clear, sky-blue, so transparent they were almost colorless. They were the same color as her mother's father's eyes.

No one could forget the uniqueness of those eyes, and here they were, echoed in massive orbs within this strange creature's face. His skin was light in color, almost green. It reminded Mary of tidal pools on a clear day. Faint swirls and strange, unfamiliar patterns were inked across his cheeks, and a violent, ragged scar ran from his forehead, across the bridge of his wide flat nose, and ended at the edge of his cheek.

"I'm sorry for your loss, miss," he said.

"You speak English and not Gaelic, sir," Mary answered.

"Aye," he nodded. "Did you think we hadn't noticed the way of things was changing? We have not survived for this long, hidden in the waters, by being simpleminded."

"I'm sorry, sir. I didn't mean to offend. It's just … I didn't quite know what to expect."

The cousin waved his hand in dismissal and looked at Mary long and hard. Mary felt a chill run down her spine as his gaze came to rest on her abdomen.

"Ah, I see the lineage is continuing." He raised his gaze to hers and said, "You are with child. We shall meet again, be it in this life or the next."

Mary was stunned. She could do nothing but stare at her cousin's strong, gaunt face, her mouth ajar. She had not thought herself swollen enough to alert others to her condition. Instinctively, maybe even protectively, her hand went to her belly. There was much she did not know of her distant, watery family.

"You will not need to concern yourself with me or my kin any longer. My betrothed and I seek passage on a ship bound for the new lands. Now that this business is done, and my mother has been laid to rest, I have nothing here to hold me."

The creature's eyes widened, a sight that brought fear to Mary's bones.

"Is that so?" he asked. "You think the expanse of the Atlantic will keep us from our duty? As much as I would like to dissolve the contract between our side and yours, that is naught for you or me to decide. We have an agreement. The Cantillons of the sea honor the Cantillon branch of the ground—wherever that ground might be."

"But how will you honor us, when we are so far away?"

"You will travel above the sea on a vessel, will you not?"

"Aye," Mary answered.

"We need no such vessel," he said, and he turned towards both the waves and his retreating brethren. "Safe passage, miss," he called over his murky green shoulder.

"Wait!" Mary called, and the merrow stopped and turned. "How will you know when our dead have passed, if we are so far away?"

Her cousin stopped and turned to face Mary. "A Keeper, one who tends the outer lands, will contact you."

Mary had so many questions, but their discourse appeared to be at an end. She watched as this creature, her cousin, approached the roar of the surf. He threw himself into the water and the sea accepted and devoured him with a splash of spray.

Mary watched the water where her relatives had just been and then scanned the beach. She was completely alone. Her mother was gone, never to be seen again.

Older Mary's retreat from this realm had occurred while Younger Mary and her cousin were speaking together. The certainty of this knowledge carved a hole deep in Mary's chest. Even though she had made her farewells to her mother earlier in her own way, the knowledge of her mother's absence filled Younger Mary with an exquisite sadness that cut deeply into her heart.

Mary shivered in the wind while her hands still grasped at the life swimming inside her own body.

What if the child within her *was* developing its own talons, its own sharp claws that would rip Mary open from the inside?

None of her shawls did a thing to warm the cold that Mary now felt. Letting the air out of her lungs as slowly as she could, she tried to be practical, tried to breathe away all her fears and unwanted thoughts. It would do no good. What was done could not be undone.

The wind died down, and the sky grew pink and flushed like a newborn's skin. Mary Fiona Riley, the last living earth-dwelling member of the Cantillon lineage, sat down on the sand and looked out over the waters. Far in the distance, she saw something surface. Squinting, she made out a head, then shoulders. The figure raised an arm to her. Mary raised her own arm in return.

A flash of white and gray distracted her, a seagull swooping into the surf. Mary glanced at the bird for a brief moment. When she returned her gaze to the water another moment later, a solitary hand was all that remained of the floating figure.

Slowly, as she watched, the hand joined its bearer and slid beneath the waves.

As the sun climbed into the pale pink sky now smeared with building, bruised storm clouds, Mary stayed on the beach, both hoping and fearing her watery kin would return.

But they never did.

11

New Pawtuxet Cemetery
Pawtuxet Village, Rhode Island
March 9
7:51 PM

I must have dozed off. I dreamt of fish and a torrent of jelly beans hitting me in the forehead. I dreamt of my brother, Richard, his face inches from mine screaming words I could not decipher, over and over again, until I finally understood him.

Evie! You are a hunter! The door has always been open!

I woke up.

At least I think I did. It was so dark I couldn't see my own hand, and I was sure I was waving it in front of my face.

And man, it was cold.

I'm pretty sure my breath came out in one white puffy cloud after another. To put an end to the endless darkness, I fiddled around in my pocket in search of my flashlight, but instead, I found my lighter.

See? Smoking does come in handy.

After dropping the lighter, cursing the lighter, then searching all over the freezing stone floor to find the lighter, I finally struck the flint wheel and looked around.

Still in the tomb.

Now what?

I considered my options.

Did anyone know I was here? Did I tell anyone where I was going?

The answer was a resounding, *no*, to both questions. I was royally screwed. And who shoved me in here? Oh, wait. I had a good guess.

Nomia.

Or was it *Aunt Catherine?*

Aunt Catherine took my baby and led me to believe Nomia had taken her. That did not make sense either. And what did Aunt Catherine know about Nomia? It didn't seem likely that their paths would cross.

So why did she go through all the trouble of putting wet footprints on the floor?

Well, I had plenty of time to ponder these questions and more as I sat and familiarized myself with hell.

"I'm going to die in here!" I said out loud and started to choke. Then I hyperventilated.

There's only so much oxygen in here!

Preventive measures were in order. I lit a cigarette. Inhaling deeply, I felt the nicotine surge through my veins, numbing the truth of my own demise. In time, I calmed down and remembered my dream.

Richard. It was weird that I had thought of my brother. It

had been more than twenty years since I had last seen him. We had no reason to talk. Once our parents were gone, what was the point? We had never gotten along anyway.

He was so different from me. Handsome to my hideousness, fit to my unfit, sober to my—let's call it self-medicating revelry, shall we? He was always well-liked by everyone, while I was— you got it—not well-liked.

Except when it came to our parents.

They hated both of us. It was the only thing he and I had in common. Maybe hate is a strong word. It was more like we were invisible to them. My father was gone all the time, and even when he was around, he wasn't really around. My mom was so self-absorbed that it was unthinkable to believe she knew we even existed. Neighbors, teachers, other family members praised Richard for his academic and athletic achievements. My parents hardly noticed at all.

As for me, I had no achievements to speak of. Well, I did have a few. Puking at a pep-rally from too much Schnapps— that was a good one. But no one patted me on the back for that. No one did anything.

Richard was white to my black, light to my darkness. Darkness, I know thee well.

Richard, where are you now?

Time passed. I wallowed. I slept. I smoked. Hours passed, I think. Then my phone rang.

No shit.

Why hadn't I remembered the cell in the pocket of my sweater?

Why? Why? Why? Who knows?

"Hello?" I sobbed into the phone.

"Evie, *mo rún*! Where are you?"

"In a tomb! In New Pawtuxet Cemetery!"

"Evie, what are you doing in a ... oh, never mind. Why do I still question you? You're insane, woman. I'm coming."

I sat on the couch, piled under at least four blankets with a wool cap on my head and two pairs of socks on my numb feet.

I just couldn't get warm.

In contrast to my cold constitution, the house smelled warm and deliciously wonderful. Paddy had picked up magical Chinese food. Not real *Chinese* Chinese food but rather the over-salted, over-fried, MSG-filled American kind. The Caucasian American's soul food. You know—the good, starchy stuff you eat twice because of the MSG craving.

It has no culture, just like me. It was just what I needed. Still shivering, I used gloved hands to shove forkfuls of Lo Mein noodles into my face.

Paddy was nose-deep in his combination-number-eight plate with a side of *Pu Pu Madness*—an appetizer for eight to ten people.

My man can eat.

"Evie, I've been thinking ..."

"A dangerous pasttime," I mumbled over my noodles.

"Har, har," Paddy replied. "No, seriously. You've been under a lot of, uh, pressure lately, and I think it might do you good to head to the island for a spell. You go on and take some time. Take a whole bunch of those shitty vampire shows you love, some of your trash novels, maybe even that knitting project you started and never finished—you know the blanket for Savannah that's still no bigger than a wee napkin?"

I slammed my noodles down on the coffee table and looked him dead in the eye.

"What are you getting at, big man?"

"Well, with today's newest folly ..." he started to say.

"What are you talking about? Someone locked me in that tomb!"

"Evie," he sighed. "I don't know why you stole the key to the family crypt or why you were wandering around in there, but when I got there, the door swung right open. No one locked you in. The wind probably blew the door shut."

I was so tired of being made the fool. I was so tired of the disappointing looks from Paddy. Something was very wrong, and I was being shielded from it.

The last straw of resolve in my dark, little soul snapped, and I let the air slowly whistle through my teeth. I needed to face the facts. My child had been taken from me, for Christ's sake. It was apparent that I was circling the drain. Maybe I needed to just give up.

"Fine," I muttered as I toyed with the fringe on one of the four knitted blankets on my lap.

"I'm sorry?" Paddy cleared his throat, his caterpillar eyebrows arched as he tilted his hair-filled ear in my direction. "What was that?"

"I said, '*Fine,*'" I huffed. "I'll pack a bag tonight. Tomorrow I will make my way over to the house and sit out my allotted isolation sentence. Happy?"

"Yes, and no," he muttered and looked at me. "I just want you to take some time and think about what has happened. I also want you to be safe."

"What do you mean? I'm not safe here? Are you finally ready to acknowledge what happened at the yacht club?"

He sighed and gently placed the white styrofoam take-out container on the coffee table. "I'm just saying I want you safe. Is that so wrong—to want safety for my wife?"

He looked like one of those pathetic, droopy-eyed hound dogs on the posters my fifth-grade teacher had in her classroom.

"But," I started to protest.

"No," Paddy cut me off. "No more questions, *mo rún.* You need to let go and trust me on this one. There are things going on ..." His voice trailed off.

"Yes?" I felt my own eyebrows rise, urging him to continue, to let me in on what was happening, on what was making our world chaotic and dangerous. To explain why our daughter was no longer under our roof. To explain why I was being put in a Siberian time-out. "Go on."

He dropped his gaze and toyed with the remnants of his dinner. "Just go to the island, Evie. Let me take care of things here. Savannah is where she needs to be, for now. I need to know that my girls are … Go make a blanket, binge-watch television, read, try yoga, for Christ's sake. Just go and know that I love you with all my heart."

The wind howled as I waited to drive aboard the ferry. Drumming my fingers on the steering wheel, I glanced into my rearview mirror. No vehicles were behind my Land Rover. And no one sat in the pink car seat behind me.

A lump formed in my throat, and I forced my gaze away from the empty car seat filled with Cheerios, cracker crumbs, and a tiny, stuffed baby doll.

I missed *my* baby doll. But I knew I had to trust Paddy, and maybe, to some extent, I had to trust Aunt Catherine as well. I was not well and maybe I did need a time-out to think things through. Also, something wicked had come this way, and the more I thought about it, the less I wanted to be a part of whatever it was. I wanted my mundane life back. Maybe this little excursion was the right thing to do.

Maybe.

I took out my cell phone and scrolled through my contacts. I found what I was looking for in the B section, *Bitch Face.*

I pressed the call button and waited. It rang and rang, then went to voice mail. *You've reached Catherine O'Connor. Please leave a message.* I hung up and dialed again and again and again. Then, on the ninth try …

"What is it, Evie?"

"Why hello, Catherine. How are you? Do you think you could find it somewhere in that cold, cold heart of yours to let me talk to my daughter?"

"She's a toddler. How do you propose she use the phone?"

"Just put the phone to her head, Catherine. She's *my* child, and I have every right to talk at her," I barked, and then I composed my voice to a more genial tone. "Please, Catherine. I am begging you."

There was a long pause. I checked the phone three times to make sure I still had a connection. Then I heard heavy breathing and gurgling.

"Hey, baby girl! It's your mama! I love you, and we'll be together very soon. Be good for that mean old witch, okay?"

More heavy breathing, then the line went dead. I sucked in both of my lips and watched the windshield turn blurry.

"Damn it," I mumbled to myself as I wiped my eyes on the back of my sleeve. Somewhere, a seagull screamed, followed by a curt horn beep. Glancing in my rearview window, I saw a man in a beat-up station wagon giving me two hands up in the air, as in *move it.*

"All right, all right!" I yelled at my own dashboard and looked ahead. One of the crew members was waving me on board, so I put the car in gear. The angry station wagon and I were the only ones going to the island. Of course we were. It was a summer destination. In late winter, the only people headed over to the island were the ones who commuted to and from the island to work on the mainland and vice-versa, and there was no one commuting to the island at three o'clock on a Wednesday.

I got out of the car and walked to the back of the ferry. In time, we shoved off and I watched the mainland retreat. Even though my heart felt like it was tied with a tight elastic band stretching all the way across the Bay to Savannah, a small part of me felt good about being alone for a few days. Inhaling the salt air, I resolved to try and make the best of my situation. Paddy said he would call me every evening around seven to see how I was faring.

Sometimes it's better to be alone. I'm one of those people who doesn't mind eating at a restaurant, seeing a movie, or sitting at a bar alone. I don't think all women feel this way. But really, what's so bad about being by yourself? We come into the world alone, and we sure as hell head out alone. Why not enjoy yourself?

You're all you've got.

Until, of course, you give birth. Then you're responsible for another human being who relies on you for everything, and you wonder if you'll ever be alone again.

Well, there I was—alone.

I found an *everything* bagel in my pocket and—in an attempt to keep my tears in check—I proceeded to devour it. Stress-eating. I brushed the crumbs off my lap and wondered why it was called an *everything* bagel. It's not really filled with *everything*. Who would eat a bagel with *everything?* It's not filled with booze. I think I would welcome an *everything-bagel-including-booze*.

I sighed and wandered back towards the parked cars in the

wide open cargo bay. Glancing around, I checked to see if *angry guy* was looking. He was not, so I left a few crumbs of bagel on his windshield. You know, for the hungry seagulls that might, or might not, poop all over his nice, clean hood.

As I always say, don't get mad, get even.

The ferry ride passed quickly, and before long, I found myself bumping along the old, unpaved roads towards our home on the western side of the island. Our house is so isolated we don't have any visible neighbors. I pulled onto the lawn-cum-driveway and killed the engine.

Maybe this was a bad idea. Normally, I loved a trip to our summer cottage—any time of year. But now, with everything going on, I was suddenly feeling a little less sure. I mean, really, an *island?* An *isolated house?* Why did Paddy think this was a *good* idea? *Why did I?*

Well, it's not like I'm known for my *good* decision-making skills, and it was too late anyway. Might as well make the best of it.

Everything looked the way we had left it. A large wrap-around porch greeted me as I grabbed my bags and headed up the stairs. I unlocked the front door, and it creaked open as the house welcomed me back. A stale smell with notes of mold and moth balls wafted towards me from the empty, dusty rooms, and I smiled at the familiarity of the scent. I busied myself with the reoccupation task list—turning on the heat, sending a silent blessing to Paddy for remembering to have the oil delivered and the boiler serviced, pulling the dust covers off the furniture, plugging in the fridge, turning on the hot water heater, and *blah, blah, blah.* All the chores necessary for my time-out until my husband decided to let me come home.

No, no. Only positive thoughts. This is a vacation. Right? Right.

While I emptied my groceries into the fridge and cabinets, I heard the comforting hiss and clang of the old radiators heralding the return of heat. Once I had squared away all my supplies, I realized there wasn't much else left for me to do.

I glanced around. The place looked spooky in late winter. I took in the mismatched furniture, the peeling wallpaper, and the cat clock on the wall, the one with a tail that swings the seconds and the eyes swish back and forth.

"Hey cat," I mumbled, mostly to hear my own voice. I put my hands on my hips and considered making a snack. Maybe I would read, too.

Yeah, a sandwich and a book. Sounds good.

I imagined myself with a yummy sandwich, all curled up in one of the sun-filled windows, a trashy romance novel open in my lap. I couldn't remember the last time I had read something decent. Really, few things are better in life than good food, a sunny window, and an exciting book.

Invigorated with my decision, I walked over to the fridge with renewed purpose and put all the fixings for a big sandwich on the counter. I smiled to myself. This was nice. Making food is a healthy thing. Then I reached into the cabinet to grab a plate and pulled out a plastic one, a pink plastic one with unicorns and stars on it.

I stared at the unicorn for a long time and could not get the image of tiny hands smearing apple sauce all over the unicorn's mane as the summer breeze stirred wispy, fine hair barely a year old.

Goddamn it.

I decided to go for a walk. I ditched my sandwich-making and left everything on the counter. I couldn't bring myself to put anything away. I just wanted out.

Wrapping a scarf around my head, I went down the front steps and made my way towards Narragansett Bay. Thick woods, nearly impassable in the height of summer, surrounded our house. Someone—one of our neighbors, I guess—always bush-whacked a clear route to the water in the summertime. It wasn't necessary this time of year. All the lush greens had shriveled and retreated with the warmth of the sun, leaving whatever remained gray and dead.

The bleakness echoed my soul. I glanced down at my ugly mom shoes, brown clog loafers, *cloafers.* They were both prac-tical and repulsive.

Shoes, at one point in my life, had been important to me. No matter how fat you get, your feet don't change much. A gal could put on a pair of sexy shoes and dream a little dream of seduction. Savannah had been the product of one particular pair of red vinyl pumps.

Now, the cloafers did their job and delivered me over the winter path. Leaves crackled and twigs snapped in my wake. The deeper I went, the quieter it got. The intermittent twitter of birds ceased, leaving the occasional groan of overgrown trees chaffing one another in the light wind.

I shivered and zipped up my coat, but I kept moving towards the beach. I had no interest in returning to the warmth of the house. Not with that plate sitting on the counter.

In the distance, I could see the remains of a stone wall, crumbled and forgotten. Farm animals, long gone, had once been penned in by the wall. It went on for miles. Stone by stone, one farmer, probably working alone, had moved each and every rock into place. What a pensive, painful endeavor. I nodded to the wall, to the farmer, and to the memory of the animals, thankful to have something other than my pitiful life to ponder.

The dull roar and retreating hush of waves crashing on the rocky beach filled my ears as I approached the Bay. The island was not known for pristine beaches with endless white sand, hunky lifeguards, and beach umbrellas.

Heartier beach people headed here, people who didn't mind traversing difficult terrain or the risk of breaking an ankle on slippery, smooth stones. This place was for rugged travelers, those who came by kayak, sail boat, or even powerboat.

Many came to avoid the overpriced fried clam shacks and lobster pounds of South County and the too-chic-for-thou beach boutiques of Newport. Some came maybe just to escape.

There was very little to do here. There's only one store, one school, one ferry. It's why we went, to unwind and think of nothing. There was no internet, no cable, no landline phone. This place was for sitting on a rocky beach and considering one's life.

I sat on the cold, gray stones until the icy winds crept down my neck and my fingers went numb. It was too windy to even light a cigarette, which pissed me off to no end.

With an unlit cigarette in my mouth, I sat there and scanned the Bay. Far to my left, I could see the Newport bridge arcing itself across the water to Jamestown. The strong, tall pillars looked eternal and ominous, making the cold seem even colder.

I remembered when Paddy told me about a distant relative of his who had died making the bridge. The poor man had fallen into the half-built column, his body sliding into the wet cement, never to be seen again. It was hard to believe. Yet when I looked at the immensity of those supports, I had to wonder ...

How many other souls were trapped in there with him, and why couldn't they get him out?

After Paddy told me this happy little nugget of trivia, I never looked at the bridge the same way again. The knowledge that a man's bones helped hold me up as I traveled from island to island haunts me to this day.

To the west, I saw Prudence's smaller, sister islands, the one named *Hope* and the tiny rock pile known as *Despair*, which was just north of Hope. Unlike Prudence, both were uninhabited.

Our cottage had been in the family for generations. That's how it was with most of the island's homes. They were family owned, passed down through time.

Our property had a dock, and we kept a small craft moored there. It was beat up, because we always forgot to bring it in for the winter. Maybe the person who cleared the forest path was the same person who eventually beached our boat, out of pity.

Once, when Paddy was on an exercise kick, we used the

small dingy to get to Hope Island. We wandered around the island, enduring cuts and scratches from overgrown trees and bushes, laughing at how stupid it was to try to be healthy if this was the reward.

Stumbling among the trees, we burst into a clearing and found the remains of a home. Its foundation was neglected, rotten, angry-looking. As we explored, a hush fell between us. It was several degrees cooler inside, and it smelled of mold and decay. Scattershot graffiti flourished like rampant, brightly colored mold all across the walls. Animals had come and gone, leaving their waste behind.

It was not a happy place.

Without warning, Paddy shoved me out the door, "Time to go."

"Why are you shoving me?" I whined and pushed his meaty hand off my shoulder.

"Don't look in the corner, Evie. Just head back out the door."

I looked up at him and smirked. Then I bolted for the corner.

I mean, really. *Don't look in the corner, Evie?* I was supposed to be compliant? I was supposed to ignore whatever horror might be too awful for my innocent eyes? What the hell did he take me for? Maybe it had been the wine at the picnic, making him all chivalrous and shit, but come on. We work in the funeral industry. We're not fucking florists, for Christ's sake.

It was bizarre. I've seen a lot of gruesome stuff. But this was weird. Bones littered the floor in piles, mostly fish bones, but there were others, too. I know Paddy had seen them. He knew what they were.

"Paddy." I turned and looked at him. "We need to tell someone about this."

He stood in the doorway, rubbing his giant hands across his pudgy face. "Yeah," he said. "I know."

Then it hit me.

"Oh." I suddenly felt sober, and it wasn't pleasant. "This is going to ruin our vacation, isn't it?"

"Yeah," he muttered.

"Maybe we didn't see this."

"Yeah."

I looked at him and saw the pull of morality on his face. Paddy is a good man, an honest man. This was not in his nature. Me? I don't have too many scruples. It was our vacation! There was mold on the bones. They had been there a long time. Why was it our responsibility?

Paddy sighed heavily and shook his head. Bits of leaves fell from his thinning hair.

"It's my duty, Evie."

It was my turn to sigh. Our vacation had been ruined. We returned to Prudence and started the arduous process of calling the proper authorities. It took forever to get ahold of the local law enforcement. It took even longer for them to confirm that Paddy was who he said he was. Then Forensics took their sweet time getting to Hope Island and finding the abandoned building. When they finally arrived, they found nothing.

There were no bones. There was no sign of what we saw. The team mentioned the scene seemed *tidy*. It was the only thing Paddy could glean from the local police.

Paddy kept coming back to that one, little word—*tidy*. Someone had been there after we were and had made things *tidy*.

I couldn't remember the last time I had really thought about the event. It had been so many years ago. Sitting there on the beach, sucking on my unlit cigarette had brought it all back.

Hope and *Despair.*

Those words had been my banners lately, although *despair* was much larger than *hope* at the moment. I'd had it with the wind, with the bad memories, with despair.

I turned towards the cottage in the failing light. The memory of what we had found all those years ago on Hope hunkered down in my mind like a gargoyle brooding on a ledge. Anxious to put some distance between me and the sea, I hurried back with a renewed quickness in my step.

The warm cottage embraced me, and hunger beckoned from my gut. Famished, I finished making my sandwich from earlier. I tried not to notice the unicorn on the pink plate staring at me. After a few minutes of its glares, I shoved it back in the cabinet and pulled out a white ceramic one.

With the sandwich hanging out of my mouth and crumbs flying everywhere, I pulled the sheet off the makeshift entertainment center and shoved my disc into the decrepit VCR/ DVD combo machine we had saved from our first home. I settled into the couch and wrapped an old afghan over my shoulders. While I chewed and waited for the FBI warning to get the hell off the screen, I wondered about the origins of the word "afghan" as it pertained, specifically, to a woven blanket.

In Afghanistan, do they refer to blankets as *americans?* As in, *Hey, I'm cold. Can you hand me that nice chartreuse american?*

The front door smashed open before I could laugh at my own joke.

Sandwich matter flew everywhere as I bolted off the couch and backed up against the living room wall. The foyer was next to the living room. I stared at the fringe on the beaten rug on the foyer floor. Tattered and neglected, it fluttered in the wind blowing through the open door. The living room wall blocked my view of the doorstep.

My heart beat rapidly in my throat. Nothing happened. Only wind and nothing.

I wrapped the afghan over my shoulders even tighter. Arming myself for the worst, I grabbed a heavy pitcher from the side table. I must have looked like a real badass with my purple yarn blanket and ceramic water pitcher at the ready as I crept towards the door.

The frigid air made the spit in my mouth evaporate as I neared the foyer. I shivered and continued forward. The corner of the wall edged closer and closer as my view widened to expose the empty porch.

The gathering night collected along the railing, and the last beams of sunlight leaked through the trees in the woods. There was no one around, just the wind.

I shuddered violently and reached for the handle to close the door. As if I had suddenly cut myself, my hand recoiled, and I sucked in a sharp breath. I brought my hand closer to my face and examined the dampness that clung to my frozen fingers.

The handle was wet and it wasn't raining. Even if it had rained, the porch had a roof.

I looked down at the worn, gray boards in front of our door. Water pooled and shimmered in the fading light. I wished I had grabbed something more violent than a water pitcher.

I backed into the house and with as much force as my shaking hands could handle, I slammed the door shut. Then I did something I never do on the island unless we're leaving the island. I locked the door.

"It's nothing," I muttered to myself. "Not a damn thing. Just the wind, Evie. Just the wind. Go watch your show."

Adjusting the blanket on my shoulders, I noticed, for the first time, just how many windows faced the porch. Many. Too many.

As I sat down, I looked at the TV, the menu screen looping over and over, waiting for me. Beyond the screen, the three porch windows changed from portals to the outside world to mirrors of the house's interior. I saw myself huddled on the couch. My eye sockets were deep, dark holes in my pasty face. I looked small and frightened. The balance of daylight had completed its shift and left me like a goldfish in a highly illuminated bowl.

"Why didn't we ever get blinds?" I yelled at my reflection, my mouth changing into a yawning hole of black with each word.

I felt naked and vulnerable. Rising from the couch, I walked to the windows and checked all the locks. It was nearly impossible to see into the darkness. *And what did I expect to see?* I preferred not to answer that question and instead rescued my sandwich from the floor. No longer hungry, I tossed it towards the coffee table where it landed with a *plunk* on the white plate.

I reached for the remote.

I was going to watch my vampire show, damn it. Whatever would happen would happen. Unease surrounded me, but I pushed it aside. What could I do anyway? Not a whole lot. I was in a bad situation. I was alone on an island in the woods where I would be safe. What a masterful plan. Best not to think about it.

I hit play and eased into the suspended reality that TV so lovingly delivers. A good vampire binge fest would cure anything.

I enjoyed the first show. I took a snack break, chucked the sandwich, and threw some popcorn into the microwave. When it was popped, I doused it with Sno-Caps. If you don't do this, you should. It's divine. The second show started, and I shoved handful after handful of nonpareils-coated popcorn into my eager mouth. My mind went numb, and I let my reality, my history, my current events slide off me like water off a duck's ass.

I had my shit together. Then my pocket buzzed, and I skyrocketed off the couch.

"Jesus H. Christ!" I shouted.

It was my cell phone. I stabbed the answer button and held it to my head.

"Yeah?" I shouted.

"What's wrong?" It was Paddy. Must be seven o'clock.

I took a deep breath and composed myself. "Oh, hey!" False cheer made my voice rise. "I just broke a plate. You know me, so clumsy. How's it going over there across the Bay? Can I come home now?" I tried to make my voice sound as sing-songy as possible.

"Don't bullshit me. What's wrong?"

"I ... I ... I ..." I stuttered, "I broke a plate. That's all. So did anyone interesting die?"

"Do I need to come over there?"

I sighed heavily.

"No. Really. I'm fine."

"I can be there in an hour."

"Really? And how do you propose to do that? You don't have a boat, my love, and the ferry doesn't run at night. I'm a prisoner on an island. I can do no harm. Listen to me. I made a sandwich, and as I was sitting down to watch my—*what do you call it?*—'shitty vampire show,' I dropped the sandwich plate. That's all. So if there isn't any news—and I am sure there isn't because I called your bitchy aunt, and she graciously allowed me to talk to Savannah, so I know she's fine—what more is there to tell?"

"Nothing, I guess. So, you're all right then?"

"Yes!" I said, exasperated. "I'm fine. Can you let me get back to my supernatural smut?"

"Okay. I love you, Evie."

"Love you, too."

I hit the *end call* button. I wanted him to come over right away. I wanted him to leave me the hell alone. I wanted to be home. I wanted to be on a tropical beach with a nice cocktail in my eager hand. A torrent of conflicting thoughts paralyzed me while the DVD menu music framed the background of my stupor. I shook it off and resolved to make the best of my situation.

Hours linked themselves together. Time passed in terms of episodes. I must have dozed off somewhere around midnight, I think.

The DVD menu was back on again. The familiar theme music filled the living room, playing and replaying in an endless loop. I stretched and yawned, wincing at the uncomfortable crick nestled deep in my neck.

Flicking popcorn off my chest, I reached for the remote. As my finger hovered over the menu button, the window behind the television exploded.

12

Cove of Cork
County Cork, Ireland
April 21, 1834
5:32 AM

Mary shielded her eyes from the early morning light and stared up at the enormous ship. It towered above her and creaked against the dock where she stood. The wooden beast was Mary's new home, at least for the next few weeks. The crowded dock teemed with passengers and their kin, crew members, and merchants. It was a hive of activity, bustling and noisy. Large gray gulls swooped above, circling, searching for food, sniping at one another as they fought for a rare scrap. They added their raucous sounds to the impatient and urgent calls of the crew and the nagging advertisements of the merchants. Vendors yelled at the waiting passengers, hawking their wares, seeking out those with a spare coin, preying on their needs.

Bolts of fabric here! Finest in Ireland! Take a piece of home with you! Good bread, low cost! Get your bread here! Don't want to be hungry on the seas, do you?

The morning light made diamonds on the sea, blinding

Mary. She composed herself, making her swollen body as small as she could. The thought of touching some of the other travelers was as revolting as eating her shoe. As she waited for her journey to begin, she tried to focus on something simple to take her mind off the daunting trip. She settled on watching the seagulls as they congregated on the pilings wrapped in thick ropes. The giant coils looked like sea snakes, groaning and creaking with the tide.

Shuddering at the thought of what lay ahead, Mary rubbed her belly and fussed with the buttons on her sleeves. Seamus put his arms around her, and she inhaled his warm, familiar scent. Her shoulders relaxed a bit, and she took the opportunity to lean into his large, strong torso. She could never make this crossing without him.

The pair had been married in December. It had been a simple affair. Seamus' parents and siblings had been the only wedding guests. At the time, Mary's pregnancy was still unannounced. Although her clothes hugged her swelling body, no one said a word. Perhaps they attributed Mary's fuller form to premarital overeating. Or perhaps no one noticed anything at all.

The baby would not arrive until the newlyweds were far across the seas. Mary and Seamus thought it best to keep their growing development to themselves. Better to spare any unnecessary fretting or feelings of loss from Seamus' family and avoid potential attempts to sway the couple into remaining in Ireland.

Following the wedding, Seamus and Mary undertook the difficult and lonely task of hiding their unborn child from Ireland.

It had not been easy. But thus far, Mary had been blessed with an easy pregnancy. She knew she had been fortunate. But just how well her body would respond to being confined to a wooden, floating city remained to be seen. Comfort may not be a priority for anyone—crew or passenger. That was fine. She had been uncomfortable her whole life. This should be no different.

Shifting her weight from foot to foot, Mary surveyed the scene, her gaze taking in both the people who were leaving and those who would stay behind. Men, women, and children were wrapped in various shades of gray and brown, their faces not much different from their clothes. An occasional ruddy face and shock of red hair would differentiate one from another, but for the most part, the crowd looked like one large group of similar individuals, all sharing the same heritage, all bound for a new life.

The look of too much drink and not enough sleep was prevalent—the aftermath of an *American Wake*. It was common to celebrate the loss of a loved one. Even if said family member was not dead.

Not many returned once they answered the great call from across the seas. Passage to America was no different from passage to the heavens. It was a one-way journey, a journey in need of traditional Irish celebration, with great revelry, story-telling, and, of course, drinking.

Mary was surrounded by the aftereffects of this tradition— the swollen-eyed stare of those who had overindulged and then indulged twice again. They leaned on one another and fought to keep their eyes open. Some were still drinking and carrying on, occasionally breaking into song, then sobs, then laughter, then more sobs.

No such revelry took place for Mary. She was the last of her kind to leave. No one would mourn for her.

Her husband's family was absent as well. None of the McFagans had come to see Seamus for the last time. As Catholics, the McFagans did not approve of *self-imposed exile*, the label they chose for the young couple's plans. No McFagans would be present to see their Seamus leave the Emerald Isle, nor would any McFagan indulge in the opportunity to make revelry.

What good was it staying in a land where the life was being choked out of it? There's change in the wind, but they don't feel it.

Mary looked down at the trunk she and Seamus shared. All of it was useless. She needed only the clothes on her back, the love of her husband, and the hope of a new life. The rest they would acquire when they found work in the new lands.

An old woman with a bad limp and a face like a weathered potato sobbed into a yellowed handkerchief. She broke her cries long enough to cough something thick and visceral into the murk surrounding the dock. Her gnarled hand gripped the worn and tattered sleeve of a young man. He had her nose, but nothing else.

The young man leaned down and whispered something to the old woman, who nodded, a solemn look upon her road-mapped face. The look lasted only a moment, then it was gone. She took to crying all the harder.

Returning her gaze to the large ship, Mary watched the decks above. Sailors buzzed like bees, set to the tasks at hand, preparing the vessel for its long journey to the southwest.

"I see a friend of mine from school, Mary," said Seamus. "Why don't you sit a spell while I go over and say 'hello'?"

Mary glanced down at the trunk, sighed, and sat down. She was seven months along, and she felt enormous. A few weeks past, Mary had made a secret visit to the local midwife. Laying down a few extra coins to guarantee secrecy, Mary had then explained her reservations about traveling across the sea with her tiny passenger.

The crone had waved away Mary's concerns with one gnarled hand, then leaned in to examine Mary's midsection. She clucked and clucked, turning Mary's body this way and that. Then the old woman chuckled some nonsense about twins. Mary left the woman reassured about the voyage but agitated by her comments. She was pregnant with Seamus' child. That was all she needed to know. There was no point in speculating about sex or multiples. What good would come from speculating?

Too many possible outcomes lay ahead—too many variables, too many things beyond her control. Would she even survive the journey? Would her offspring? Would she survive the birth? And who would deliver her child? Would the child or children—if she was to believe the village crone—survive in their new home abroad?

Mary shifted her weight on the trunk, then rubbed her thighs with her hands. Heat flushed through her body, turning her cheeks as pink as a sunset. Lifting her skirts a bit, Mary shook them, inviting the air to cool the overwhelming, sudden warmth in her legs.

Nearby, the old woman appeared to have calmed herself enough to afford a toothless smile. It was a gruesome smile, but Mary was pleased to no longer hear the woman's wailing.

Beyond the old woman stood a solitary man. He was taller than those around him, and he carried himself with a lean, quiet strength. A deep brown cloak was pulled up over his head, obscuring most of his face. A strange pipe protruded from the shadows of the cowl, sending plumes of pale-blue smoke into the air around him. Smoking his pipe, the man stood, unmoving, facing towards Mary.

His stillness unnerved Mary. Her gaze kept returning to the place where the man stood. Several minutes passed, and he did not move. If it were not for the smoke swirling up from his pipe, Mary might have mistaken him for a statue.

And then the statue's gaze fell on Mary.

She turned and looked over her shoulder, searching behind her for the source of the man's attention. Mary saw nothing of interest, just crates piled into a great heap on the dock. Not wanting to be rude, she allowed her gaze to fall on her worn-out shoes. A few more moments passed. Curiosity got the better of her, and she raised her head to the strange man. He was gone. Mary exhaled. She had not realized that she had been holding her breath. The old woman nodded at her again, and Mary did her best to smile in return.

"Are you a Cantillon?" The sudden question came from a deep voice behind Mary.

She jumped and cried out.

Turning her head, she gasped. The inquiry came from the

cloaked man.

"Who's doing the asking?" she ventured. It was not practical to give her name to strange men in dark clothing.

"One who is concerned with the Cantillon name. You are Mary, are you not?"

Mary stared up at the man and saw his eyes for the first time. They were the wide eyes of her aquatic cousins, unmistakable with the unnaturally large eye-sockets and light-colored irises.

He was a merrow.

Mary shivered. The flush of heat in her body was replaced with the same cold dread that had gripped her on the beach in Ballyheige Bay. She swallowed hard and stared at the merrow, trying to discern if he had been one of those who had taken her mother's body into the sea. It was difficult to tell. *Was he kin?* They had all looked similar to her.

Mary nodded in answer to his question, then blurted, "Why are you following me?"

He looked down at her from his great height, his eyes roaming over her swollen mid-section, settling on the trunk beneath her.

"You need to make your way south from Boston. Do not linger in that dirty city. There are better waters in Narragansett Bay. Once you are settled, find a place on the Bay where you can leave a lit lantern at night. It must be visible to anyone in the Bay. Near the lantern, leave three piles of rocks. Beneath the first, leave a coin. Beneath the second, leave a shell. Beneath the third, leave this."

The man handed Mary a small piece of rope tied in intricate knots.

In the center of one of the knots was a blue stone. It caught the early morning light, reminding Mary of a clear autumn sky.

"A lantern, a coin, a shell, this rope—remember these things. These actions will establish contact with the Keeper in the Bay. He will leave a feather in place of the coin to acknowledge your presence. When you collect your lantern every morning, check for the feather. Once you find it, return to meet the Keeper that evening. He will instruct you further."

If she had not watched men from the sea take her mother, she would have thought this man deranged. But she had seen the unbelievable, and there was no unseeing it now.

She nodded. Mary would honor the promise she had made at her dying mother's side. She would honor her merrow lineage.

Looking down at the knotted rope in her palm, Mary passed her thumb over both the smoothness of the stone and the roughness of the knots. *Such a contrast of textures, much like the contrast between our kind and theirs.*

Mary raised her head to the man, questions dripping from her eager mouth, but the merrow was gone. Searching the docks, she saw nothing.

A moment later, Seamus returned. "Hello, *mo rún*," he said, a broad smile spreading across his face. "What have you there?"

Mary looked down at the knot work in her lap and tucked it up into her sleeve. "Oh, it's nothing. Something I found on the docks, perhaps some superstitious nonsense."

"Then why are you keeping it?" asked Seamus.

When Mary had returned from her encounter with her aquatic cousins, Seamus had listened with patience and sincerity until Mary finished the telling of her strange tale. He had then helped her into bed and dutifully tucked her in, warming her poor cold form with all the quilts he could find in Mary's hope chest.

Neither the subject of Older Mary's remains nor the merrow had been spoken of again. Mary was sure Seamus had not believed her, but she also believed he was probably too afraid to admit his doubts to either her or himself.

The knowledge of Seamus' disbelief did not bother Mary. In fact, it made her love her husband all the more. A man who would overlook the unnatural possibility of sea creatures in the family bloodline was a true gentleman—a man worth keeping.

She looked up at him. He winked, then recounted his visit with his school friend. The friend was there to wish his cousin farewell. Mary listened but heard nothing. They soon made their way up the gangplank, leaving their entire world behind. As they went, Mary searched the sea for any sign of the merrow.

The great ship with its precious cargo safely aboard left the Cove of Cork and eventually rounded the small islet known as Fastnet Rock, the southern-most point of Ireland, also called *Ireland's Teardrop*. It was the last piece of land the emigrating Irish passengers saw of their home.

Unlike the other sentimental travelers, who lamented leaving their loved ones, their small scraps of landholdings, their heritages, Mary kept her eyes on the water, searching for something, for someone else.

Off on the horizon, far to the northeast, a being broke the

surface of the water and lingered there, watching the ship's departure. Perhaps it was a seal.

Perhaps.

Mary raised a hand to the floating object. Seamus saw her strange gesture, then scanned the expanse of water. Finding nothing, he looked down at his bride, a queer smile spreading across his face. Mary let the small, knotted rope slide down her sleeve into her palm. She rubbed her belly, then turned her back to the sea. As she ran her thumb over the knots once more, she looked up at Seamus, her husband, and said, "When we reach America, we need to make our way to Narragansett Bay."

13

McFagan Cottage
Prudence Island, Rhode Island
March 11
12:04 AM

Shards of glass burst into the room like shrapnel, slashing into the back of the television, the sofa, my face. Cold air blasted through the window, biting into my fresh wounds. Amidst all the glass, the skeletal remains of a half-eaten bluefish lay on the floor, staring at me with its one soulless eye.

I screamed. I couldn't help it. It just flew out of my mouth while blood dripped down my face and the stench of dead fish filled the room.

I couldn't move. I couldn't stop staring at the fish, even though every instinct in my body wanted to see who had thrown the carcass. But I couldn't do it. I just couldn't raise my battered face.

The shrill sound of laughter echoed into my frigid living room, and now I looked up and through the wreckage of what used to be my front window. The faint image of trees and darkness filled the ragged window casing. Then more laughter, shrill laughter joined by another cackle just as wretched as the first, drifted towards me. It didn't sound like Nomia, but there was something so familiar about the laugh, something genetic, something sinister. It had to be someone or something like her. Another goddamn mermaid.

Not one, but two? Two laughing bitches throwing dead fish at me? Really?

The laughter was retreating. I looked at the fish. I looked at the ruined sofa, the destroyed window, and then at my lifeless television.

And they wrecked my television!

I snapped. Everyone thought I was making up this merbitch nonsense. Everyone thought I was crazy. Everyone thought I was a shitty mom. It all boiled in my soul and purged forth like a vomit-filled rage as a primal scream tore from my throat.

I had had enough.

Jumping up from the sofa with new purpose, I glanced around the living room. I spied the fireplace poker next to the ash bucket. I grabbed it and dramatically shook it over my head, channeling my inner Amazon woman.

"I'm a warrior, goddamn it! And you trashed my television! I'm coming for you!"

I ran out the door, onto the porch, a banshee scream tearing from my open mouth. I got halfway across the front lawn and stopped.

"I need shoes, damn it."

I returned to the house, shoved my feet in my ugly cloafers, grabbed my parka, and headed back out the door screaming the whole way. The sources of the laughter were gone, but I had a good idea about where they had headed.

I turned towards the beach.

When I got there, most of the screaming fight had left me—left me with a wheeze and a strong desire to get back to my couch. Then I remembered what my living room looked like, and the anger surged anew.

With enough ambient light from the full moon, I could see the beach sprawling out before me. I scanned the twinkling surface of the water. Far in the distance, heading towards Hope Island, two figures broke the surface and then disappeared into the inky-black water.

Right. Game on, bitches.

The silhouette of our lame little boat sat farther down the beach. I trotted towards it, pushing up the sleeves of my parka. Scanning the Bay a second time yielded nothing, so I got to work. The wooden dingy made a soft grating noise as I pushed it into the water and then climbed aboard, soaking my cloafers in the process. I made a face of disgust as I wiggled my toes in their damp confines.

The front of the boat (*Prow? How now prow? I have no idea what the hell it's called ...*) splashed against the waves, making a wet sloshing thump as the water hit the old wood. Yeah, I know what you're thinking.

Chunky girl in a boat with a smoker's cough. This should be good.

Well, I am going to disappoint you. This chunky girl, believe it or not, is an excellent rower. I may not get much practice, but for some strange reason, I enjoy rowing. Paddy is always amazed with my oar-handling prowess.

So suck it.

I set my course for Hope. It took forever to get there. Yes, you were right. Chunky girl with a smoker's cough does not an Olympian rower make. It took some time. I aimed my small craft for the dark beach, rowing in as far as I could, pushing the boat up on the rocks. The fireplace poker made a loud *clank* when I tossed it onto the beach. It bounced around on the rocks, smashing and rebounding, making more and more *clanks*.

So much for stealth.

I hopped out and scanned the beach. *Nothing*. Not that I could see in the dark, but I stopped and listened. Still nothing.

I wandered along the rocky coast and headed in the direction of the island of Despair. The wind had died down, leaving a steady, frosty temperature. I tried to keep my footsteps light on the rocks while attempting not to drag the über heavy fire poker behind me like a lost child dragging a blankie.

I considered lighting a cigarette as I walked, but reason intervened—both the smell and the light might give me away. Oh, a hot toddy would be lovely. I shook off the desire. I needed to move beyond alcohol.

The rhythmic sound of the waves came from my right as I stumbled along the rocky coast, cursing every time my damp cloafers caused me to stumble on the uneven surface of the beach. But I kept moving. I was a woman on a beach, at night, with a fire poker, on a mission.

Fearless and stupid.

I heard them before I saw them—*them*, as in more than one.

It was hard to swallow. One Nomia was frightening, but several? Snarling, yapping, splashing. The noise started off faintly, but the closer I crept to where Hope meets her sister island the louder, more ominous, more terrifying it grew.

Clicks, trills, and some ungodly, thick snapping sounds floated over the sea into my ears. My blood turned to ice water, and my limbs felt like logs soaked in swampy, river water. But I couldn't stop myself from seeking the origins of the noises.

I had to see. My anger and drive gave way to some sick, morbid curiosity that demanded satisfaction. I was Pandora, with my fingers on the box handle—at the point of no return.

I wanted to know what was in that box!

I dropped to a low crouch. Rocks and pebbles bit and gaffed my hands and knees as I crept forward. I winced but kept moving. Not far ahead, a low outcropping of sturdy, time-worn boulders faced north towards the rock-pile known as Despair Island. As I inched my way painfully towards my destination, the sounds grew louder and more intense.

I reached the boulders and climbed into a sort of crevasse between two enormous rocks, each the size of a European compact car. From my new, cradled position among the freezing rocks, I could see Despair.

What I then saw will stay with me until my dying days. The images, the sounds, the smells that wafted along the calm waters to infiltrate my nostrils and leave a permanent scar on my memory were the things of horror movies.

Except it wasn't a horror movie. It was me, Evie, on a beach in the middle of the night witnessing the stuff of nightmares.

I never was able to count how many of them there were. They would appear and reappear, bobbing on the surface of the water. Some would climb out onto the rocks, grab what they wanted, tearing it from its source, then slip back beneath the gentle, black waves.

The moon was at its apex, bright enough to illuminate the atrocities on Despair. They seemed to be all female. Their long hair, stringy and damp like rotten seaweed, clung to their twisted, harsh faces and bare breasts. Their sharp, almost filed-looking teeth flashed in the low light as they snarled at one another. It was like a Nature Channel scene in which alpha wolves establish dominance over a fresh carcass.

Oh, the carcass. I've seen cadavers. I'm no stranger to dead bodies. But this was so different. So, so different.

I had never witnessed a limb being ripped from a torso, and I hope to never do so again. I have never witnessed a human— *stop right there.* To call them human is wrong. They are a close approximation to humans, with human-like faces and human-like upper torsos. They hold the essence of humanity in their altered-parallel species, a species that feasts on the flesh of what was a human but was now reduced to human sushi.

I almost vomited in my mouth. The reverse of popcorn and Sno-Caps burned the back of my throat, but I held it together.

I shifted uncomfortably in my rocky position and hoped I wasn't visible. If these were the perpetrators of the flying fish incident, I was counting myself lucky. As in much luckier than whoever was now part of the aquatic food chain over there.

I squinted hard to look for my favorite mermaid amidst the chaos, but I didn't see her. I blinked and everything disappeared. The oily and slick surface of the water appeared vacant. Only the corpse remained, one leg drifting in the subtle waves.

Where did they go?

The world was still. Water lapped, waves shushed, the corpse nodded in the gentle current. I held my breath in the quiet, interrupted only by the low whine of an engine coming closer.

My brain screamed at its divided self. One side wanted to yell to the oncoming, innocent boater rapidly approaching hell's sixth or seventh level. The other side screamed, *Shut the fuck up, Evie! What the hell are you going to do? Yell to them, expose yourself, get the both of you killed? Maybe you should beat it now. Go get help.*

That sounded like a grand idea. I wanted to run back to my little dinghy, but I had grown frigid roots that had attached me to the rock. I couldn't move at all.

The approaching craft cut the engine, and the sound echoed across the nearly still waters. I really wanted to warn them— really, really, I did. This poor person (or persons) was probably out looking for lobsters or something similar. The rock pile of Despair would be a logical location for lobsters, especially since those delicious crustaceans are scavengers, fond of any tasty leftovers they find floating around in the ... *Oh my dear God.*

Mental note: I will never eat lobster again.

I watched from my rookery, hoping for the best, fearing the worst.

A figure appeared at the front of the boat, a tall slender

figure in a hooded coat. The person placed a hand on either side of the small craft and leaned forward a bit, head back, inhaling the air, to ... *smell?* A sniffing sound emanated from the figure, who then reached up and pulled back the hood on the coat. With a practiced grace, the person shook out long tendrils of hair and tossed them around like a stupid shampoo commercial. This foolishness was followed by a long, rich honeyed laugh.

I knew that laugh. I will *never* forget that laugh. Nomia.

Nomia turned away and looked down into the boat. She barked something sharp and commanding, then turned back to the sea and raised her fingers to her lips.

Two short, shrill blasts echoed off the rocks where I was hidden. Nothing happened at first. Nomia made the sound again— two more blasts.

I held my breath and watched the surface of the sea. It had become a slick, obsidian expanse of glass. Smooth and placid, like a membrane covering the unknown.

Then one appeared. A head broke the surface of the moon's mirror, rising unnaturally, shoulders following. Then another joined the first, then another, and another, and another, until the water was teeming with floating heads, all watching the boat, watching Nomia. They waited, swaying in the gentle ebb of the sea.

Nomia spoke to them with a series of clicks and trills. Whatever she said seemed to please the heads. One raised a terrible arm, and I saw its claw-like hand. The moonlight glowed between both the webbing and the long, translucent talons that emerged from each digit. A gargled cry came from the talon-raiser, and the remaining heads echoed the sentiment. Each one raised its nasty hand to the moon and emitted an awful sound. Some seem to launch themselves higher, perhaps using their tails to propel themselves upwards, like dolphins in one of those tank shows.

Nomia trilled back and then disappeared below deck. She emerged seconds later with a heavy bundle slung over her narrow shoulders. The bundle was moving and making a low mewing sound like a cat in distress.

Nomia laughed and chucked the bundle over the side of the boat.

There was an enormous, noisy splash. Seconds later, the contents of the bundle broke the surface of the water. Arms appeared—human arms, belonging to a man who appeared to be in his mid-twenties. He sputtered and choked as he flailed around, trying to tread water.

All of the creatures in the water dove forward at once. Their bodies arched as they submerged, spiked tail following spiked spine, until they all disappeared without a trace, gone beneath the dark surface.

Mr. Bundle seemed a little more with it now. He was turning in circles, coughing and looking wildly to his left and then his right, until he spied the boat.

"*Why?*" Mr. Bundle screamed at Nomia.

She just laughed.

Mr. Bundle leaned forward and started to swim towards Nomia's boat. She disappeared from view, reappearing with a long fishing hook-grabber-pole-thingy—the kind used to pull a heavy catch into a boat. I had seen one on a fishing show. Nomia aimed the hook at Mr. Bundle and struck a hard blow into his right shoulder. He cried out but kept up his pursuit. She struck him again, this time on his left shoulder.

"I'm bleeding, you bitch!"

She covered her mouth and giggled but stopped short. All the sinister mirth left her, and in its place was a placid, almost blank look of concentration. Mr. Bundle stared up at her. She tilted her head to the side, listening to something only she could hear, then threw the fishhook down onto the deck, climbed up on the side of the boat, and dove into the water. The darkness embraced her, swallowed her whole.

Mr. Bundle jerked his head around and looked at the spot where Nomia had entered the water. There was no sign of her. Droplets flew from his hair, glistening in the moonlight, as he whipped his head and shoulders around, scanning the slick surface.

Get in the boat! I wanted to scream. But I knew better and kept silent, hidden among the rocks. Maybe Mr. Bundle heard my thoughts. He splashed his way towards the back of the boat. He never made it.

He took three, maybe four, strokes before his body jerked suddenly. His head disappeared beneath the surface of the water, a startled cry bursting from his lips. He resurfaced, gasping for air, and tried to swim again. *Determined bastard, good for him.*

Mr. Bundle's body skidded to the right, then the left, then the right again, before he disappeared underwater. A burbling cry left his lips before I lost sight of him. Seconds later, he reappeared a good twenty feet from where he had just been.

Mr. Bundle screamed. The sound filled the night air but was lost in the isolation of our location. I shivered in my hiding spot, frightened tears threatening to leak down my frozen cheeks, but I was useless to this man. There wasn't a single thing I could do to help him. I'm not a strong swimmer, and even if I did charge into the water—like some macho, deranged life guard—who knew what was teeming just beneath the surface? Wouldn't they just love to tear me limb from limb?

Mid-scream, he went under again. The night was eerily quiet without his frightened cry. Waves lapped against the rocks, a gentle rhythmic pulse, while the wind rustled some of last fall's leaves behind me on Hope. The silence felt endless.

I had given Mr. Bundle up for dead when his body broke the surface of the water and flew through the air. Useless and weightless, his arms pin-wheeled as water streamed from his heavy clothes. He disappeared once more, and the water stilled. The empty boat drifted in the pale light while the impassive moon watched from above.

I held my breath and counted. *One, one-thousand, two, one-thousand, three, one-thousand, four* ... I got to fifteen when Mr. Bundle was suddenly once again launched into the air. His arm stuck out at an odd angle, and one of his legs was missing from the knee down. I wasn't sure if he was alive or not, until I saw his hand—the one on the good arm—cover his face before his body slammed into the water.

This would be a good time to go.

My heart raced, and my breath came out in a series of short, ragged gasps. I had just witnessed something out of *Shark Week*, except it wasn't on cable and Mr. Bundle wasn't a seal.

I eased out of my hiding place, praying and hoping my graceless nature did not call *any* attention to my whereabouts. A lump formed in the back of my throat as I thought about Mr. Bundle. I let his demise be my warning. I wanted no part of his fate. I scampered away from the rocks as fast as I could.

My little dinghy was right where I had beached it. I shoved it away from the shore and climbed in. My cloafers filled with water and my legs prickled as the icy wetness soaked into my pants, but I didn't care. I wanted to put as much distance between me and the horrors as possible.

Fear-soaked adrenaline coursed through my veins like meth through an addict. You bet your cheese hole, I picked up those oars and rowed like a maniac. My arm muscles burned from both the trip over and general underuse, but I ignored them. The image of Mr. Bundle flying through the air as if he were a sadistic child's plaything motivated my sorry ass.

I glanced behind me and could see the shore of Prudence. I was almost there when I heard the engine. A low moan escaped my lips, and I began to tremble all over.

"Please, dear God. I know I've been awful, but please, don't let me be a chew toy! Please!"

I rowed faster and faster. The oars noisily spanked the water as I crept along. The sound of the engine grew louder and louder with each stroke. I didn't look up. I kept my head down and rowed. I stared at my shoes, the inside of the dirty boat, my knees. My shoulder sockets were on fire, but I didn't stop. I glanced behind me—only a few more yards.

I abandoned dinghy.

The icy water pushed a scream from my lips, and I couldn't catch my breath, but I found the strength to slog my way to shore. The motorboat grew louder and louder until I heard it slow and idle. It could go no farther without dragging the motor on the rocky bottom.

I never looked back. I ran. My sodden cloafers and soaked jeans slowed down my out-of-shape ass, but I didn't stop. Wet fabric chafed my inner thighs, burning red hot with every step I took. Adrenaline surged through my body, spurring me towards the tree line. Behind me, the idling engine purred like a big hungry cat, a cat with razor-sharp claws and an appetite for human flesh. The sound faded once I moved into the trees.

I ran through the woods with tears streaming down my face, my breath like an old man's. Little high-pitched sobs and moans punctuated my uneven gasps. Branches scraped my already-torn face and ripped at my clothes, but I still didn't stop.

I stumbled out of the woods and saw the house ahead of me, lit up like a lighthouse beacon, calling me forward. The wind had picked up, and the curtains were sucked out the shattered window, flapping in the frigid breeze, reminding me that this was not a safe harbor.

I took the steps two at a time and attempted to kick the door open. No, of course it didn't work. I'm no action hero. I had to use my shaky hand to turn the knob.

I rushed in, grabbed my purse, and ran back out into the night towards the Land Rover. It roared to life, and I threw it into reverse. Tearing up the lawn, I spun the wheel hard and aimed for the road.

Two figures stood just beyond the reach of my headlights. Their features were masked by the shadow of the trees. They looked at me, and I at them.

I threw the Land Rover into gear and slammed my foot down on the accelerator. I shifted into third and gunned it.

At the last second, just before my headlights illuminated the figures, they dove left and disappeared into the woods. I roared by and kept going. The clock on the dash read 4:03 a.m.

There was a 6:25 a.m. ferry.

I pulled into the first position in the queue. My hands shook on both the steering wheel and the stick shift. Then my whole body joined in and shook just as violently as my hands. Sobs wracked my frame, and tears spilled onto the steering wheel. I screamed and cried until I could do nothing else. I must have collapsed and slumped forward because the next thing I knew, that same asshole in the station wagon, bird shit all over the front of the hood, was beeping at me to move forward. I couldn't get on the ferry fast enough and, once on board, I never left my car.

I didn't want to be anywhere near the water. I didn't want to be anywhere near any water ever again.

14

In the accumulating darkness, Aiden O'Conner stood on the ill-named Rock Island, a misnomer for a long, jetty-like causeway. Rock Island was not an island at all, but a series of rocky islets connected to the mainland at one end and jutting out into Narragansett Bay at the other. The jetty was popular with fishermen, bored teenagers, and the occasional geologist. The latter came to investigate a prevalent rumor of rare fossils, which they never found.

Aiden had his own reasons for being on the causeway at the end of a beautiful spring day. He faced east, a beer in his hand, a tuneless tune drifting from his lips. Across the Bay, like a tall, big-headed ghost, the East Providence water tower stood on the far side, its red lights winking.

A jetliner roared overhead, and Aiden followed its path. The passenger plane flew from East Bay to West Bay. Aiden heard the engine whine and change pitch as it prepared for descent.

The plane was headed for its final destination, T. F. Greene Airport or PVD, for Providence.

Another piece of Rhode Island misinformation. The airport was never in Providence. It had always been in Warwick. Aiden smiled at this tidbit and shook his head. He turned, keeping his eyes on the giant bird, and faced the forest behind him, Salter Grove. Beyond the Grove was Narragansett Parkway, a scenic thruway that slithered along the coast, making its way into the Village. Aiden could see his truck nestled just below the Parkway. The failing light bounced off the windshield, creating a blinding beacon.

Taking a long pull from his Narragansett beer, Aiden swallowed deeply and turned his gaze north, towards the Village. He squinted, searching for his own home, farther up the Bay. It was no good. The night was gaining a foothold, making long-distance visibility null and void. He took a deep breath, spread his arms wide, and exhaled. His beer can tipped a bit. The amber fluid flowed down to the rocks where it foamed and fizzed.

"Oops," Aiden said, chuckling to himself.

Since his arrival on the jetty, he had enjoyed the pleasure of two beers. In the parking lot, before he stumbled out onto the rocks, he had polished off two or three, and on his way home from the boat yard, perhaps there had been one or two more.

Earlier in the day, while he was on his boat, his cooler had been filled with two shiny new six-packs. Now, just one lonely beer swam in the melted ice at the bottom of the dirty, white container.

Aiden cursed under his breath. This little covert mission of

Catherine's required more adult beverages, and he was running low.

"Ah, Catherine." Aiden raised his next to last can. "Here's to you. You make my life a living hell, but I love you anyway."

Catherine was a rule-follower, a by-the-book, this-is-the-way-we-do-things type of woman. Back when they had been young and full of hope, this stability, verging on rigidity, had attracted Aiden to Catherine. Now that they were old, all their hopes and energies were as stagnant as an unused sewer pipe.

It was all Aiden could do to stay out of his wife's way, ducking her mercurial moods, finding solace anywhere he could. There was plenty of solace to be found in the bottom of a shiny can with a slogan that read, *Hi Neighbor! Have a 'Gansett!*

"I think I will," said Aiden to himself.

It was a sad day when a man had to take his kindness from a beer can slogan. But there was comfort in knowing that he was—most likely—not alone. As the soothing fluid slid down his throat, he joined the brotherhood of *neighbors,* united under the grand Narragansett Brewing Company.

"Here's to the brewers."

An audible crack followed by a long satisfying hiss echoed in the quiet evening as Aiden popped the final can. The smell hit him before the liquid touched his tongue. The experience was so reassuring, so comforting. He smiled as he drank. Both taste and scent brought back memories of his grandfather, another hardworking *neighbor of the Narragansett Brewing Company,* now long gone, a permanent season pass holder to the hunting grounds in the sky.

"And here's to you, Pappy!" shouted Aiden, raising his can once more and sloshing beer all over his extended arm. Aiden glanced around the rocks. No one was around—just a man and his beers—on a mission for his dear wife.

Great Aunt Margaret had died, and ever since the old bag had passed, Catherine had been impossible to live with. In an act of self-preservation, Aiden had done his best to avoid his bride at all costs.

Catherine had not tended any false flame on Margaret's behalf. She couldn't stand her. For the past ten years, week after week, she had driven the twenty miles, alone, to Margaret's nursing home to fulfill her visitation duties. Each time, she toted a just-the-right-size tissue box and some just-the-right-size hard candy for Margaret—along with donuts and coffee to appease the poor nurses who the woman abused and ridiculed to tears during Catherine's absence.

It was grueling.

Aiden went once. That had been enough for him. He hated the smell, an old, feeble odor that reminded him of Lysol, bedpans, stale breath, and death. It was not a positive place for a strong man—such as himself—and besides, Margaret was prissy and opinionated, and she had hated him from the moment she had laid eyes on him. Looking back, perhaps he should have been more supportive of Catherine. Maybe he should have accompanied his wife on her mercy missions, but he hadn't.

Well, it was a brand new day.

Starting tonight, he would make it up to Catherine. He was here—wasn't he?—taking responsibility for this bizarre little ritual. This would show Catherine how much he loved her. And he did love her, even though sometimes—okay, a lot of the time—she was infuriating to live with. Even though sometimes being alone might be preferable to one of her week-long freeze outs, when she didn't speak to him beyond a head shake or a nod.

"Today I become a husband again!" shouted Aiden, startling a flock of nearby seagulls. Their cries made him grimace. He hated those god-forsaken birds.

Rats with wings.

After Catherine received the call concerning Margaret's passing on Friday morning, she had put the phone down, told him the news, then stared out at the Bay.

"You all right?" Aiden asked.

She did not answer right away. No tears filled her eyes. This was unsurprising. Her relationship with her aunt had been one of formal obligation, not one of familial love. She continued to watch the gulls swoop down to the water and then resume their endless circling.

Aiden thought she was ignoring him when she suddenly jerked her head up and looked his way. With a look that bordered on fear—something that had surprised Aiden—she opened her mouth to speak.

Maybe she'll cry after all.

But no tears appeared on her white cheeks. Instead she said, "Tomorrow is the recital."

Aiden didn't know what to say. This was tricky ground he was standing on. Each step came with the possibility of falling into a hole he had never known was there.

"Yes," he ventured. "The recital is always the Saturday of Mother's Day weekend."

He felt he had said the right thing, a way of demonstrating to his wife that he did occasionally pay attention. By stating the known, he reinforced to Catherine that he was a man who knew what was going on—even though he could not, for the life of him, make a clear connection between the recital and Margaret's death.

Arrangements needed to be made, but Paddy would handle all that, and a Friday death did not necessarily mean a Saturday wake. Sunday or Monday would be sufficient, *should* be sufficient.

Aiden felt the ground shift beneath his unsteady feet. He was missing something, and missing something meant he was stupid. Catherine made him pay when he was stupid.

Think. Think, Aiden, think!

His brain hurt as it whizzed though all the implications of a Friday death and its subsequent impact on the Saturday recital.

Catherine looked at him expectantly. Aiden stared back. He blinked twice.

Catherine broke the silence between them. Her hand slammed down on the table. The sugar bowl flipped on its side, spilling its contents all over the lace tablecloth.

"I cannot leave the recital," she said with conviction in her voice. "It's impossible."

Aiden nodded. Still on shaky ground, but this much he understood. The dance school was everything to Catherine. It lived and breathed because she did. Without her, it would die.

She had built it that way, to be ever reliant on its founder's existence.

The arrival of their large teenage nephew aside, they had never had children of their own. In fact, after countless doctors' visits—and seemingly endless, violating tests—they had been informed that they were medically unable to have children of their own. As a way to grieve her childlessness, their childlessness, Catherine had opened the studio. By having the recital on Mother's Day weekend, she had created a distraction for herself, a way to cope with what was—and what was not.

She looked back out the window at the water, then back at Aiden.

"I'm going to need you to do something for me. You will need to do it *exactly*. No questions asked."

The last of the sun disappeared over the horizon far to the west, leaving Aiden to bask in the glory of the May half-light. His second six-pack was gone, and an ancient lantern swung from his right hand. He needed to light the lantern and then make some rock piles, or something like that.

No, not something like that, Aiden. Think! You need to do it right, or she'll be madder than shit.

Right. He remembered. Three piles—one with a hundred

dollar bill in a plastic baggie at the bottom, which pissed him off to no end, one with a seashell, and one with a … a … *shit.*

He forgot to bring the little rope with the blue stone.

Goddamn it!

How could he forget the rope? He could see it in his mind's eye, sitting on the dining room table, right where he had left it.

He cursed again and stomped his feet on the rocks. He would have to go back and get it.

Damn. Damn. Damn!

Aiden left the lantern and the seashell at the end of the rock jetty and stuffed the money into his faded dungaree pocket. No way was he was leaving the cash behind.

The money had caused an enormous blowout. He argued that they barely had enough to put gas in their cars, and she wanted to put his hard-earned cash under some god-forsaken rock? For what? For some goddamn tradition to honor an old bag that neither of them cared about? Catherine had only stared at him with those cold blue eyes of hers.

Now here he was, doing what he was told to do and screwing it up, as usual. "Goddamn it!" he shouted, sending one more curse word to the heavens for his stupidity.

Aiden stumbled towards his truck in the growing darkness. Cursing, he tripped down the causeway, his vision now lit by the dim parking area lights. His vehicle was right where he had left it, and soon he was tearing through the streets of the Village on his way back home.

Sure enough, the stupid rope with the little blue stone was right where he had left it. He scowled at it and then snatched it up, stuffing it in the same pocket as the money.

On his way out the door, he stopped in his tracks, backtracked into the kitchen, and grabbed another can of beer from the fridge.

One for the road, and for my troubles.

Aiden retraced his route back to the Salter Grove parking lot. He parked his truck and made his way to the stone breakwater. It was fully dark now. Aiden was without a flashlight.

"You're a real ass-hat, Aiden," he said after returning to his vehicle to search the glove box, which yielded his registration and an empty beer can.

With only the lights from the parking lot as his guide, Aiden stumbled back into the darkness towards the narrow causeway. As he squinted at the rocks in his path, he imagined himself on his porch, another beer in his hand, and Catherine by his side—smiling.

"Fat chance of that happening," he mumbled. "Time to face the music and get this shit done."

Aiden took in a deep breath and straightened to his full height. Walking with purpose, he made his way towards the end of the narrow strip of rocks and scanned the last flat rock for the lantern.

It wasn't there.

"Shit on a shingle," he yelled to the dark sea. "There's no goddamn wind, where did it go?"

Aiden stood there. There was no way he could go home and face the disgusted, disappointed look on his wife's face when he told her how he lost her family's stupid goddamn lantern.

Shaking his head, he put his hands on his hips and sighed.

The water lapped against the rocks, a soft lulling gurgle. The gulls were gone, and Aiden could make out the faint sound of an engine far across the Bay.

Probably someone out night fishing. Wish I was with them, lucky bastards.

The boat faded into oblivion. Once it was gone, Aiden snapped his fingers, then dug into the back pocket of his dungarees. Tucked neatly in his pipe pouch were two matchbooks.

"Right!" he said drawing out one of the matchbooks. He returned the pouch to his back pocket and opened the heavy folded paper. One match remained. Tearing the last stick off, Aiden struck the match on the faded strike pad. Pinching the match in his oil-stained fingers, he searched the rocks for the lost lantern, cupping the flame with his free hand.

"What the ...?"

The stones from the three piles had been reconfigured. Shards of glass, which he assumed came from the lantern, circled a large X of smooth flat stones. In the center, something dark and visceral glistened in the fading light from his match.

"Huh?"

Aiden stared down at the handiwork, then looked around the empty jetty. The match burned down to his fingers, then went out.

"Ouch! Damn it!"

He dropped both the burned-out match and the empty matchbook then shook the stinging pain from his fingers.

The darkness was all encompassing. Aiden's eyes had not

dilated with the light change. He was blind. With his eyes no longer useful, his ears went into overdrive. The waves slapped at the jetty, sloshing and licking at the rocks. A bell chimed on a channel marker, far across the Bay. Something rustled behind him followed by the sound of something shifting, sliding, as whatever it was tried to be silent.

Aiden dug out his pipe pouch in a hurry. The zipper sounded like a jet plane as he opened it. He winced and, with trembling fingers, produced his backup matchbook. He kept the matchbook in his palm and returned the pipe pouch to his back pocket.

Ripping another match from the brand new book, he struck the head on the back of the matchbook once, twice, three times. On the fourth strike, it caught with a faint hiss, the flame burning brilliant white, then fading to a warm orange glow. The smell of sulfur burned the hairs in Aiden's nose as he lifted the lit match above his head.

The flame didn't produce much light—just enough to make the blurry shadow of Aiden's head dance around his feet. He turned left, then right, his hands above his head, shielding and directing the flame to cast some light on the source of the noise. He saw nothing.

Must have been a rat.

But unease and a slight tremor had settled in his soul, nesting there, squeezing Aiden's heart with icy fingers. Returning his attention to the rearranged rocks at his feet, he crouched down to examine the handiwork of the unknown vandal.

Holding the second dwindling match with his left hand, he extended his right forefinger and poked the thick substance pooling in the center of the X. With a scowl on his face, he smeared the gunk against the pad of his right thumb. It was sticky.

He brought his fingers to his nose and inhaled deeply. Aiden's eyes grew wide. He knew that smell. Blood.

Something's not right.

Aiden stood. The second match was almost out. The rustling sound returned, this time from his left, off the edge of the point.

Aiden turned, swinging the match light to illuminate the source of the mysterious rustling. He saw nothing. But the noise continued. It was more of a whisper this time, more like the bubbling of liquid escaping down an old drain, gurgling as it hit the filth of the pipe on its descent.

It was coming from just beyond the lip of rock that jutted out into the Bay, just beyond the light of his match.

Aiden took a deep breath and chucked the match over the rocks. It flew end over end, then landed with a *pfft*, expiring as it hit the surface of the sea. Aiden was sure he saw something in the water just before the match died. A large shape that disappeared the instant his eyes registered its presence.

Aiden struck another match and crept over to the rock's edge. The flame danced and shimmied as he tried to keep his hands from shaking. He got down on his knees, both hands in front of him, directing the flame to what lay beyond the boundary of the rock. Aiden held his breath. Holding out his hands, he stretched the light towards the water. The ever-moving surface of the sea lay four feet below him.

The blue-green liquid shimmered and swayed while tiny flecks of aquatic life flitted in the small pool of light, but there was nothing else to see.

Letting out his held breath, Aiden leaned closer, his third match threatening to expire at any moment. The noise came again. This time it was right below him.

Using the lit match, Aiden set his entire matchbook on fire, creating a miniature torch. He leaned forward, his torso over the surface of the water and looked down.

Two hands, two clawed hands, and a face, a face of nightmares, raced towards the surface of the water. Towards Aiden.

He never had time to scream.

Across the Bay, a bell chimed, lulled by the gentle rhythm of the incoming tide. In a nearby cove, gulls napped on pilings, waiting for the morning light, waiting for the opportunity to scavenge for whatever might be floating on the cold surface of Narragansett Bay.

15

McFagan & McFagan Funeral Home, Inc.
Pawtuxet Village, Rhode Island
March 11
8:18 AM

I couldn't move.

I sat in my car in the driveway and stared at my home. It looked the same as it always did—a neat sign on our pristine lawn indicated that both death and comfort could be found within our walls. The engine idled, growling in the background, while a honey-voiced woman on public radio explained something newsworthy, something that evaporated as soon as it hit my ears.

My hands hurt. White and shaking, my fingers were death-gripping the wheel at ten and two. My brain told them to let go. Nothing happened. My gnarled and rigid digits ignored my brain and continued clutching as if the act of driving could erase all that had happened. If only.

I was too stunned to allow my string of well-loved, dog-eared curse words to fly out of my mouth. Instead, the words remained internal, bubbling in the back of my throat, waiting for the next chapter of horror to begin.

It was after eight o'clock in the morning, but the shades were still drawn, as if no one was awake. Paddy's post-toast morning usually consisted of making the rounds, moving from room to room, opening shades with one hand while sipping coffee and juggling a folded newspaper with the other.

Paddy is an early riser.

My breath started to hitch and hiccup, and I felt as if someone was holding a warm pillow over my face—pressing, pressing, pressing, pressing. I gasped for air, like a fish out of water. It was a full-on panic attack—the kind that feels as if you are experiencing a heart attack. Ask anyone who's ever had a panic attack. Once they dig deep enough, they discover the source of their panic, and it's usually some heavily buried shit.

My shit was right there, floating on the surface of the bowl with a tail, claws, and friends—lots of friends.

Something was not right.

Leaving the Land Rover still running, I bolted into the house. My suspicions were confirmed even before I reached our entrance. The back door to our living quarters was wide open. I couldn't help it. Like a ninny, a tiny sob escaped my lips, "Oh, Paddy, no!"

I stumbled up the stairs towards our kitchen. It was a mess. The kitchen table was overturned, and chairs lay broken and askew. It looked like a breakfast massacre. Toast, butter, and coffee were splattered all over the walls, the floor, the cabinets.

As the tears spilled down my face, I surveyed the scene. One small consoling thought crossed my sleep-deprived, tortured mind as I took in the complete and total destruction of my home.

Paddy had put up a good fight.

Frantic, I raced from room to room screaming his name. It was hauntingly quiet, my hysteria the only sound. But my search yielded nothing. I returned to the kitchen and reached down to right a fallen chair.

They had taken him.

There was nothing left for me. My home was not a home without my family, and I needed to put things right.

As I made my way back to my car, I discarded the notion of calling the police. And for whatever reason, I first processed and then dismissed the idea of calling my estranged brother. I couldn't deal with the outcome of how my words might be received, how disgust and misbelief would ooze from each and every one of his rebuffs.

I threw the Land Rover into reverse and headed towards the only ally I could think of. Five minutes later, I arrived. My ally was waiting at the window with Savannah perched on her bony hip.

Let me tell you something. If that wretch had not had my daughter in her arms, I would have wrecked her—I swear it. And another thing, I wanted to roar at her, scream at her, tear out clumps of her whiter-than-white hair, then mess up that perfectly composed, calculating face.

But I didn't.

"You know why I am here, don't you?" I asked through gritted teeth. "He's gone. My Paddy is gone."

She nodded. Fear and despair swam and pooled in her blue eyes.

Savannah was squealing, her arms outstretched as she made a repetitious, "Muh," sound.

I lost it. Tears and snot poured from my face. I snatched my child from her great aunt and dissolved into a puddle right there in her doorway. I held my daughter tight to my heaving chest, burying my disgusting face into her clean, sweet smelling hair, and I cried and cried and cried, pausing only to inhale the wondrous smell that permeated her small, fragile form.

She smelled exactly the way she always did. It made me cry all the more.

I felt tiny, chubby fingers crawl across my face. I looked down. Concern and the most innocent expression you have ever seen were scrawled across her sweet, diminutive brow. Returning my gaze, Savannah reached up and put her fingers on my mouth, then shook her head. Her angelic curls bounced like coiled springs around her sweet face. It must have been awful for her to see me in such a state.

"Okay," I whispered, then snorted up the snot threatening to further pollute my face.

"Come inside, Evie," Aunt Catherine said. "It's time you understood the Cantillon family."

I looked up. There were tear tracks in her make-up. "My dear God. Aunt Catherine, you do have tear ducts after all."

Catherine's home was like a museum to things no one but old people care about. Doilies, knickknacks, teacups, mundane crap in embroidery hoops crowd every available surface. Flowered wallpaper bloomed all over the place like a greeting card garden, each room a different shade of pale pink. I usually find this environment repulsive, but that day I didn't. My whole world felt upside down, and a trip to Catherineland was unexpectedly what my soul needed.

She sat me down at her linen-covered table, made me tea, and wrapped a shawl over my shoulders as if I were a crime scene victim. Catherine then disappeared into the kitchen again.

Savannah cooed and squirmed in my arms, comforting me with her warmth and oh-so-Savannah smell. I looked at her small face, her shiny blue eyes, the rosy cheeks. She was a wonder, a miracle, the physical result of my dedication and devotion to Paddy. I choked back a sob as the thought of my husband in peril filled my mind.

Savannah grew quiet and stared at me, then laid her head against my chest. She raised her small thumb to her mouth, while her other hand sought out my ear. It was something she had started recently, a way of soothing herself. She would rub my earlobe between her thumb and her forefinger while she sucked her other thumb. I, too, found it comforting.

I sat there, holding my child, trying and failing to block the worst-case-scenario sequences running through my imagination.

Please, God. I know we're not tight, but let my husband live. Please? I ask this for Savannah, not for me. Please?

I sighed and rocked my baby girl. Somewhere in the kitchen, I heard the familiar clinking of metal on metal, the sizzle of an egg hitting a hot pan, and then the sudden jolt of toast popping out of a toaster.

Without asking, Catherine had made me breakfast. She placed a plate of eggs, toast, and sausage in front of me. She gestured to Savannah, offering to take her from me with her open arms. I shook my head. It had been some time since I had eaten a meal with my little one on my lap, but I just couldn't let her go. Not yet.

Catherine smiled at us and didn't press me with questions. She sat down and lifted a teacup to her lips. She looked tired.

We sat in silence while I made a weak attempt to eat break-fast one-handed. Savannah lifted her head, grabbed a piece of toast, then lay her soft curls back against my chest. She made little murmuring sounds as she nibbled on the warm bread. I wasn't very hungry and soon the eggs grew cold while the sausage fat congealed into a white mass.

In time, Catherine asked to put Savannah down for a rest. I hesitated, then relented when I saw the telltale yawns and eye-rubbing, all signs of the morning ten o'clock nap. But once she was gone from my sight, I became agitated. My breathing was irregular, and my arms ached and burned for my sweet baby girl's return.

Catherine came back and sat across from me at the table. She turned the baby monitor my way. It crackled, and within seconds, I heard happy gurgles followed by the soft breathing of a child, my child, sleeping peacefully.

Dabbing at her eyes with a napkin, Catherine delicately used the edge of the cloth to eliminate the smear of mascara marring her otherwise perfect face.

"What the fuck is going on?" I growled.

"There's no need for such language. My goodness, you swear like a sailor, and it is so unbecoming."

"Fuck that. I want answers. You know what's going on, don't you?"

"I do." Catherine poured herself another cup of tea. I watched as the steam rose gently, swirling and disappearing into the air. My own cup sat in front of me. I toyed with it, but I wasn't in the mood for tea.

"We have a history, those of us who carry the blood of the Cantillons," Catherine said. She dropped a single cube of sugar into her tea and then raised a spoon, her pinky finger extended, stirring slowly. Each clink of the spoon against the side of the fine china cup startled me. I was struggling to stay awake.

"No one knows when they came out of the water," she continued, reaching for the flower-festooned creamer. "But they came nonetheless. They came out and joined their family to ours. The sea-dwellers forever changed their fate when they decided to bind their bloodline with the land-dwellers."

"Catherine," I said. "What the hell are you talking about? Are you on some new, old lady drug? Land-dwellers? Sea-dwellers? I have not slept in days, my husband is missing, and you are making zero sense."

She stopped stirring and looked me dead in the eye.

"You know exactly," she said, and then she paused before

asking, "*How do you say it?* Oh, yes. You know *exactly* what the hell I'm talking about. You've met Nomia—am I correct? You've met Nomia's family, and I'm not talking about David and their half-breed child. You've met her true family. The family that lives in the Bay. The family of females who has lived in the Bay for centuries, and you've caught their attention. I cannot even begin to explain how dire this situation has become."

I opened my mouth to tell her *exactly* just how dire my situation had become when I noticed that she was no longer present, no longer consciously aware of me, of her surroundings, of anything.

Aunt Catherine's home was on Pawtuxet Cove. She had an amazing view of the Bay. Her gaze veered to the window overlooking the little cove that had seen so many, many events over the years. It wasn't far from the very spot where her gaze fell that a handful of brave Americans had set out to burn a British ship.

Catherine's eyes scanned the surface of the water as if she was looking for something—something sinister. Then she shook her head and returned her gaze to me, and I saw fresh tears in her eyes.

Her voice cracked and broke when she spoke again. "They're beyond evil. They're nothing like us, and they need to be stopped."

The next thing I knew, a small sob escaped her, and I barely made out her next four words, "They took my Aiden."

"What are you saying?"

I remembered Tony's words.

He went out into the Bay, and he never came back.

I didn't voice my thoughts. I was too flummoxed by the sight of this woman, whose stone veneer would rival Margaret Thatcher's, crying and sobbing like a character in a soap opera.

I gave her time to compose herself before I said, "So the rumors are true. Aiden was killed. He didn't die in his sleep as I was told."

"What rumors? Who told you that?" she sniped.

"I have my secrets, and apparently, you have yours. What else do I need to know? Wait ... *what are you telling me?* Is Paddy *dead?*"

Panic filled me with both doom and adrenaline, and I snapped the handle off my china cup. Blood dribbled down my hand onto the white tablecloth while I stared at Catherine. I hoped and prayed that she knew he was okay, that she would reassure me of his well-being just as easily as she had put a shawl over my shaking shoulders.

"I don't know," she muttered, dabbing at her eyes again while looking down into her teacup. She stared at it as if the answers were in the dark liquid, floating just below the surface. "I've put out word to our contact. He should be in touch soon."

"What contact?" I sobbed. "Why are you speaking in riddles? Just tell me the straight up truth, goddamn it!"

Catherine slammed her hand down on the table so hard that her tea splashed up into the air and hovered as if it was free-falling. I jumped back in response.

"Speaking of these things is forbidden!" She bellowed. "There are only three, maybe two of us left! *You* brought these troubles upon us! *You* were not supposed to know *anything!*"

I lost my shit.

"Anything? *Anything?* I'll tell you what I know, sister! I know that there are things in the water that are not supposed to be in the water! And those *things* are about as subtle as a great white shark! In fact, I would rather take my chances with the shark! At least the shark would have the decency to NOT visit the same goddamn playground as I do and pose as a mother-fucking mother! In fact, an aquatic apex predator would also have the decency to leave my loving, fat husband alone in our kitchen where he belongs! So don't tell me I don't know anything! I've seen way too much! I'm going to need a goddamn lobotomy if I plan on sleeping *ever* again!"

Catherine stared at me for a long time and then, as if a switch had been flipped, she leaned forward, slammed her hand down again, and said, "You're right."

Bless the Saints of Small Sleeping Children that Savannah took a four-hour nap. In that time, I persuaded Catherine to brew me her strongest tea and add a dash of whiskey for good measure. We both drank deeply as she relayed all she knew about her fishy past.

Don't think I didn't point out the fact that I was the normal one. Me, with my crass mouth and fat ass. I was a square compared to the fish paste stewing in the Cantillon DNA.

I gained a rudimentary understanding of an entire secret culture known as the *merrow*. The merrow prefer this moniker over mermaids, because there are also *mermen*—go figure. Catherine's merrow, both male and female, hail from Ireland. Yeah, you got that right. Apparently, merfolk come in different

flavors and varieties. It seems that Nomia and her kind are orig-
inally from Scandahoovia somewhere. At least that's what Catherine gleaned from her Keeper—a sort of ancient *aqua-angel*
who has watched over Catherine's family for generations.

And no, she did not find my *Trapper Keeper* reference amus-
ing or understandable. She was so old, she didn't even know
what a Trapper Keeper was. Hey, I tried, but mostly she just
stared at me and then said something like, "You finished?"

She went on to explain how her family arrived here from
Ireland, how they keep in contact with the main clan through
the Keeper, yadda, yadda, yadda. She talked a lot, and most of
it sank in, but I was so damn tired, it was hard for me to keep
the details straight.

Four hours passed, and Savannah awoke from her nap. For
the rest of the afternoon, I would not let her leave my arms. I
think I slept. I remember being on the couch, reading a book
about a bunny to Savannah, and then it was night.

I sat upright in the darkened living room and listened.

Catherine was singing softly to Savannah in the kitchen. I
could not make out the words of the song, because they must
have been in Gaelic, but the tone and the melody reminded
me of a lullaby. I waited until she finished and then cleared
my throat. A kitchen chair squeaked and groaned as it was
pushed backwards. Catherine appeared in the doorway of the
living room. Light framed her silhouette, making her features
unrecognizable, but I could see the small shape of my sweet girl
in her arms. She was leaning into her aunt, a sleepy satisfied
pose.

I must have slept the early evening away.

"Say good night to Mommy," whispered Catherine.

Savannah mumbled something, then raised a chubby hand. She yawned, then snuggled back into Catherine. I smiled and waved back. The pair disappeared. I waited on the couch, listening to the crackling of the baby monitor.

For the first time in my life, I was grateful for Catherine. She was a grandmother to Savannah, kind, loving, generous with her time. I had been selfish to not realize this sooner. Catherine was more important to my family than I ever admitted, and I felt ashamed for the way I had treated her over the years.

She returned to the living room and sat across from me in an old, flowered easy chair. Doilies graced the top of the chair and both of the arms. She sighed heavily, and I smiled at her.

Then something burbled to the surface of my consciousness, anxious for release. My smile faded to a frown.

"Why did you go through all the trouble of staging Savannah's kidnapping, then leave evidence pointing to mermaids— excuse me—*merrows?*"

"I had nothing to do with Savannah's disappearance from your home."

"Don't bullshit me, Catherine," I said.

So much for the warm fuzzies.

"You had her the next day. How did she get to your house? She crawled out of her crib, packed some essentials, then hitch-hiked on over? Is that what you would like me to believe?"

"No, that's not what happened. I guess you have a right to know what happened. Would you like to hear the truth?"

"Yes. It would be refreshing."

"Nomia broke into your home."

I knew it!

"But Ronan interfered."

"Who the hell is Ronan?"

"I am." A deep, raspy voice came from the behind me. Catherine and I froze, looked at one another, and then slowly turned our heads towards the speaker.

A tall, slender man stood alone in the doorway.

And he was naked.

Coastal waters between the
future-named Rhode Island
and Block Island
July 20, 1636
4:43 AM

Ronan Cantillon watched the scarlet sun rise from the ocean's surface like a brilliant ball of fire. The silhouette of a ship drew his attention and snapped him from his morning ruminating. It moved silently through the waters, heading southwest towards an island three leagues off the coast.

He regarded both the ship and its progress with interest. It was not uncommon for merchant ships to transverse these waters, trading for goods needed farther inland. There was money to be made off colonists whose needs could not be met in their new, raw surroundings. It was a tranquil scene, and Ronan felt at ease.

Ronan hung on the rocks and watched the dawn split the velvet night from the ocean's surface. He inhaled and savored the rich salt air, admiring the mildness of the morning compared to the intense heat that had haunted the area for the past few weeks. It was as cool as it was going to get for a July day. The humidity was not yet awake enough to plague the land dwellers and not oppressive enough to bake the warm wool clinging to their sweat-soaked backs.

Looking east, Ronan thought of Ireland and his distant clan. It would be full light in their waters, their daily life already on its way towards midday. He nodded to himself, feeling secure in his decision to leave his sea-dwelling family. The ocean was a large place, and he had always felt the pull of distant tides, distant shores, distant vistas.

He had proved himself a competent swimmer and hunter, and when the time came to declare his place among his people, Ronan surprised everyone when he announced his desire to be a *Seafarer* or possibly a Keeper. Both trades were solitary ones, positions that rarely allowed for a family of one's own or participation in clan life.

Seafarers were drifters—spirited individuals whose lives seemed always full of adventure. They spent their time traveling the currents, visiting and exploring the wide world beyond the Irish shores.

A Keeper was a lone merrow who occupied a remote outpost in the ocean and kept tabs on land-dwelling clan members, those who had chosen to leave their native lands for opportunity elsewhere. Keepers relied on the infrequent visits of traveling Seafarers to provide them with news and gossip as the Seafarers also served as messengers, carrying information long distances in a type of primitive, pan-oceanic message service.

Ronan had been a Seafarer for many years. He had seen a

great deal of the world but had recently found solace on the northeastern shores of what the land-dwellers called the *Americas*. He experienced a sense of nostalgia in the topography of the ocean floor and the shores above.

But change was coming. Ronan kept his distance from the ruddy natives of the land. They had their own problems with colonists from Europe. Ronan did his best to keep his profile minimal, as was his species' natural inclination.

The far-stretching Bay wound its way deeply inland, into wooded forest. It was perfect for his kind. The rocky waterway had many islands, inlets, and coves well-suited for hiding and hunting. It was clear why the ruddy ones came here to fish. Few natural predators threatened the area, leaving it ripe for hunting.

Ronan was in awe of these strange land-dwellers. Their skin was much darker than he was used to, and they wore warm, soft animal hides. Their sea-crafts were swift, designed to slice across the rough waves of the Bay, carrying lean hunters to the deer-rich island off the coast.

Ronan liked to observe the quiet woodland people. They moved with almost no sound, their lives still in line with the natural world. They were so unlike the land-dwellers he had left behind in Ireland. His cousins on land were farmers and fishermen, hardworking people, but he would not describe them as quiet.

The merchant ship before him glided towards the rising sun. He watched in wonder, as he always did.

How could something so large move so quickly?

His eyes followed the ship's progress. It was swift, strong, and steady. The wake caught his attention. At first, he thought the sun was playing tricks on his large, over-sized eyes, which were more accustomed to the ocean's murky depths. Bright sunlight bothered him, as it did most of his brethren.

Shifting his position on the rocky outcropping, Ronan used the shade of the rock to improve his daylight-vision.

There was something in the waters behind the ship. It was moving fast, too fast for a porpoise or seal.

It broke the water, and he saw what it was. It was not an *it*. It was a *she*. And *she* was not alone. Several female merrow aggressively trailed the ship.

One of the merrow pulled ahead of the others, leaping out of the water and intermittently blocking the sun. She was bound for the prow of the vessel. Then she disappeared.

Ronan was fully alert now, his languid mood gone like the dawn. Straightening up in the water, Ronan strained to see if the swift-moving craft had struck down the lone merrow.

A quick glance aft of the ship rejected that possibility. The pod of merrow continued trailing.

He heard the shrill call of the boatswain's whistle and watched as a six-person crew swarmed the prow of the ship. They gathered to one side, all facing east.

He concentrated and used his keen hearing to focus on the voices of the sailors. Ronan discerned excitement in their cries. Following their gestures and the direction of their gazes, he peered across the waters and found the source of their animation.

A woman—not a merrow—was floating on the surface of the water, far ahead of the ship. Both her skin and her hair were as pale as the moon. She lay motionless, her naked form bobbing and ebbing on the gentle tide while her hair floated like a halo around her head.

The crew scrambled to slow the vessel's course, and a smaller craft was lowered over the side of the ship.

Two men occupied the smaller boat. One of them had a strong back and thick, powerful arms. He rowed with vigorous speed towards the unmoving woman. The other man clambered to the front of the dinghy. His anticipation of gathering the enticing flotsam in their path was evident in his eager, anxious mannerisms. They made good time reaching the woman and drawing her limp form into their tiny craft.

The remaining crew dropped the anchor while the would-be-heroes gathered their bounty. Each link of the enormous anchor chain made a loud clang as it slipped over the railing of the vessel and splashed into the dark waters. Once their task was complete, the crew returned to watch the small boat as it crawled its way back to the main ship.

The woman had been revived. The anxious man was no longer anxious. A broad, dumb smile spread across his face while the naked woman, who seemed not to notice her immodest state, wrapped herself around his body.

Girlish laughter echoed across the water and filled Ronan's ears. The sound set chills up and down his spine.

That was no girl. *That* was a merrow.

Movement near the back of the ship, where the large anchor

chain entered the water, caught Ronan's eye, and he re-directed his attention away from the rescuers.

The iron anchor couplings were teaming with merrow. They hoisted their scaly, gnarled forms, arm over arm, upward along the metal links. Their tails hung useless, swaying as they slith-ered up the back of the ship. The giddy crew's attention was elsewhere, their eyes riveted to the naked woman.

Ronan watched in horror. His kind did not participate in raids on land-dwellers. They kept hidden, revealing themselves to their land-cousins only when circumstances presented dire need.

This was unnecessary. These waters were overflowing with food. What could this pod possibly need from a ship?

Ronan watched as the merrow transformed themselves into human women just before vaulting the railing and soundlessly landing deck-side.

A shout rang out from above the attacking women. Ronan spied two young boys in the crow's nest pointing to the deck below, their voices filled with alarm and warning.

It was too late. The women moved with speed and agility, tossing two crew members overboard, their bodies hitting the water with loud splashes.

One of the merrow, a dark-haired beauty, attempted to climb up to the crow's nest, eager to get at the young men far above her head. The boys saw her, then disappeared into the mock safety of the barrel-shaped perch. The merrow climbed with great speed and was soon within grasp of the barrel's lip. One of the boys stood, his head and torso visible. He was wielding a knife. Yelling, he swiped the blade across the merrow's hand. Blood appeared, shimmering in the sunlight, and she cried out, releasing her grip.

The merrow plummeted to the deck below. Ronan thought she was dead. Her body lay inert for several moments while the boys peered down from high above, both of their mouths fixed into dark, gaping circles.

She sat up suddenly and shook her head. Dark hair whipped around her face. She examined her badly damaged hand and screamed with rage. Vaulting to her feet, she attempted to climb the mast again, but someone stopped her.

An enormous merrow, larger than any Ronan had ever seen, strode into view and pulled Dark Hair from the mast with one wide hand. Dark Hair fell to the deck like a rag doll, then looked up at the pale merrow towering over her.

The aggressor was whiter than sinew, whiter than bone, whiter than white. From her skin to her long, ragged hair, no color interrupted the endless span of ivory. Her hair hung in long knotted clumps. Braids, seashells, and possibly bones were tangled in the wet mass that hung nearly to the backs of her legs. Her face was not elegant. No masterful trick of symmetry organized this one's features into an eye-pleasing arrangement. She was born for fear and terror.

There was an exchange between the two, and then Big White kicked Dark Hair hard in the ribs, once, twice, three times.

From across the expanse of water, Ronan heard the impact of the blows. Several of the other merrow paused to watch the interaction between the tall, pale being and the dark-haired beauty.

Big White walked away, leaving Dark Hair in a heap on the deck. Another, slightly shorter, fair-haired merrow approached Dark Hair. Smaller White was not as tall as Big White, but she was just as muscular and lean, and her facial features were more palatable than those of the ivory giant.

Ronan thought for certain that Smaller White would help her sister to her feet. She did not. Smaller White wound up and kicked Dark Hair with her bare foot then spit on the fallen merrow's naked back.

Dark Hair screamed and scrambled to her feet. She clutched her stomach with both arms but could not stand to her full height. Ronan could not decipher the words she spat at her sisters, but he understood their sentiment—*I hate you! I hate all of you!*

The gathering crowd of female merrow laughed openly at Dark Hair, shouting and jeering as she limped to the railing of the ship. Dark Hair looked back at them, a scowl on her beautiful face, then made a weak dive into the waters below.

Ronan did not see her again. Both Big White and Smaller White disappeared from view. Ronan caught an occasional glimpse of their tall, pale forms in the background of the ship from time to time, but there was so much else on his mind, so many other atrocities to witness.

On the dingy far below the deck of the main ship, the golden-haired beauty who had been rescued reverted back to her natural state, startling her two heroes who shrieked in surprise.

She made quick work of them. Her claws swiped at one, then the other, tearing out the poor men's throats. The she-beast threw back her head and screamed, a blood-chilling howl that echoed against the ship and lodged itself deep in Ronan's psyche. Then she bit into one man's shoulder, tearing the flesh away with her powerful jaws. He had heard of this but had never witnessed it.

Feasting on human flesh.

Ronan's elders had whispered rumors of this abomination. Some said it could lead to an extended lifespan, others said it created virility, strength, speed. More sensible clan members believed these latter statements to be false. They argued the practice of eating human flesh could cause madness, aggression, and vicious cruelty.

As Ronan watched the atrocity of wasted human life, he saw the truth for himself. They were aggressive. They were cruel. They were mad.

In time, the screams, the sickening snap of bones, and raw tearing of human flesh faded.

Ronan gripped his rock and endured the horrific event. It lasted until mid-morning. The barnacled rocks bloodied his hands. He could not move. He could not call out. He bore witness and committed all he saw to memory. Ronan stayed where he was, a petrified observer until the bitter end.

He remembered the way some of the bodies—or body parts—were cast aside, wasted flesh floating and bloating on the tide. He remembered the putrid smell of human carnage, how it baked in the growing heat of the day. He remembered the shrieks of the seagulls as they maniacally called and screamed at one another in anticipation of their ghoulish meal.

Once the satiated merrow pod had finished feasting, they turned to Big White, who spoke and gestured around the ship. In response, a cry went up from the women. They dispersed and then tossed the dry goods and other useful cargo overboard. Their intentions—*spite? angst?*—known only to them.

He kept watch for the two boys hidden in the crow's nest. They, too, had witnessed the tragedy and savagery of the day's events. He doubted those two young men would ever be the same. Ignoring his own hunger and fatigue, Ronan waited and kept watch for the boys, who stayed hidden.

The cannibals left under the direction of Big White. They dropped, one by one, into the sea and did not surface.

Late in the day, a fishing vessel happened upon the unfortunate merchant ship. The fisherman saw blood in the water and called out a warning to the massacred craft. There was no reply. Keeping a safe distance between their smaller boat and the eerie merchant vessel, the fishermen waited for signs of life.

Their hail went unanswered and the smaller vessel steered its course back the way it had come. But before they caught the wind, a tentative call came from the crow's nest. The frantic boys saw safety in the smaller fishing boat and waved their arms, crying out to the passing men.

When the fishermen boarded the larger vessel and surveyed the deck, they stopped in their tracks—their heads slowly turning from left to right. A few of the men raised shaking hands to their mouths. All removed cover, and held their hats to their hearts—a sign of solemn respect for the remnants of the dead. Seagulls swarmed overhead creating a white shrieking cloud of feathers that swooped and swelled above the deck. The scavenger birds took offense to the newcomers and made aggressive attacks on the fisherman who yelled curses and swatted at the angry birds.

Hearing the voices of the men now onboard, the boys called down from their roost. One of the fishermen stood beneath the mast and coaxed the shaken, sobbing boys down with offers of shelter on the smaller ship. Ronan could only imagine the tale they told.

The rest of the men continued their inspection of the vessel, swatting the seagulls as they went, stopping every now and then to look down and shake their heads. One of them vomited overboard. He leaned his elbows on the railing and held his head in his hands. The sickened man did not move for some time.

The tide changed and the wind picked up. Ronan clung to his testimonial rock, unable to leave. The fishermen attempted to tow the merchant vessel, but after several tries, they gave up. They scuttled the ship, waiting for it to sink to the depths, and then moved on with the rescued boys safe below deck.

Before the sun set on that fateful day, Ronan made a decision that would forever change the course of his life.

Should his land-cousins ever choose to make ground near these waters, Ronan vowed to keep a vigilant watch over his brethren and do his best to keep them from the dangerous pod of merrow he had just witnessed.

Ronan had found his life's purpose. Ronan Cantillon of Ballyheige Bay, County Kerry, Ireland, would from that day forth become Ronan Cantillon, Keeper of Narragansett Bay.

17

The waters of
Narragansett Bay, Rhode Island
March 14
6:42 PM

It was one of those evenings best appreciated from a deck somewhere, a cold drink in hand, a good friend by your side. The brilliant, red sun approached the water. *Or did the water approach the sun?*

We humans on Spaceship Earth are always moving, always turning, while the unforgiving sun stays inert, unflinching, judging us from afar, scowling down upon us—burning, burning, burning us with its one red eye.

The same could be said for Catherine. She stood at the front of our craft, her gaze fixed on the horizon, a scowl creasing her fair, aging face. It was as if her eyes were setting fire to the waves, making their crimson surface flame with the heat of her anger. My stomach was in knots as I watched her from the safety of the bench. I could feel Ronan's strong presence behind me as he steered the small watercraft towards our imminent doom.

Savannah was safe—for now. That morning, Catherine had surprised me and called Tony.

"Yes," she said, false charm dripping from her voice. "This really *is* Catherine, Tony. No, you're right. *I* am calling *you*."

Bouncing Savannah on my hip, I had rolled my eyes and hoped Tony didn't take a heart attack.

"Family emergency," Catherine continued, wrapping the phone cord around her gnarled finger. She was the only woman left in America with a rotary phone. I had no idea how she made calls. She probably guilted the phone company into allowing her to continue with her ancient ways of communication.

"Six o'clock would be grand. Savannah just adores you, Tony, and besides, she's just a dream to take care of."

There was a pause.

"Oh, okay," said Catherine. "Sure, Joe can join you. See you at six then. Goodbye."

It was comforting, sort of, to know that my daughter was in capable hands. *Of course if we didn't return ...* No. I was not going to complete that thought. Best to stay positive.

The future hung like the setting sun. It was inevitable, but uncertain. Would the weather change? Would the sun return the next morning, or would there be fog? Would Paddy, Catherine, or I or even Ronan be ripped to shreds? Would any of us see the next sunrise?

I swallowed and stared at the heavy knife in my lap. Its weight and presence introduced even more questions. Would I be able to wield a weapon when and if the time came? I shook my head at my lap. Ronan, Keeper of Narragansett Bay and of the Cantillon lineage, had placed the knife in my hands three days before.

"Wouldn't a gun be more effective?" I had pleaded.

Ronan responded with a cool stare. Oh yeah, he was definitely related to Catherine.

"Three days time 'til the Summit. Gather your courage and prepare for the meeting, Evelyn."

"Um, yeah," I had answered. "Have we met? Oh, that's right, we haven't. Here's my bio—I'm a short, uncoordinated screw-up. Three days isn't *nearly* enough time for me to be battle-ready against a pod of homicidal merrow."

More frowning from Mr. Stoic.

One of Nomia's relatives had approached Ronan. Their request was simple. "Turn over the non-Cantillon. She's wanted for retribution." As in, they wanted me.

"What the hell did I do? That bitch has been harassing *me* since October! Can't we all just get along? And how do we know they won't just kill all of us? You, me, Catherine, Paddy? Huh? Where's the insurance policy, Aqua-Man?"

"We don't know anything beyond what I was told," was all Ronan would say.

My husband was out there in the ocean being held captive because of me. I gripped the knife harder and turned to look at Ronan.

"How much farther?"

His gaze broke from the horizon and fell on me, cold and steely. It was still hard to look at him directly. His appearance was eerie. He passed for human, but there was something about him that was off. Something about the way he held himself, so straight and alert, his sense of hearing tuned to things beyond the human scope while his gaze remained intense.

When he stared at me with eyes infinitely lighter blue than Catherine's and Paddy's, it was as if he was seeing all the way into my soul. I felt naked, bare, vulnerable in his gaze. As far as I was told, Ronan's family was not carnivorous. But when he looked at me, it was akin to how any prey must feel before it succumbs to a dominant species. I had seen the other side of the coin, and there was indeed a tendency towards killer instincts. It was there in Ronan, even if it was simply a choice towards a veggie/pesca lifestyle.

"We'll be there in time. Prepare yourself," he said again and then returned to his gaze to the Bay.

I thought about mumbling some smart-ass retort but then thought better of it. Instead, I stared at the passing shoreline, trying to decipher the landmarks. It was like trying to see your home from an airplane. By the time you've oriented yourself, the moment passes and familiarity is gone, leaving you searching for a new point of reference.

Wait, was that Wickford Harbor?

I saw a few restaurants with docks out front, nestled into a small cove. Lights were coming on, illuminating the empty, seasonal moorings. Then the scene was gone, and the light was fading. It would be full dark soon. We were headed south towards an area near Jamestown. The air was mild. It had been one of those rare, warm March days when Mother Nature throws New England a bone and says, *Winter's almost over, little darlings, and as long as PMS doesn't strike me and I don't irrationally curse you with a freak snowstorm, you might get more of these nice days to make you forget all about the wretchedness of winter.*

But as the sun disappeared from view, the temperature started a rapid death spiral towards the lower forties. I pulled up the zipper on my parka and glanced back, once more, at Ronan. In his ridiculously threadbare t-shirt and blue jeans, still barefoot, he seemed completely impervious to the dropping temperatures. It was as if he were wearing clothes solely for our benefit.

Catherine also seemed completely unaffected by the oncoming cold. This didn't surprise me. I never thought she had anything other than ice in her blood.

The spray of the waves sent a fine salty mist into my face. I licked my lips, tasting the seawater, and said another silent prayer (the zillionth one since Paddy had been taken) that my big man was safe, warm, and dry.

I knew it was a lot to hope for.

So many questions raced through my mind. *Was Paddy still alive? Would they kill all of us? Why did we have to wait three days?* Every time I asked Ronan the last question, he looked over my head as if I had never spoken at all. It was beyond infuriating.

Gingerly, I stood. I felt the boat rising and falling as it careened along the relatively calm seas, slamming up and down on the gentle rolling waves. My knees buckled, and I almost pitched forward. Reaching for the thin metal railing running along the side of the craft, I righted myself and made my way to Catherine. When I stood by her side, she didn't look at me.

"They might kill us all," she said. Her voice was just loud enough to be heard above the engine and the endless slapping of the boat against the surface of the sea.

I didn't say anything in return.

We were somewhere in the middle of Narragansett Bay. The shoreline was rocky, angry, secretive. I understood how a bunch of savage, man-eating mermaids could find this sort of place attractive. How many smugglers, fishermen, sailors, and the like had met their doom under their scaled, clawed hands? I shivered and said another silent prayer for those poor souls, may they rest in *pieces*.

Without warning, Ronan cut the engine. The boat reeled to a stop, and I almost fell overboard. Somehow, Catherine, in her infinite grace, held strong and never even flinched as the forward momentum of the boat halted.

In the distance, an outcropping of large rocks jutted out towards us like a menacing tooth. The shoreline wrapped around the boulders. It was difficult to see much more. We were surrounded by a stillness, and the eerie silence encapsulated our tiny boat, making our presence seem alien and unwanted.

A soft shuffling sound came from behind me, and I turned to see Ronan standing behind me, his arms outstretched, pushing a set of oars in my direction. And he was naked again.

"Um, thank you?" I offered and took the oars, trying to keep my gaze on his disturbing eyes. I tried not to notice his body. Taut and muscular, it rivaled that of any young, male Olympic swimmer. I had no idea how old Ronan was. *Fifty? Two-hundred and fifty? Should I count the years by the lines on his abs?*

"What do I do with these?" I asked.

"You row," he answered and pointed to the dark shore on my right. Then he turned and walked to the edge of the boat and climbed up on the railing.

"Stay in the shadows," he said as he rolled his shoulders backwards, like a swimmer on a starting block. "This isn't your fight any longer."

He rocked his head from one shoulder to the other. I heard a crack, and then he became very still. In an explosion of movement, he jumped into the air and entered the water without a sound. He barely disturbed the surface of the sea. It was as if the Bay had swallowed him whole.

He was gone.

"Well," I said, turning to Aunt Catherine, "I guess we row."

After examining the rear of the boat, I saw that Ronan had already pulled in the engine. I took the right side, and Catherine took the left. Together, we worked in unison and paddled our way across the water to the shore.

When we reached the rocks, I looked at her, and she at me. Neither of us moved. Finally, I acquiesced with a shake of my head. I removed my pink polka-dot wellies, rolled up my pants, and jumped over board. The water was freezing cold, and I gasped as soon as my feet hit the water. I swallowed hard and towed us into the shore. Like a dainty belle of the ball, Catherine swung her legs over the side of the boat and hopped delicately to the pebble-strewn beach.

"Now what?" I asked as I shivered.

"We wait," was the only answer I received.

Catherine wandered over to the rocks, then disappeared into the darkness.

I sighed and climbed back aboard the boat. Stumbling around in the darkness, I found what I was looking for—my pink rubber boots and the knife. I stuck the knife in the inside pocket of my parka and threw my boots overboard to the beach. Being nowhere nearly as graceful as Catherine, I jumped down to the shore and landed with a thud, my back making contact with a few sharp rocks. Grumbling to myself, I got to my feet, then went about finding my boots.

I located them and pulled them back on. Looking around, I could not see Catherine anywhere. I was alone. There was nothing for me to do but try to follow her into the darkness.

She was waiting for me above the large boulders I had seen from the boat. When I climbed up beside her, she didn't say a word. Instead, she started walking. We stuck to the shoreline, picking our way over rocks.

It was slow-going.

Every now and then, we would stop and listen, but there was nothing to be heard. We were traveling with the water to our left. *What if we were supposed to be heading in the opposite direction, keeping the silent Bay to our right?*

I was just about to ask Catherine how she knew which way to go when she stopped. I crashed into her like a drunken elephant.

"Shhhh!" she whispered.

I complied, at first wondering why the hell she had stopped, but then I heard it, too. It was a faint splashing. It reminded me of a flopping fish.

We listened and held our breaths. "We need to get closer," whispered Catherine.

She was right. I resisted the urge to whine and instead followed close behind as she headed towards the source of the noise. The splashing grew louder. I could make out a large pile of boulders up ahead of us. The splashing came from beyond the massive rocks. We needed to climb.

Catherine surprised me. She made swift work of the ascent. As for me, I cursed myself for not bringing gloves. My fingers had only just thawed from the paddling. The hand-over-hand climbing did nothing to warm my frozen digits.

The splashing grew louder and louder as we neared the summit, and a subtle glow emanated from the top-most rock. It looked like light creeping out from below a closed door, a door that leads from a well-lit room to a darkened corridor.

Catherine reached the summit first. I'm so glad it was her and not me. She gasped, ducked down, and grabbed me by the sleeve.

"Steel yourself, Evie," she whispered. "You cannot cry out."

I just looked at her. I saw terror and fear in her eyes. A cold stone developed in the very bottom of my stomach. It stayed there—heavy, icy, completely unwanted.

"It's Paddy," I whispered back. "Isn't it?"

She nodded, motioned to the summit, and put a single finger to her lips. I took a deep breath and then slowly let it out.

This is it. This is where I see my dead husband.

I stifled tears, sobs, and angry curse words as I made my way towards the light. I thought of how much I loved him, how

much he meant to me. I thought of all the times I was shitty to
him and how he had forgiven me, had gracefully forgiven me,
knowing full well that I would probably do something shitty
again, and yet he loved me regardless.

"*Múchadh is bá ort, mo rún*," I muttered. "Smothering and
drowning on you, my secret love."

Please, let it not be so.

I held my breath as I came to the crest of the rocks. I kept my
eyes tightly shut. Like a child, I could pretend I was invisible,
that this whole ordeal was not happening. If I just closed my
eyes, I could imagine that when I reopened them, we would be
in our sunny kitchen. Paddy would be reading the paper with
toast crumbs in his chinneck. Savannah would have her cereal
bowl on her head while she shoved Cheerios into her sweet little
face, and me—I would be there, and I would be happy.

Instead, I was on a rock pile, freezing my ass off, waiting to
see the fate of my better half. I opened my eyes and almost fell.

There he was, and—thank his green namesake—Patrick
McFagan was still alive. He was not in good shape, but I could
see his large, blubbery chest rise and fall with the ragged
rhythms of one still breathing.

He lived! But for how much longer?

Below me, a large cove curved around like a giant backwards
C. Across an expanse of water the length of two football fields,
Paddy was held captive. A small beach was tucked into a nook
of rocks that rose above him. The beach was narrow, maybe ten
feet wide, and it wound along the rocky embankment, disappearing a hundred yards to Paddy's left.

My poor, big man was chained to one of the boulders. Both of his hands were above his head. His wrists were bound in iron manacles. By his feet, several torches were shoved into the sand, casting an eerie warm glow on his body. He was bound and lit up for a specific audience—me. Even though I could not find the humor in it, Paddy reminded me of King Kong—captured, defeated, displayed for the entertainment of others.

Enhancing his degradation and humiliation, someone had stripped him naked, all except his dingy tighty-whities.

I raised a shaking, torn hand to my mouth and bit down hard. I wanted to run down the rocks, jump into the water, swim across the expanse of sea separating my love from me, and rip those shackles off his fat wrists. I would cover him with my body as best as I could and get my man back home.

The splashing had stopped. I scanned the cove but saw nothing. It was too dark to see below the surface of the water that reflected the orange glow of Paddy's torches and little else.

I glanced down at Aunt Catherine. Our eyes locked. We, too, were bound—bound in our mutual feelings of hopelessness and despair. This must have been what she went through with Uncle Aiden. How absolutely wretched and horrible.

But I sure as shit wasn't going to allow Paddy to endure the same outcome as his late uncle. And even if he didn't make it out alive, I vowed then and there on that cold, cold rock that I would make them pay.

I would make them all pay.

I channeled my fear and despair. I imagined that it was coal in my gut—frigid, heavy, and lifeless. I willed the coal to become fuel, to become energy and heat. Where I was going, I would need both.

The jetty curved into the darkness, away from Paddy, and then disappeared to the right of my vantage point. The rocks surrounded the cove as far as I could see, creating a high wall.

There must be a way to get to him from here. I just need to climb down, get to the jetty, and make my way there.

I eased the knife out of my parka, and when I pulled out the blade, Catherine's eyes opened wide.

"What do you plan on doing with that?" she whispered. Her eyebrows crawled into two querulous arcs.

"I'm going to get my man. If anyone tries to stop me, I plan on sticking them with the pointy end. You stay here. If anything goes wrong ..." I couldn't say it. I started to choke up.

No, Evie. Fire in the belly. Get Paddy back.

"If anything goes wrong, Catherine, you are all that Savannah has left. Be good to her. I know you will."

She didn't say a word. She just nodded, and then she did something she has never done—she reached out and pulled me to her chest, embracing me tightly.

She hugged me so hard I almost gasped. Then the moment was over.

I looked at her one last time. Her eyes were wide like saucers, filled with tears. I reached over and squeezed her arm, then started my descent.

I headed down, then veered off to my right. I would make my way around the cove, using the high rock wall as my cover.

My hands were bloodied and ragged from the rocks, and it

was hard to climb while holding a dagger. I put the blade in my mouth. I looked like some half-crazed soccer mom/pirate. It would have been a better idea to place the blade back in my pocket, but I wanted to be ready for anything.

As I disappeared below the rocks, so did the light from Paddy's fire. It made the going slow. I couldn't see shit, and I was deathly afraid of falling into a gap between the rocks.

That would be bloody wonderful. It would also be the end of it all.

I chose my path carefully, using the toe of my boot to feel around for footing and then pushing down with my foot to verify the level of slipperiness and solidity of each rock. The goddamn kelp was not helping at all.

After twenty minutes of climbing, moving onward to my right, I decided to approach the summit of the rock wall and check on Paddy. I clambered up towards the stars, then stopped.

The stillness of the cold, dark night was shattered by a roar.

I had heard a facsimile of this sound once before. Paddy had been down in his morbid realm, preparing a body. A crash boomed throughout the house, shaking the foundation and rattling the dishes in the cabinets. The sonic boom was followed by a tremendous bellow, like that of a wounded, ferocious beast.

I had flown down the stairs, and there was Paddy, underneath a massive casket, one reserved for a large person. The occupant was inside, his arms lolling over the side of the heavy mahogany box, while my poor big man was in an awkward pile beneath the giant stiff and his massive forever-box.

The bellow now was the same, except it was laced with fear

and desperation. I clambered as fast I could, slipping once and almost embedding the dagger into my face. Good thing I had placed the blade facing out. Otherwise, my big mouth might have grown a whole lot bigger.

Removing the blade from my mouth and placing it back in my parka, I peeked over the top of the rocks.

Two merrow, both females, stood on either side of Paddy. They were naked and possessed human legs, but their arms were still greenish and their hands ended in razor-sharp claws. Their dark hair hung limply down their backs like stringy seaweed, obscuring the backs of their legs.

Fucking hags.

I hoped one of them would catch fire, stumble into the other, catch that one on fire, then gracefully unshackle my husband. It didn't happen, but I wished it all the same.

The taller one on the left reached back with her right claw. It swung high up over her shoulder and flew towards Paddy's fleshy mid-section. He cried out as four long gashes opened and bled freely on his whiter-than-white gut. He had a matching wound on his face.

The other merrow laughed, a loud screeching howl, and stepped towards Paddy. She cocked her head to the side and poked him in the face with one of her long fingernails.

Paddy raised his head and looked at her. The merrow said something, and her head moved as if her jaw was working. Then she laughed. Her face was inches away from Paddy's. Suddenly, he reared his head back and performed the only act of defiance he could. He spit in her face.

The merrow punched him in the gut, making him bleed even more. Then she bent her head and licked the blood from the wound on his side. Paddy recoiled, turning his head away from her, his eyes squeezed shut. She raised her arms in triumph, then spun around to face her sister who laughed in response.

Tightening the grip on my knife, I imagined hurtling it across the distance, end over end, until it embedded in one of their skulls.

Fire in the gut, Evie. Keep it stoked. Nothing you can do from this distance. Keep your fat ass moving towards the man. You can do it.

I did not want to take my eyes off him, but I could not remain crouched and useless any longer, witnessing my husband's abuse. I needed to take action. I continued my slow, crab-like journey around the cove, enduring my husband's screams. They grew louder, more anguished, and my heart felt as if it were in an ever-tightening vice grip. My teeth hurt from clenching them. I winced each time he cried out. His screams sounded more and more ragged, as if his defiance was waning like the tide.

Then he stopped. I paused and listened. I heard the *shush* of the surf, the lapping of waves against rocks, but nothing else. Something had changed. It was too quiet.

I needed another gruesome peek.

When I reached the summit again, everything looked different. My vantage point had shifted. I was no longer facing Paddy. Instead, I was looking at his profile.

He was alone, his head hanging down to his chest, and I

wasn't sure if he was still alive. I counted in my head. *One, two, three, four, five ...*

I made it to twelve before he finally took a deep, ragged breath.

I let out a breath of my own, one of relief. He was still alive.

But, oh my God, he was so bloody and torn up. Ribbons of blood crisscrossed back and forth across his massive torso. His eyes looked bruised and swollen, probably from the blow I had witnessed and from countless others I had not. He was all alone. Those tormenting bitches were nowhere to be seen.

This was my chance. I looked down and could see that if I climbed down the embankment, I could make it to the sandy beach stretching all the way over to Paddy. I lifted one leg over, then the other. I blew all the air out from my lungs and started down the steep barrier separating me from my love.

It didn't go so well. I climbed down five feet and then fell. My body careened off the sharp rocky edges like a tennis ball falling down stairs. I think I hit every single rock on my way down.

I hit the ground with a loud thud and a wheeze. All the air left my body, leaving me with blinding pain. I attempted to take another breath, but nothing happened. Then all at once, it did happen. I let out a high-pitch scream that could rival any tea kettle.

My head lay on the sand, and fortunately, it was facing Paddy. As I fought to remain conscious and force air back into my squashed lungs, I watched him slowly lift his head. He squinted, but the firelight masked whatever lay beyond those godforsaken torches.

"It's me, Paddy! I'm here!" I tried to shout. But nothing came out. I couldn't do anything beyond wheezing. And oh, the pain. There was not enough Ibuprofen in the world for the aches I had. I tried again.

"Paddy! I'm here! I'm coming, my love!"

I watched him struggle to speak as I scrambled to get to my feet.

"Evie," he mumbled. I could see that word—my name—drop from his cracked and bloody lips.

It was all I needed. The fire in my gut sparked anew, and goddamn the pain, I got up, located my knife, and started running, screaming the whole way, "I'm coming!"

"No," he said, quiet at first, and then louder and louder followed by another word—one I couldn't, for the life of me, make out.

Was it *hat? Why would he be looking for a hat?*

He said it again. I was almost there. I could see his eyes peering at me through their swollen lids, getting wider with each step I took. He said it once more, and before the word entered my ears and registered in my brain, it was too late.

He was trying to say, *trap*. As in, *it's a trap*.

The next thing I knew, I was underwater, and the flames from the torches were receding away from my vision. I had only re-educated myself on how to breathe a few seconds ago, and now I would never breathe again. I was going down. I had been here before, so I let it be. I had tried my best to be a hero. But I was underwater—again.

Everything hurt, and I was so tired. I was being held under, and I felt a strong arm tighten its grip on my neck. Then I remembered something. I had a knife in my hand.

I had a knife!

Wielding the blade with all the ineptitude of one who has never wielded a blade—much less underwater—I slashed at the arm holding me down. I swiped over and over again, making random cuts as deep as I could until the arm let go, and I kicked my way to the surface. Gasping and choking on frigid water, I exploded into the night air, only to be pulled back down again.

This time, I was pulled down by my ankle. My head went under, but I had the foresight to take a deep breath before I disappeared beneath a wave. My back smashed down on something solid, and so did my left hand.

I had hit a rock on the sandy bottom. I could stand. It wasn't that deep. The darkness and the suddenness of being pulled under had disoriented me into thinking I was in deep water.

I spun around and kicked out with my free leg, connecting with something soft. The impact of my foot into what I hoped was my attacker's face loosened the grip on my leg. Pinwheeling my left arm and firmly holding the knife with my right, I reached back and grabbed the rock behind me.

And I kept on kicking.

The gentle pull of the tide swayed my attempts, but it worked. The attacker let go, and I pulled myself backwards, clinging to the rock. I resurfaced and gulped at the air, scrambling to get up on the rock and out of the water.

I crouched there, like an animal, my hair dripping water into my eyes, and my clothes hanging on me like cold, dead weight. But I was poised, knife in hand, ready to strike. I spun around, keeping my crouch, and waited. Whatever had messed with me did not burst forth to drag me back under. I took a chance and glanced back to where I had last seen Paddy.

He was gone.

"No!" I screamed. They must have taken him under, too. I judged the distance from my rock to the shore. It seemed to be about thirty feet. I couldn't stay where I was forever, and I needed to figure out a new plan.

Dear God, what if he's dead?

Before rational thoughts could enter my mind, instinct took over. Adrenaline coursed through my veins as I dove back into the dark, frigid waters, my blade in hand, ready to rescue my man. I opened my eyes and felt the sting of seawater. There wasn't a lot to see. The dim light of the beach torches did little to illuminate the surf.

I could make out shadows swimming past at great speeds. One passed nearby. It was large and fast. I followed its path until it hit another dark shadow that was even larger than the first. The shadows collided.

The water became murky, and silt from the bottom was swirling towards my face. I could hear thrashing in the water. There was something going on. I squinted and strained my eyes, desperate to make out more details, but I was running out of air. And something narrow was heading straight for me. I screamed, and a torrent of bubbles escaped my mouth, fleeing towards the surface.

Time slowed down. The water muffled everything, making

my head feel stuffed with cotton. Whatever it was, it was coming, and it was intended for me. My mouth formed the letter O. I was out of air and the long, straight, sharp object was still coming.

At the last second, I turned sideways and watched it sail past me. It was a spear, and it had just missed me. I watched it continue its trajectory, then lost sight of it in the clouded waters.

My vision doubled, and my mind screamed for oxygen. Out of habit, I tried to suck in air, and water flooded my lungs. The pain was a searing contradiction to the icy ocean. I needed to breathe. I started to descend towards the bottom of the sea. Both the surface, which was only a few feet away, and the starry night receded from my vision. I was dimming with each second. Then I jolted forward. My back hit bottom. Kicking my legs down, I stood and gasped for oxygen, coughing up seawater.

Standing, I spun around and searched for Paddy. The beach was now an explosion of activity. Male and female creatures fought, chased, stabbed, screamed, killed, and died right in front of me. Confusion filled my mind.

Who are those males?

I drew in a sharp breath. While still clutching my knife, I wrapped my arms around my chest. I was so cold. My hair hung down into my eyes. Not wanting to remove my arms from my core, I tossed my head to the side so I could see better.

Where are you, Paddy?

What was I to do? I stood shivering in the water and glanced around. If I stayed in the water, I was at risk for hypothermia. As I thought about this, a water creature burst from the waves like a great white shark hurling itself skyward with a seal firmly pinioned in its ferocious jaws. Except it wasn't a shark. It was a merrow. A male merrow, and it had *part* of a female merrow in its taloned hands.

I think I threw up in my mouth a little bit. Then I looked towards the beach.

Make a decision, Evie. The water is not a good option right now.

I looked to the rock embankment where I had fallen earlier. That seemed like a good place to hide.

Go. Go now!

With lumbering steps, I sloshed my way towards the rocky shore. It was the longest walk of my life, but I made it. Screams, roars, and splashing filled the night sky. All I wanted to do was find Paddy and get the hell out of there. But I couldn't see him. As I crept towards the safety of the rocks, I kept shooting glances over my shoulder. I scanned the torchlit beach filled with fighting males and females, searching for my big man. It was difficult to see with all the movement, and I could not find him.

I reached the rocks and crouched down. My body twitched and jerked, spasms shaking me in the dampness and the cold. My muscles tried their best to generate heat on their own, but it wasn't working. I couldn't feel my toes any longer, and my fingertips were numb, useless. I held on to my blade. There was no way I was letting that slip out of my poor, bloodless hands.

There was nothing I could do but watch the fighting from the pseudo-safety of the rocks. I mean, really, what was I supposed to do? Run out there and show off my non-existent knife skills? Yeah, that sounded like a grand idea. So I hid there in the darkness. Watching. Waiting for a hero.

The battle before me was vicious. I watched in fear and thought about the severity of early warfare. We are so far removed from the battlefield. We kill each other with computers and drones. This was something entirely different. This was savage.

One barbaric female warrior stood out from the others. Her hair was blonde, the kind of blonde you see on women born and raised in winter. It was a white kind of blonde—the color of snow, the color of nothing. A long scar sliced across her left eye, ending near her chin, but the scar tissue did not seem to affect her vision. A chunk of muscle was missing from the outside of her right thigh but did not impede the strength of her stride. She had a swagger to her step, an arrogant confidence in her every move. She was paler than the others, and her head was shaved on both sides. A long braid started at her hairline and swung all the way down her back. Every four inches, the braid was wrapped with leather straps.

This Scar Eye moved with speed and accuracy. She carried a net and a long ragged knife that she held with the blade pointing down. When she slashed, she used a backhand motion. Her kills were swift and brutal, and she didn't stop. The males fell at her feet, she stepped over them, whipped her braid over her shoulder, and moved on to another opponent.

Again I wondered, *Who are these males? Do they know Ronan? Where did they come from?*

The males carried spears, knives, nets, and other rudimentary weapons. All were tall and muscular—athletes built for hunting and swimming. Much like Scar Eye, their heads were shaved on the sides, leaving only a long strip of hair that grew from their foreheads down to the nape of their necks. Braided and interspersed with bones, their hairstyles were similar to the Native American mohawk. All had tattoos across their faces. Blue markings swirled around their wide flat noses making their enlarged eyes even fiercer.

Scar Eye had found a new target—a guy with a spear. Holding his spear in his right hand, Spear Guy reached out with his left in an attempt to snatch the net from Scar Eye. Scar Eye slammed Spear Guy in the throat with her right forearm while simultaneously sweeping his left leg out from underneath him with her right leg. Still holding the net, she stepped backwards and smirked as Spear Guy hit the rocky beach.

As his back made contact with the hard surface, he released his spear and spread his arms wide, slapping the ground. Sand flew into the air, and the *smack* of his impact echoed off the rocks around me. He rolled on his right shoulder, grabbed his spear, and popped up into a defensive stance.

Scar Eye was ready. Still holding her knife, she let out slack from her net, the loose web of ropes swaying as she bobbed back and forth on the balls of her feet, waiting for Spear Guy's next move.

He never had one. His chest exploded as a large blade came through his rib cage, splattering a mist of blood on Scar Eye's face. Spear Guy fell forward, sliding off the weapon. His killer stood in his place, grinning, her brown hair whipping in the wind.

"*Nomia!*" I screamed at the same time as Scar Eye.

Nomia was not alone. She held a rope in her hand, a leash wrapped around a large figure's neck.

Oh my dear God! It's Paddy! He's still alive!

I couldn't breathe. In addition to the rope around his chin-neck, his hands were bound and so were his ankles. His skin was gray and bruised. Blood still streamed from the claw-marks on his chest and, my God, he looked like shit. He looked ready to give up. Both of his eyes had swollen to puffy slits. His lip was bleeding and his nose looked crooked.

Scar Eye screamed at Nomia. Nomia screamed back, the grin gone from her stupid face. Scar Eye swung her net high up over her head, readying it for Nomia. But she was stopped mid-throw. The tallest woman I have ever seen grabbed Scar Eye's hair and yanked hard. Scar Eye stared up at the night sky, her stomach protruding forward from the severe bend in her spine. Nomia lunged, her knife aimed at the exposed, pale flesh of Scar Eye's unprotected belly, but Tall One reached out and smashed Nomia in the forehead with the butt of her hand, sending both Nomia and the still tethered Paddy reeling backwards.

They fell in a heap on the sand. Within seconds, Nomia was on her feet. She jerked Paddy forward, and he stumbled into an upright kneeling position. Nomia pulled on the rope and the noose tightened around Paddy's chinneck. Even though I was thirty yards away, I heard him gasp.

Stifling a cry, I watched, helpless, as Scar Eye recovered and made a lunge at Paddy. Tall One put out her arm and stopped Scar Eye a second time, shaking her massive head. This enormous woman towered over the other merrow, her skin even paler than Scar Eye's. She was devoid of all color, her skin the absolute *absence* of color, making Scar Eye look bronzed as she lurked beneath the larger merrow. Tall One's hair was matted and nappy-looking, as if it had never been brushed. Bones, shells, and things I could not recognize, did not *want* to recognize, festooned the rat's nest of her pale locks.

She was enormous, almost bear-like. All her limbs, her hands, her feet, and her skull were beyond the limits of comprehension. Never in my life had I witnessed someone that large. I had always thought Paddy was big. Next to this she-beast, Paddy seemed child-like.

She placed her enormous hand on Scar Eye's shoulder. The two looked at one another, communicating with their eyes. An agreement must have passed between the two because they grew still and calm. In unison, they turned and faced Nomia who stared at them expectantly. I heard Tall One say something in a deep gurgling voice. Nomia smiled.

Stepping around and facing Paddy, still on his knees, Nomia raised her weapon high up over her head—execution-style.

"*No!*" I screamed and jumped out from my hiding place.

Screaming the whole way, I raised my own knife over my head and ran towards Nomia. Startled, she stopped and turned to face me. Tall One and Scar Eye did the same.

Scar Eye made a move as if to run at me, but Tall One stopped her with a firm grip on her shoulder. A scowl covered the fair merrow's face, but she did not move. Scar Eye stood, waiting as I approached.

Confusion, then mirth filled Nomia's face as she realized who was coming towards her. She dropped the rope in her hands. Paddy lifted his head, but his eyes were so puffy, I knew he didn't recognize me.

"You! You're the one I want," yelled Nomia. "Come on then!"

Her words flew across the beach to my ears. She beckoned to me with one clawed hand, while the other hand twirled her blade. I didn't care. Adrenaline coursed through my body. I felt its warming effects fill my veins, heating my muscles. A cold sweat broke out under my arms.

I screamed an unintelligible battle cry and sprinted forward, moving faster than I ever had. Yes, she might have killed countless individuals, but she had messed with my family and I had had enough.

I crashed into the bitch with all the speed and weight of a freight train. The force of our collision tossed both of our weapons into the air, leveling the odds. It was just me against her. Blinded by my rage, I disregarded all the bad possible outcomes of my actions and pinned her down to the sand. She might have been craftier, but I outweighed her.

I raised my fists and brought them down. Over and over and over again, I smashed and smashed and smashed. She did her best to shield her face from my blows, but I was enraged, unstoppable. She had awakened my inner mama bear, and I wanted a pound of flesh for all my troubles, for all the fear and danger she had brought to my house and to my loved ones. Each and every time my fist connected with her body, I felt more and more powerful. There was no nausea this time, only red anger.

Nomia howled like a wounded animal, or maybe that was me. I didn't know and it didn't matter.

Then everything changed. I hurt. I hurt a lot, and the source of the pain sprouted in my left shoulder.

A primal scream tore from my throat and I looked down. A spear protruded from my body. It stopped inches from Nomia's bloodied face. A few of her sharp teeth were cracked, bruises were developing on her cheeks, and her wide eyes looked even wider. Her gray irises darted from my face to the spear's point, then back again.

My body leaned to the side and I slumped over, off of Nomia. Then I fell forward, and the spear hit the beach and slid five inches farther through my body. I screamed again, a high-pitched howl. With a shaking right hand, I reached up and gingerly touched my new appendage. I cried out. It hurt like a motherfucker! Blood seeped down onto the sand, a detail I noticed through the blur of my tears.

That's my blood. I'm dead now.

"Evie."

I cried and cried.

"Evie!"

The adrenaline was sapping away, leaving a wake of white pain. I could hear my husband. I lifted my head and saw him. My love was there in front of me. The ropes were still around his chinneck, wrists, and ankles. He fell to his knees and put his giant, meaty hands on my right arm.

"Evie," he said. "There's something in your shoulder."

I just looked at him and felt the last of my strength slip away. I was beyond sarcasm.

"How did you get free?" I asked.

"Don't worry about me," he said. "We need to get you to a hospital."

I looked past Paddy. Nomia was still lying on the beach, but she was farther away from me now. A smooth path was left in the sand, formed when her body had been dragged fifteen feet away. She rolled on the beach in pain, clutching her arm and moaning. Tall One and Scar Eye were standing over her. Tall One's brow creased as she looked past both Paddy and me. Her gaze fell on the waves.

"What's going on?" I whispered to Paddy and then winced.

I looked at his face. He had turned his gaze towards the water. It was hard to see past the torches, but his grip on my good arm tightened, and when he looked back at me, there was a blankness on his face. It wasn't quite fear. It was something else, something like awe.

"It's over," was all he said.

"What's over?" I asked. I had no idea what was going on. I knew we were not safe, and I knew I desperately needed medical attention.

"Paddy," I said. "We need to get out of here."

"We can't leave yet, *mo rún*," Paddy said and moved to sit beside me. He was so warm and I was not. I was freezing again, still soaked to the bone, and I was bleeding.

"We need to see how this ends," he said.

I felt sleepy and I had no idea what he was talking about, so I put my head on his shoulder and let the heat of his large body seep into me. He was alive. That was all that mattered. The enormity of the horrific events weighed down on me, and discovering the truth was beyond the scope of my concerns. I just wanted to disappear into the oblivion of sleep. I must have slumped, because I cried out at the fresh pain in my shoulder. The spear had made contact with the beach or something.

"Try to stay awake, Evie," said Paddy.

"I don't know, Paddy," I said. "I'm just so tired."

"Evie, you just kicked the shite out of Nomia. You can do this for me. Stay awake."

"I did that for *you*!"

"Oh, my love," he said. "It was so very brave of you."

"Who the hell threw a spear at me?"

"I believe it was one of our guys," he said and turned to stare at the water.

A stillness fell over the beach. The fighting had ceased, and the air felt different. The hair on the back of my neck stood up. Paddy must have felt it, too. He leaned closer to me, nudging his bound arms towards my frigid body. There was an electricity in the atmosphere, the way the world feels before a lightning storm—charged, pensive, aggressive.

I tried to lift my head to see what everyone was staring at. I managed to look up, and then I saw them, too.

Beyond the torches, a collection of male merrow emerged from the water. Steam rose from their bodies as they stood. In the surf just behind them, twenty heads, followed by shoulders, followed by torsos, emerged from the inky water. They were hideous—half men, half fish, their faces and forms ragged and scarred. They used their arms to push their torsos up from the surf. The beings then rose from the water, standing as their legs formed.

The transformation of tail to legs, solid and sturdy, took only seconds to complete. Seawater rolled off of the battle-worn creatures and dripped into the receding waves. Several more stayed in the water, but I couldn't keep my eyes off the ones coming closer and closer to where we sat.

One of the shorter ones looked at Paddy and nodded. Paddy nodded back. Then Ronan stepped into view. He rushed over and cut Paddy's binds, then examined my wound. He turned his head back and forth, muttering something I couldn't understand.

From behind the warriors came three ancient-looking male merrow. Their heads were not shaved as high as the younger warriors' heads. They wore their hair long, in neat braids down their backs. Pale blue, sometimes green, skin was visible a few inches above where ears would be, but in place of ears were small holes, and ... *were those gills?* It was the first time I noticed their gill slits, long gashes traversing their necks. They looked feathery, like pale eyelashes.

Wincing with the burning pain in my shoulder, I turned and looked at Tall One and Scar Eye. They were no longer alone with Nomia. More than fifteen female merrow had gathered behind them. They were all still, unmoving, like statues.

Fierce-looking statues. They crowded together and stared at the approaching males.

One of the elders strode past us. He glanced down and nodded to Ronan, then continued on, stopping in front of Tall One. The two regarded one another for a moment, and then the smaller male extended his arm up to the mammoth female. She waited a few moments, then returned the gesture. They grasped one another's forearms and shook.

It was so quiet, but I needed to know what was happening.

"Ronan," I whispered and then sucked in my breath. Speaking hurt. Everything hurt. "What's going on?" I all but wailed.

"The fighting is over. Our clan and theirs will decide what happens now. There will be a tribunal. Hush, Evelyn. Let me examine your shoulder."

Tall One and the elder male spoke with short words and hand gestures. Nomia rolled into a ball at their feet. She clutched her sides and rocked back and forth.

Good, I thought, then cried out as Ronan touched and prodded the spear in my shoulder.

He made clicks with his tongue and murmured to himself as he looked me over. Then he paused and looked up at his elder, listening intently.

Ronan whispered, "We need to get Catherine and go. But first I need to do something about this spear of yours."

While Ronan busied himself with his field examination, the tallest of the male merrow came over to us and looked down at Paddy and then at me, his face coiled into something foul, as if he had just stepped in shit.

"I need that back," he said. His voice was deep and carried Paddy's Irish lilt, but his words sounded gurgled, gravely, angry. He looked down at me expectantly. I didn't know what his words meant, until he gestured towards the spear in my shoulder.

"You? You speared me? Why the ... Oh, no way," I stammered and looked at Ronan.

Ronan put a reassuring hand on my right shoulder and smiled at me. I felt at peace, lost in the deepness of his gray irises.

Then he grabbed the spear with his right hand and yanked hard.

I sucked in all the air around me and then let it out in one, long scream. It came from the depths of my being, the absolute bottom of my soul. Blood poured from the wound like a geyser, and the last thing I remembered was Paddy's horrified face, hovering over me.

"My dear God. Will she be okay?"

My eyes would not open. Many voices spoke at once, all echoing, reverberating in my head. I heard the surf pounding the rocks, an endless splashing and shushing. I heard the echo of dripping water falling into a puddle or pool. I was aware of dampness and cold, the smell of brine and wet stones—and something on fire.

Me. I was on fire. I was burning from the inside out. The fire consumed me whole, searing through all other thoughts, dragging me from the solace of unconsciousness out into the heat of a thousand suns.

Fuck!

I could not shape my lips into the necessary shapes to let the curse fly out. Didn't matter. My throat was a barren desert. It *all* hurt the most. No, not all. My nose was fine, but the rest—*oh the rest*—was nothing but exquisite, mind-blowing pain.

I fell. I fell down a rock-strewn embankment. I was almost drowned. Then there was the impalement.

I revisited each event, identifying their aftereffects, noting how they bloomed over my body, like weeds flourishing across an abandoned lot. I shifted my weight and gasped. My hip exploded with an undiscovered injury, forcing me to lie still and practice opening my eyes.

You can do it, Evie. Just flick those lashes.

"I think she's trying to wake up."

Aunt Catherine?

"Be still, *mo rún*," said a warm, familiar voice.

I smiled, then winced. My face hurt, too. Then I did it. I opened my eyes. Paddy. My Paddy, alive and by my side. I smiled despite the pain. He knelt down next to me, his form barely covered by a dark men's trench coat many sizes too small. The belt was missing and three belt-loops hung down, useless, like broken feathers. The front of the coat hung open and the fabric puckered away from Paddy's chest. His skin was a mess. Shredded slashes and long coagulating scabs crisscrossed his torso. I tried not to make a face, but it hurt to look at his wounds.

"It's all my fault." The words scratched their way out, damaging the already tender tissue of my throat.

"Hush now," said Paddy. He reached down and stroked my hair. I wanted to melt into his touch. "None of this is your fault. Save your strength. We need to stay here awhile longer."

I tried to sit up and decipher our whereabouts, but the pain in my shoulder pounded me back down like a tidal wave. I raised my hand to my wound. The spear was gone. In its place,

I felt thick padding, perhaps cloth or, no, wait—it was slippery. *Seaweed?*

"Ronan took it out, dear," said Aunt Catherine from my other side. She and Paddy placed their hands under my upper body and eased me into a sitting position. I almost vomited from the intensity of the pain.

"I've never seen a wound dressed before," she said. "Certainly not like this. Another merrow aided Ronan. Once the spear was out, they packed the hole in your shoulder with a rope made from kelp. Ronan smeared some balm over the entry and exit wounds, then wrapped you in more kelp." Catherine shook her head and *tsked* under her breath. "I hope and pray you don't get an infection."

"No need for worry," said Paddy. "Ronan said as long as we irrigate the injury, nothing will get into Evie's system. It's all quite impressive. I once read an article about dentists using alginate dressings in extraction procedures. There is something in the seaweed—naturally occurring polysaccharides, I think— that form a gel-like barrier, allowing the granulating tissue to form naturally without being disturbed. There's no need to change the dressing, hence the importance of the irrigation. It's all natural. Absolutely fascinating."

"Paddy," I croaked. "Shut the fuck up and tell me where we are."

Paddy smirked and looked at Catherine. "See? She'll be fine." Then he looked down at me. "We're in a cave, love. I'm not sure where exactly. I was too consumed with your well-being after Ronan removed the spear. There was a lot of blood.

It all happened so fast. Many of our merrow carried you here. Someone was kind enough to give me this coat."

"So," I said, my voice still full of gravel, "do you believe in the killer mermaids *now*?"

"Oh, my love," he said with a heavy sigh. "I've always believed you. I just couldn't say anything until I knew what was happening for sure. Catherine and I were waiting for word from abroad. Honestly, until the night on the docks in Stillhouse Cove, I knew very little of the merrow. I took care of our family's fake funerals, but I never questioned the empty caskets. I was told not to ask. Until recently, my experiences of these creatures consisted of children's stories—fairy tales, really." He glanced over his shoulder and winced.

We both needed some heavy-duty painkillers.

"*These*, I don't know what to call them. The word 'creatures' seems so rudimentary. They didn't seem like this in the stories I heard as a child in Ireland. In those tales, the merrow always wore little red caps. All their magic was in their caps, and if you took a merrow's cap, you owned him—or her."

"I remember the cap stories," said Catherine. "My favorite tale was the one where a merrow stole the souls of fishermen and kept them in cages beneath the sea."

I shuddered. In my mind, I saw the poor young man off Despair Island torn to pieces and eaten. They stole more than his soul. Did the maker of the soul cage story witness the brutal dismantling of a fellow fisherman? Was the story his way of cautioning others? If it was, the storyteller gave the G-rated version. The R-rated version would have put an end to the fishing industry.

"Well, these merrow are far more complex than the ones from my childhood fairy tales, and, as I've recently discovered, they're my kin. Nomia and her kind have been causing problems in Narragansett Bay for centuries. I'm truly sorry she interfered with our lives, Evie. But everything happens for a reason. If not for you, my love, she would have caused even more mischief, stolen and ruined more lives. But she crossed the wrong family. She's brought the force of the Irish Cantillon clan to these waters, and now she'll pay for what she's done."

Where were *Nomia and her kind?*

I tried to turn around. The pain in my shoulder burned.

"Are they all dead?" I asked.

"Who, Evie?" asked Catherine. "Are *who* all dead?"

"Nomia and her kind. Did that asshole with the spear and his mer-buddies kill them all?"

"No, *mo rún*," said Paddy. His face was solemn and filthy. I reached up, licked my thumb, and tried to wipe some of the soot and grime from his face.

"Och!" cried Paddy. "That mom-juice thing you do is disgusting, Evie. Please, let it be." He grabbed my hand and held it between his giant bread-loaf hands. "After you passed out, when the spear was removed ..."

"Uh, you mean torn from my body as if I was a martini olive on a toothpick?"

"Yes," Paddy chuckled. "That's the very thing. Well, after that, our side pulled our dead from the waters and burned them in the fires on the beach. Nomia and her kind left. We weren't told very much. Ronan said little. He disappeared after tending to you and then returned with Catherine. After that, we were brought here, to this cave."

The cave was large and spacious. Torchlight bounced off the ceiling where condensation gathered and dripped down into tidal pools scattered around the cave floor. To my right, the cavern disappeared. The ceiling sloped into the dark, and any light attempting to illuminate the diminished space was devoured by blackness. Far to my left, I heard the sea crashing against rocks. It must have been the opening to the cave.

I tried again to turn my sore neck, this time towards the entrance, but it wasn't easy. Jagged rocks concealed the opening. Each enormous shard burst forth from the cavern floor, partially obscuring the world beyond. Towards the top of the opening, I could see the velvet sky, crisp and clear in the frigid night. In the vast blackness, stars, like fairy lights, danced. I had no idea such a place existed in Little Rhody, but I've been wrong before. Take, for example, my belief that humans are the most evolved species on earth. Wrong.

Really, what the fuck do I know?

Naked, tattooed men meandered around, lit torches, congregated in groups, spoke in hushed voices. It was like pictures I had seen on the internet of Comic Con, except no one was wearing a cape. And there were no females. So, yes, it was just like Comic Con. I recognized some of the warriors I had seen on the beach, including the bastard who had impaled me with his stupid spear. He glared at me as he walked by. I did my best to sneer in return, but it hurt too much to sustain it for very long.

"Where are all your *girl* merrows?" I asked.

"Ronan says they're back in Ireland," said Catherine. "They send their men-folk to deal with issues abroad. The females do not concern themselves with foreign clan members. They see no point in honoring those who choose to leave the motherwaters."

"They sound stubborn," I said. "Nothing like you, Catherine."

She surprised me with a wry smile, which faded as swiftly as it had arrived. Her gaze was elsewhere, inspecting our new location.

"What are they doing?" I asked.

A central fire was lit, and three individuals sat on beat-up lobster traps.

"They're preparing for the tribunal," said Ronan, appearing from the darkness behind us.

I looked to Paddy for an explanation, but his gaze was distant. His face was beaten and swollen, and his eyes had a sadness to them. I wanted to get home, to *our* home. I wanted to put all this behind us, get some medical help, grab our daughter, and have a decent cup of coffee. His face was my everything.

How did we end up here?

"It's for Nomia," explained Ronan.

"While you were unconscious, the two sides met and agreed that a trial would be held for her crimes against our family," said Catherine. "There will be retribution for my Aiden." She shivered in the cold of the cave and moved closer to me for warmth.

"No one knows if she was the one who killed Aiden, Aunt Catherine," said Paddy. He reached across me and put a hand on her arm.

She turned to him with a look that could wither a cactus. "Who else would have done it? She's a wicked thing. Her mother should have drowned her the day she was born."

I was about to question the likelihood of a drowned merrow, then thought better of it.

"I've watched her for centuries," Ronan continued. "She's done nothing but lure men to their graves. A council has been formed. The elders of both clans will determine Nomia's fate."

"Both clans?" I asked. "I only see our side."

"The females have not arrived yet," said Ronan. "They are tending to their dead and wounded and should be along shortly."

Ronan knelt down beside me. "Twas a bold thing you did there on the beach."

"It was indeed," said Catherine. "I watched you from above, Evelyn. I saw you try to save my Patrick."

Catherine stood and moved behind Paddy. She put her frail arms around her nephew's mammoth neck and lay her silver head against his own giant one. Then she closed her eyes. Strange how supernatural catastrophes bring out the best in people. She must have murmured something in his ear, perhaps some sweet endearment because Paddy smiled a small, sweet smile and nodded.

Catherine came around and also knelt down next to me. Taking both of my hands in her own she said, "Our merrow came from the Bay. I heard a commotion in the waters, and I looked beyond the cove, out to sea. The water frothed as they moved through the waves. It was as if they wanted their enemies to feel their arrival, the arrival of larger predators. They out-numbered the female pod four to one. When you dove in, you entered an underwater war zone."

Catherine shuddered. I could feel her body tremble through her frail fingers. She looked so tired. I'm sure I didn't look much better. Within the cave, all sense of time was lost. I had no idea how long I had been gone from Savannah. It felt like days and I felt like shit.

Catherine continued, "I cannot believe you attacked her like you did, Evelyn."

She reached out towards my shoulder. Her fingers hovered there, just above my wound, and her face crumpled into itself, like a flower near the end of its fragile life. Watery one moment, and then, as if a switch had been flipped, her eyes cleared, and her face returned to order. A small smile graced her crinkled lips.

"I was so proud of you! Who knew you were a prize fighter! You walloped her right good, missy." Nodding with approval, she patted my hands, then stood and returned to the empty space beside Paddy.

Around us, the conversations grew louder, more raucous. The elders stood, and a hush fell over the room. Everyone turned and faced the entrance. I turned to Paddy. He, too, raised his head.

"They're here," he said.

Two Cantillon merrow, spears in hand, both naked, ran to the cave entrance and disappeared behind the rocks.

I knew who was coming. The familiar nausea claimed me, and I doubled over, clutching my gut.

I turned to Catherine and said, "Do you feel that?"

"Feel what?"

"You don't feel like you're about to vomit?" The pain was excruciating, acute and sharp, like food poisoning.

Catherine made an annoyed arch with her eyebrows and turned her eyes back to the cave entrance. Paddy looked down at me and drew me closer to his large, warm side.

"You all right?"

"No, Paddy," I said. "I'm not. I can feel her. Why does she makes me so sick?"

He looked down at me and from the crunch of his caterpillar brows, I knew he did not understand.

"Whenever Nomia is around, I feel nauseous. It's so strong."

Concern blanketed Paddy's face, and he squeezed me again. He looked to Ronan.

"I've never heard of such a thing," replied Ronan.

"Brave new world we're living in," I croaked, swallowing the bile that threatened the back of my throat. "Brave new world."

I couldn't help thinking, *Why* does *this bitch make me so physically sick?* But I never completed my train of thought. Shrill sounds echoed off the solid ceiling and filled the cave.

A chill went down my already cold spine and settled in the hole in my shoulder. The wound ached, and not for the first time, I wished I was anywhere but where I was at that moment.

I glanced around the cave. Several of the other merrow were on their bare feet, weapons in hand, alarm spreading like fire across their large eyes.

Another loud trill filled the cave. Then nothing.

The stars twinkled above the ragged rock, the sea hushed

beyond the entrance, and no one moved. I felt dizzy, light-headed. I was holding my breath as the moment spread out, unfolded before us, wrapping us in anticipation.

An older merrow, one of the elders near the fire, moved towards the entrance. His feet made no sound on the cave floor as he glided towards the night. He lifted his head and emitted a sound like I had never heard before. It came from deep within his chest, a low bass-like growl or bellow. The call rumbled and then rippled off the cave walls.

Moments passed. We all waited and watched the opening.

A response came from outside the cave. It sounded more questioning, as if to say, *I heard you and want to know if you really meant what you said.* The elder called again. His bellow had a finality to it, as if the matter at hand was completed, and no response was necessary. When he finished, he nodded to two young warriors and then returned to his place by the fire.

The younger merrow gathered their weapons and moved to the opening of the cave. They stood motionless like sentries and then, in unison, hit their spears against the cave walls. They created a steady rhythm. It filled my ears as it gathered speed and then stopped as suddenly as it had started. The warriors ceased their movements, silent guardians of the entranceway once more.

With the sound of the spears still reverberating in my ears, I looked to the cave opening. It was no longer empty.

Two female merrow entered. Tall, willowy creatures, their skin glowed an unnatural bluish color, like jellyfish. Their gait was slow and cautious. They were naked, stunning, their presence demanding attention. I could see why so many men had lost their lives to these creatures. As women, they were perfectly formed. Both were pale blondes. Their hair hung behind them and swayed with each step they took. The females kept their chins up and scanned the cave with their large, almost colorless eyes. Glancing at one another, they stopped on either side of the entrance, almost directly in front of the male merrow sentries, and then looked back the way they had come.

I snuck a glance at Paddy to see if he was gawking, but he wasn't. His brow was set in a stern straight line, and I could see the muscles in his jaw working. These were the bitches who had threatened his family.

My cramps doubled.

Without ceremony, a female was shoved through the entrance. A mass of tangled limbs and long, brown hair cascaded over her face and shoulders, obscuring her features. I knew it was *her*. I could pick that bitch out of a crowd any day. She stumbled in and fell to her knees. A rope woven of crude, organic material was attached to her neck. It slacked when she fell, but then the holder of the leash snapped the line taut, jerking Nomia to her feet. Her arms were bound at the wrists, and she kept them above her head when her legs hit the rocky cave floor. Her face and body were covered in bruises from my attack.

Good.

Scar Eye, the merrow I had seen on the beach earlier, entered behind Nomia. As the pair moved farther into the cave, Scar Eye wound Nomia's leash lengthwise around her palm and elbow, coiling the rope tight. Nomia looked back at her captor and let out a low guttural growl that ended in a hiss. Scar Eye sneered in response and jerked the line a little harder. Nomia fell onto her stomach with a loud wet sound. The air left her lungs, and Nomia wheezed, then gasped.

I'd like to say I felt bad for her, but I didn't.

Winding up for a kick, Scar Eye was stopped by Tall One, who had entered the cave without my noticing. She grumbled something to the smaller, fair merrow who bowed her head in response. Then, reaching down, Scar Eye grabbed Nomia's bound hands and jerked her to her feet. Nomia scowled, her upper lip curling to expose her broken and chipped teeth. Scar Eye snapped her jaws together near Nomia's face, then shoved her captive forward towards the center of the assembled Irish elders.

Tall One followed the pair.

Countless female merrow, all pale, blonde, and lithe, entered the cave. They carried knives and fanned out behind Tall One, Scar Eye, and Nomia.

The Irish merrow formed a defensive guard in front of the central fire, the elders at the center looking on, impassive, unfazed by the presence of the female warriors.

An Irish elder pushed his way through the vanguard of his clan and nodded to Tall One. The two leaders walked side by side, making their way through the throng of male merrow. The crowd parted, clearing a path to the waiting fire. Several of the males stared up at Tall One, their jaws open in awe as she passed by. The elder shot a look at one gaping merrow who dropped his gaze to his feet. Spear Guy watched the leaders walk towards the fire, and then he skulked around the edge of the crowd, disappearing from view.

Pushing Nomia ahead of her, Scar Eye followed the two leaders into the crowd, along the cleared path. A low rumble, a deep baritone bellow, flowed from the crowd as Nomia passed. Several of the Irish warriors spat at Nomia's feet, but she kept her head held high and did not acknowledge their resentment. A fat, satisfied sort of smile hung on Scar Eye's face as she moved through the crowd behind Nomia.

The males stepped back farther when the small pod of females brought up the last of the procession, following Scar Eye and Nomia towards the fire. The tension in the air grew and hung like an electrical charge. Males stared down females. Females eyed back. Both were cautious of the other. All were poised to strike.

All this trouble for this bitch. I didn't get it. Why was Nomia being treated like this by her own kind? *This is all surreal.*

Catherine moved even closer to Paddy. He put his arm around her back and hugged his aunt, pulling the three of us closer. We were outnumbered. If something went wrong, odds were not in our favor. We would not make it out alive.

What would become of Savannah?

I pushed the thought from my mind and focused on the gathering before me.

"This is intense," Ronan whispered. "I've never witnessed a gathering of this size before."

"What will happen?" I whispered back.

"The females will present Nomia to the elders and a decision will be made."

One of the elders stood and motioned for all his warriors to sit down. The male merrow looked at one another and did nothing. A long, cold silence fell across the cavern until one of them set his jaw firmly, closed his eyes, and sat down. One by one, the other male merrow followed suit and joined their brother, sitting cross-legged on the floor.

The females looked to Tall One. She nodded to them and raised her arms, palms facing down, patting the air. They, too, sat down.

Nomia started to sit, but Scar Eye kicked her and jerked her into a standing position. Still holding the lead line, Scar Eye walked over to the elders and stood above them, glaring down. Some of the male merrow seated closest to their leaders growled, their hands tensing on their weapons. Tall One looked up and caught her charge's attention. The female warrior nodded to her leader, then turned to the elders. She bowed deeply, then unwound the line from her forearm and presented the rope to the elders. They took the line and nodded back to her. Scar Eye stood upright and scanned the crowd, her fierce stare daring anyone to challenge her. No one did. She walked, head held high, to the rear of the cave and sat down.

One of the elders said something to his warriors, after which a lone figure stood up and came to sit down between the elders and Tall One.

"Who's that?" Paddy whispered to Ronan.

"That is Murtagh. He spent time exploring the North Sea and learned a dialect similar to the language of this pod."

"But Nomia speaks English," I said. "Doesn't all of her pod?

I mean, they all live around here, right? And haven't they lived here for, like, forever?"

"It's true," said Ronan in a hushed voice. "From what I've observed, Nomia picked up the local language easily. She's sort of a go-between for her people. For whatever reason—inability to speak, lack of desire to speak—Nomia is the only one who speaks multiple languages. Therefore, they rely on her to make contact with the outside world. Their elder, Kolga, the tall one, certainly does not speak English or Gaelic. Murtagh will speak for them both."

"Kolga's a big girl," I muttered.

"I've steered clear of Kolga for as long as I've been in these waters. She terrifies me," said Ronan. "I once saw her rip a man's head clean from his body, then drink the blood from his neck."

"Whoa, whoa. Too much information, Ronan," I whispered.

We were surrounded by tense aquatic warriors. I did not need an image of beheading to add to my unease.

"Now you know why she scares me."

"All you have to do is look at her to be scared," said Paddy. "It's not often I feel like a wee little thing."

"If Nomia is their go-between, why do they all seem to hate her? Only a few of her sisters, or whatever you call pod-mates, seem to be looking at Nomia with anything but scorn."

"That," said Ronan, "is a long story. Nomia has been trying to leave her pod for centuries. She's a menace. She doesn't have many supporters left in her pod. If Nomia wasn't the go-between, the one with both beauty for luring men to their doom *and* language abilities, I'm sure Kolga would have relieved her of her head long before now."

It was true. When I scanned the group of females, most of them had sneers on their faces as they looked at Nomia in the center of the circle. It was as if she was garbage, something foul and disgusting that needed removal. Only a few looked at her with any type of concern. Three, in particular, huddled together and clasped one another's hands. Tears streamed down their faces, and they tore at their hair. Nomia looked to them, her face pleading and vulnerable.

The supporters were less attractive than their sisters. Their hair was the same unlikeable blonde as my own—dirty and limp-looking, almost gray in appearance. Nothing like the pure whiteness of Scar Eye's hair. There was something quite stunning about that one, even with her scar. But I could see how her deformity might be a handicap when it came to gathering food for the pod. One could surmise that the unattractiveness of the three ugly sisters was a handicap as well.

I was beginning to understand the connection between these unfortunates and Nomia. She was their source of food. They would be helpless without her.

Or maybe not.

One glance at the other pod members made me believe that there were other ways to get food, and Nomia did not need to be the solution to that problem.

Kolga spoke first. Her voice was deep. The words fell from her mouth like jagged ice chips filled with too many hard sounds and long vowels. Murtagh listened, at times nodding to indicate

his understanding, and at other times speaking and then listening again. When Kolga was in agreement with Murtagh, he
would turn to the elders and speak in Gaelic.

This discourse went back and forth for some time. I looked
at Catherine and Paddy. Both spoke Gaelic, and I watched them
lean in closer when Murtagh spoke to the elders. Their faces
told me some of what they heard, but mostly I was alone with
my thoughts. I never learned Gaelic, and fortunately, Paddy and
Catherine were respectful enough to rarely speak it in front of
me.

"What's going on?" I asked.

"They're discussing the crimes Nomia has committed."

"And?"

"This is all coming as a shock to Kolga," said Ronan. "Kolga
is saying Nomia has been trying to leave their pod for centuries,
but she had no idea Nomia has been harassing Cantillons over
the years."

"It's not just harassment, Ronan, and you know it," said
Catherine with venom.

"We're still not sure she killed Aiden, Catherine."

"What about the Potter girl?" asked Catherine.

"She never killed the Potter girl. Her suitor, Byron, yes," said
Ronan, "but not Sarah. That was a close one. I sent word to the
council when I found Byron's remains, but because Nomia did
not kill a Cantillon, there was no cause for a summit."

I had no idea who Sarah was, and I was too distracted by
Nomia to care. She was speaking now. I could hear her throaty
voice across the cavern. She spoke in the same language as

Kolga. Tears flowed down her battered perfect cheeks, and her voice was raised, pleading her case with intense emotion.

Then she turned and looked at me. Her face filled with rage, and she spat her words in my direction. I didn't understand her language, but I understood her tone.

That's when I felt my own anger rise. It started in the base of my being and boiled like an unwatched pot, building steam and scalding heat. Other merrow looked my way, their gaze filling with Nomia's same venom.

She must be telling lies! I am the victim here, not her!

The words kept coming, harsh, ugly, guttural noises all targeted at me. The boiling pot in my gut overflowed, and despite my pain, I was on my feet.

"No!" I shouted. "Whatever she tells you, it's a lie! She is evil and needs to be put somewhere where she will never bother me or my family ever again!"

Paddy and Ronan stood behind me and Catherine joined them.

The cave exploded with activity. Merrow from both sides jumped to their feet, and weapons were drawn.

Nomia screamed and ran at me. She shook her hair and tore at the leash around her neck as she closed the distance between us. Scar Eye and Tall One flew behind her.

Once again, adrenaline flooded my body. I was terrified, but there was no time to think about it. Nomia was on me. Her bound talons tore at my face, my chest, my shoulder.

My shoulder!

The pain erupted like a volcano of blinding white light, and

I screamed as I fell to the ground with Nomia on top of me. I kicked wildly and arched my back as best as I could to get her off. Her teeth were inches from my face, and I could smell her rancid breath.

My knife!

As I bucked and kicked at her, I managed to get the knife out of my jacket, but it was useless, pinned to my side from the weight of the wild creature on top of me.

Then she was being pulled away.

Kolga had ripped Nomia off me. She tossed her aside like an unwanted doll. Nomia hit the side of the cave and slumped down. I did not follow what happened to her. Kolga gripped me by my wounded shoulder and lifted me into the air.

The pain was so clear, so present, I felt myself retreating to another part of my subconscious. A low moan tore from my throat.

"Evie!"

It was Paddy. I rolled my head to the side and saw my husband looking up at me. He could not see behind him. I could. Scar Eye was about to strike him down.

"Nooooo!" I screamed.

I don't know how I did it. I don't know where it came from, but it came. I found the strength to raise my arm, my good arm, the one that held the knife. I raised it up and brought it down into Kolga's eye socket. The blade went in and I twisted it. I didn't think I was capable of doing such a thing, but I was. I twisted and twisted, until she released me and we both fell into a heap of limbs onto the cold cave floor.

I drifted. It was all a blur of faces, colors, and noise after that. A montage of images and events. Not much of it was clear. I heard screaming, high-pitched words in a language I didn't know. Scar Eye was on top of me, but then not. I was being dragged backwards away from the whiter-than-white females. One still breathing, one not. All because of me.

I remember staring at the skin of Scar Eye's scalp, her head bowed over the lifeless Kolga. I remember her eyes locking on mine. Those eyes were filled with hatred. I think I saw Nomia, running away, but maybe not. Our Irish brethren appeared and surrounded us, creating a wall of spears, nets, and knives. I was not alone in the circle of protection. Catherine, Paddy, and Ronan were all by my side. I was being carried by them—I think.

The abyss washed over me, beckoning me to hide in the darkness of my own mind, somewhere quieter than this, someplace where I could find solitude and rest. I felt myself slipping. The world around me faded, the yelling, the clashing, the screaming—it all faded.

All except her voice. Her voice was louder than all the other noises muffled by my addled brain. Nomia, clearer than anything, spoke through my thoughts. *I will find you. I will find your family. And I will take them all away, one by one.*

Then the voice was gone. The air changed and I knew we were out of the cave. I was being carried over someone's shoulder like a sack of laundry. Bouncing along with the rhythm of the one carrying me, I watched the rocks and sand of the ground pass below us both. Who carried me? Paddy? Ronan?

Another Irish merrow? It was too dark to tell. I heard splashing and then I was lowered into a boat.

"I think we're clear of 'em," someone said.

That was enough for me to let go. I closed my eyes and let the darkness swallow me whole.

When I awoke, we were moving back up the Bay in Ronan's small craft. The sun was up now, and in the golden light, the fog was burning off the water's surface. A few fishermen were returning from their early morning trips out into deeper waters. We were all headed north up Narragansett Bay. Ronan was at the helm, while Paddy, Catherine, and I sat huddled in the back of his tiny boat.

Her words echoed in my mind. *I will take them all away.*

Would I ever be rid of that bitch? Would this shit ever end?

My shoulder, my body, my everything ached, and Paddy looked worse than ever. Catherine appeared exhausted. She had cuts and bruises on her face and arms. I was worried about her. It's easy to forget that she's older and not as strong as she'd like us all to believe. I don't know what happened to her, or any of us, but I was grateful that she had all her limbs. How we escaped the cave remained a mystery to me, but we did it, and for now, it was over.

Or was it? Will I spend the rest of my life watching over my shoulder, waiting for her to attack?

I pushed the thought from my mind. I was too tired. Instead, I glanced at Ronan. He was bleeding in several places but appeared not to notice. I knew we were safe—for the moment— because of him. Thank God for Ronan. I could rely on him to be there. It was a true comfort to know he would be looking out for us, making certain we were safe.

We were all in need of rest, in our own homes, in our own beds. We all needed to embrace Savannah, to smell her curls, hear her gurgled laughter, and feel her chunky body against our own.

In the waters north of us, a tugboat materialized from the evaporating fog, and we slowly overtook her. The name on the side read *Reliance*, and she chugged up the Bay, her beautiful scarlet metal shining bright in the morning light. The captain in the wheelhouse waved to us as we passed.

He has no idea what goes on in these waters. It's just another workday for him.

The Bay looked different to me now. It was no longer a backdrop to my life but a home to another culture, a menacing culture filled with strange beings that may or may not want to eat me. I shuddered and wondered if I would ever take Savannah to the beach again.

I looked back at the *Reliance* and sighed. I needed to rely on something, someone.

"Evie," said Paddy.

I raised my head as best as I could and looked at him.

"You saved my life, not once but twice. I never knew you had it in you. You sure are a superhero of sorts."

Right. Me. A superhero.

But would I be able to save us all a third time if necessary?

I didn't know. I only knew I was tired, and I needed to close my eyes for a long, long time. So I did.

EPILOGUE

The O'Conner Residence
Pawtuxet Village, Rhode Island
Three years later

"I'll be right back," I called to Paddy as I headed into Catherine's house. Savannah and I had been playing on her new trampoline in the backyard.

Relax. It's one of those in-the-ground types. As if Aunt Catherine would allow a deathtrap on her property. *Please.*

I was exhausted and needed a break. As I opened the back-door, the musical sound of Savannah's squeals and giggles followed me and filled my ears. The smell of fresh-cooked burgers wafted into my nose, making my mouth water.

It was one of those delicious first days of summer, when the humidity hasn't set in yet, the air has warmed, and everything looks relieved to not be frozen.

Paddy called to Savannah, laughter dripping from his voice, "No, you wee thing. I will not be joining you on that deathtrap. I'll break it with one hop! You wouldn't want your da to break your tramper, would you?"

"It's not called a *tramper*, Paddy," I said before I let the door close behind me.

"Like I care what it's bloody called, woman," he answered. "Why don't you make yourself useful and go knit me a sweater, missy?" His words carried through the screen door. Then he mumbled something I couldn't understand, but I laughed anyway.

He was happy. Savannah was happy. I was happy. We were all *happy*. Even Aunt Catherine was happy.

After the cave, we had waited. We waited for her to return. We waited for any of them to return. But week after week, month after month, and now year after year, there was nothing. No news came from the sea.

It was like they had never been here at all. Except Ronan. He was still around. He kept his vigil over us, occasionally popping in, sometimes with clothes on.

Ronan had informed us that they had all left. All of them—the Irish and the females were all gone. Perhaps losing Kolga had destroyed the cohesive ties that bound the cannibalistic females together, giving them the freedom to go off on their own. Perhaps. Perhaps they were free. Perhaps they were not. We did not hear from them, and that was all that mattered.

If you're wondering if I had remorse about killing Kolga, the answer is no. I did what I needed to do. That was the end of it. Did I sometimes wake up in the middle of the night screaming, clutching my shoulder, covered in sweat? Yes. Yes, I did.

Does my shoulder still ache every fucking time it rains? Yes. Yes, it does.

Touching the scar on my shoulder, I turned and spied Catherine and Tony head to head discussing something in hushed tones. A small tender smile graced her face, and her ivory skin glowed in a way I had never noticed before. Tony looked equally pleased—*content*, I believe is the correct word. He looked content. His liver-spotted hand held Catherine's, and he patted hers in a most endearing way, as if this moment was all that mattered.

He had finally worn her down.

The two had begun dating. Their dates consisted of four o'clock dinners at the Governor Francis Restaurant (to get to the salad bar before anyone else had the opportunity to sneeze on the sneeze-guard) and then a rousing evening of Sunday night bingo at the Riviera Bingo Hall. Not to mention being next to one another at all waking hours.

I'm guessing Catherine's near-death experience had something to do with it, but really, who am I to judge?

As I watched, the white-haired pair shifted their gaze to Savannah, who had stopped bouncing and was staring back at both of them. Her chubby fingers were in her mouth, a habit I could not break her of, no matter how hard I tried. She was grinning, and her eyes held the sparkle of one young and innocent—one who knows that she is loved and loved well by many doting adults.

"I love you," she gurgled to them through her fingers.

The happy pair looked stunned in a wondrous way, as if this child was the only child on the planet, and everything she did and said was of the utmost importance.

"Come over here, you, and let me give you some smooches," said Tony as he held out his knobby fingers to Savannah.

My heart swelled, and I let the air out of my lungs slowly, relishing the satisfaction of normalcy and family love. It was a good place to be after the events a few years prior.

After we had healed, Paddy and I started a new regimen. We woke early, threw Savannah in her stroller, and went for walks around the neighborhood. We ended our walks at Heart Attack Heaven, checked in with my boys (who were relieved to hear Paddy and I had rekindled our love for one another), enjoyed a healthy breakfast, and then walked home.

Paddy had lost forty pounds, and I had lost fifteen. I was pissed that he had done better than I had, but hey, he was fatter and had a lot more weight to spare. My clothes were fitting better, and I was happy with my slow progress.

Catherine and I had reached an agreement. We were not lovey-dovey, but we were respectful of one another, more so than ever before. I saw her good side, and I saw how she loved my child and would protect her at all costs.

What more could I ask?

She still made snide comments about my appearance. I could deal. I was working on it. Did I quit drinking and smoking?

Yes.

And no.

I'm not fucking perfect, you know. I have an occasional cocktail, and I sneak a smoke in every now and then, but on the whole, I'm cutting down and focusing on my child. I even did something good for the neighborhood.

I saw this thing on the internet about miniature libraries—tiny boxes on a post, kind of like mailboxes, closed off from the elements and filled with books of the steward's choosing. It seemed like a cool idea, so I became a steward and put up two mini libraries at the Village Playground. One up high for grownups, and one down low for little peeps. An adult section and a children's section. The other moms scoffed at first, but then I saw them checking out the *Fifty Shades of Smut* I snuck in there.

That's right, everyone likes smut, whether they admit it or not.

The children's section is curated by Savannah. She's not reading yet, but she has some strong opinions about which books she prefers. She picks the ones she likes at the local book store, and I happily buy them. It's been a great bonding experience for us, and people are starting to look at me with a little more respect and a lot less disgust.

How about me being all civic-minded, huh? I'm a regular Girl Scout these days.

With my heart still pounding from the trampoline, I headed into the kitchen to check my email on my phone. I had ordered a bunch of books online and wanted to see when they were coming in. I'm trying to make books my new addiction. You know, to keep my mind off the sauce.

I sat down at the table and looked out at the Bay.

The afternoon sun danced on the surface, making diamonds of light. We own those diamonds, those of us lucky enough to see them. We become rich when we recognize them for what they are—gifts from the sea.

I hope there's nothing unsavory beneath my diamonds. Those bitches better keep clear of the Bay. That's right, skanks. Don't mess with us.

I wanted the whole thing to fade with time, like a pair of acid-wash jeans.

Sliding open the menu on my phone, I navigated to the email section and waited for the familiar sound to herald the arrival of new mail. The sound of beer cans popped three times. I had three new emails.

New smut!

I scanned the email confirmation. All the new books I had ordered were on their way. I used my finger and selected *Archive to Mini Library Folder.*

The second email was an offer for a new, local gym membership. Let's not be too hasty about this whole health thing. *Delete.*

I scrolled to the third, and my heart stopped.

It was from my brother. I waited a moment to open it. It was so strange that he would contact me. Why would he bother? Why now after so long? I had never contacted him during the merrow scandal of three years past. I barely thought of him. What the hell could he possibly want?

Curiosity got the better of me, and I tapped the line with his name on it.

> *Dear Evie,*
>
> *I know we have not spoken in a long time—much too long. I apologize for this abyss in our communication. I'm sure it's my fault. When Dad died, I just couldn't*

stand to watch you destroy yourself with alcohol, so I left. I moved to the Midwest and started a consulting firm.

I snickered at his smug words. He's still an asshole.

I've been very successful, but there has been something sorely missing from my life— family.

Recently, my business has sent me to Boston. I'm not far from you, and I believe enough time has passed. I had been waiting for the right time, the right way to contact you, but circumstances never felt right. But all that has changed. All because of one special individual. Under the urgings of this new friend—well, actually, we are more than friends; our relationship has moved to the next level and I could not be happier...

"Oh gross," I mumbled.

... I have felt the confidence to contact you. It really is such a small world. My friend says she knows you and has urged me to rekindle our relationship, dear sister. Her name is ...

I dropped the phone and ran out the door, frantically calling my dear husband's name. In the kitchen, my phone sat on the table in front of the sparkling waters of Narragansett Bay. As the screen faded to black, the last word in the email stood out. It was one I had hoped I would never see again.

Nomia.

HUNTING THE MERROW

BOOK 2:
THE MERROW
TRILOGY

HEATHER RIGNEY

1

Providence Station
100 Gaspee Street
Providence, Rhode Island
Friday, June 12
8:09 AM

Evie

The scorching train platform was overflowing with assholes. Most of them hipster assholes—the ones who wear embarrassingly tight pants, stupid old-man shoes, and slouchy hats that look as if they have been run over by a logging truck. The logger had likely pulled over, climbed out of the cab, and said, Hey, I'm not using this beard. You seem like the creative type who brews coffee for a living and owns an obscure breed of dog. I'm thinking of shaving. Do you want my beard? To which the annoying hipster replied, I own a purebred Irish wolfhound and work at Starfuck-You-Very-Much, and yes, I would love your beard—as long the product you've used to keep it supple is certified organic.

The flow of people would not stop. It was becoming

claustrophobic. A woman whose fat ass stretched out her patterned pants, which resembled a Southwestern throw blanket, talked loudly on her phone. She slammed into me as she shifted her oversized bag that looked suspiciously like a dead cat.

"Don't shove me, bitch," I muttered. The blinding heat, the unbearable pounding in my temples, the overabundance of hipsters had pushed me beyond reasonable thought.

"I'm sorry," said the Southwestern cat-killer beside me, the woman I was now imagining as a heap of goo on the floor. "Did you say something?"

I simply stared at her, making sure I held her gaze just long enough to make her marginally uncomfortable. She looked away first, continuing her inane conversation.

"I know, right? I was shocked when I graduated and there was no demand for a bio-philosophy major. I mean, I double-minored in education and web design. I thought I covered my bases."

I rolled my eyes and tried to bend my elbow. The sea of bodies was oppressive, limiting my movement and my ability to find a goddamn diet bar in my bag. That and an aspirin. I had nothing to wash it down with, but I didn't care. I would dry-swallow it. Hell, I would dry-swallow a pumpkin filled with nails if it would stop the pounding in my head.

The air changed. A whoosh of stale stench and an even hotter breeze, much hotter than the already hot-enough-to-melt-your-tits-off wind whizzing by my overheated head, swooped in from the train tunnel. The screech of brakes echoed off the stone walls, and the giant purple commuter rail train roared to a stop.

"Providence!" yelled someone official-sounding over a scratchy loudspeaker. The doors squealed open, releasing even more assholes onto the platform where I stood, helpless, drowning in a sea of sweaty, Boston-bound idiots. We pushed past one another, reversing the flow of commuters, those disembarking, those boarding, those embarking on a journey to save the neck of an ungrateful, long-lost brother.

That would be me. Evie McFagan, sister of said ungrateful, long-lost brother known as Richard Musäus. Go ahead and laugh at my maiden name. For your information, it sounds like moosehouse, and why don't you try growing up as a size extra large with a last name that refers to one of the most non-dainty animals in North America? Then talk to me, after a hellish adolescence, about how "well-adjusted" you feel.

Yeah. Think on that, Freud fans.

Elbowing my way onto the narrow train, I found a seat on the upper level of a double-decker car. A twenty-something boy in a tweed jacket was about to sit next to me but changed his mind at the last moment.

By the way, who the hell wears tweed in a heat wave? Stupid hipsters. That's who.

I watched a young mother with a stroller struggle into the car. She moved backwards, dragging the black contraption that held a passed-out toddler. Both mother and child had curly auburn hair plastered to the sides of their red, overheated faces. She paused to catch her breath and turned her head, looking in my direction. Our eyes met and I saw the fatigue, the weariness, the why-is-this-shit-so-hard? look in her eyes. I stood and hurried down the aisle towards her, then helped her wrangle the stroller into a seat near the front of the car. Her child never woke while we banged the much-abused-looking stroller into the narrow space.

"Thank you," she whispered and flopped down, instantly closing her eyes.

Hell, I don't miss those days.

I returned to my own seat and nestled in. Staring out the dirty window covered in scratchy-looking graffiti with the lovely addition of something unsavory smeared all over it, I could feel the sweat trickling into my cleavage, collecting in all the places where skin met skin. There wasn't much to see in the tunnel, except for dark, stone walls. The air conditioning was either broken or just completely incapable of keeping up with the heat.

After what felt like an eternity, the engine roared to life and, with a lurch, pulled forward. We exploded out of the tunnel as the train gained speed. Rain greeted us with a sudden shower that would probably only add to the humidity and not clear it. The drops slashed at the windows, smearing my view of the scenery beyond the milky glass.

I closed my eyes and allowed my mind to drift through the events of the previous few days. What a shit show. I sighed and pulled out my cell phone. No messages. The lock screen featured my two favorite people in the whole world. There they were, my darling husband, Paddy, and my beautiful baby girl, Savannah, now four and no longer a baby, though she would forever remain one in my heart. I wondered if I was still married and if I would see either of them ever again.

What had I done? I'm so stupid. I really am.

"But he's my brother," I had whined. It was hard to explain why I cared. I barely understood it myself.

"If you leave now, love," said Paddy, his clear, piercing eyes sending a message straight to my soul, "you will not be welcome here when you return."

"What the hell, Paddy? That's a bit extreme, don't you think?" I squeaked, trying to be brave, trying to hold my ground. I'm a big girl who can make big girl decisions, I told myself.

"I'm not going through another epic ordeal. Not ever again. And how dare you even entertain the thought of wanting to put us in harm's way?"

"You can deny the facts all you want, mister, but the truth is … the bitch is back. Your stupid, aqua family dropped the bloody ball and let Miss Terror of the Sea go. Now she's here, and she will kill my brother. Doesn't that mean anything to you?"

Paddy sat down on the bed. It was late. After receiving the email from my brother, I had plugged Savannah in, handing her a tablet and headphones, pointing to the couch. She had shrugged and gladly plopped down. The four of us—me, Paddy, his aunt Catherine, and our friend and Catherine's new paramour, Tony—had all sat down at Catherine's kitchen table and examined the email from my brother.

Recently, my business has sent me to Boston. I'm not far from you, and I believe enough time has passed. I had been waiting for the right time, the right way to contact you, but circumstances never felt right. But all that has changed. All because of one special individual. Under the urgings of this new friend (well, actually, we are more than friends. Our relationship has moved to the next level and I could not be happier), I have felt the confidence to contact you. It really is such a small world. My friend says she knows you and has urged me to rekindle our relationship, dear sister. Her name is … Nomia.

The three of them agreed that I should ignore the email.

I was not in favor. An argument of epic proportion ensued, followed by me storming out and heading home. After I poured myself a nice tall drink, I sat on the couch and clinked the ice back and forth in the glass. What did I know? Well, Richard was in Boston. And so was Nomia. Richard was blind to the fishy nature of his new girlfriend, who was most likely using my brother as bait.

This left me with two options. One, go rescue my brother, because I am so good at being a hero. I reached up and rubbed the scar on my shoulder, remembering exactly how it felt to be impaled. Yes, being a hero rocks.

That left the second option. Ignore the whole situation. Don't take the bait. Let my brother die and risk the possibility that the man-eating bitch will make quick work of him and then come after us. It had been months since we had heard from Ronan. It took time to contact him. I didn't have time. Richard, that dick, didn't have time either. I pulled out my phone and read the email again. It had been sent that morning, which meant he was probably still alive. Probably.

I got up, set my glass on the coffee table, and headed for the attic. When I returned to our bedroom, suitcase in hand, Paddy was there waiting for me.

"Where's Savannah?" I asked.

"She's staying with Aunt Catherine tonight."

"I see," I said.

"No, love," he answered. "You don't. You don't see. 'Cause if you did, you wouldn't have that suitcase in your hands."

I just didn't know how to make him understand. I couldn't tell him the things I had kept from him. I had told him the basics but left a lot out. It wasn't fun for me to discuss my shitty family. When I'd met Paddy, the orphan thing had been a bonding connection. Our isolation in the world, once revealed, was like a crappy present we gave to one another, something Paddy and I could share and compare, then screw around together to forget. When your pain is reflected in someone else, it becomes a narcissistic attraction. Quite messed up if you think about it.

At the time, he didn't need to know about my brother. I didn't even know about my brother. I hadn't heard from him in years. Richard was three years older than I was. While I was still in high school, he was starting college. Once he left home, he left home. That was that.

I had never desired to discuss the way I had been raised, the relationship my brother and I had forged out of need. Yes, we had been given everything we needed as children. We wanted for nothing—nothing like food, shelter, or college money. But things such as emotional attention, love, kindness—those were radically missing. In essence, we had raised ourselves. Our parents had been selfish and ignored us. They had never bothered to get to know us. I never wanted to discuss what Richard and I shared—our bond of emotional neglect.

Once Mom and Dad died, Richard was all I had left. He was the last link to my roots, my last tie to my grandparents, also dead, in Tarrytown, New York. Some of the happiest moments of my childhood were spent at their home, and I had shared those times with Richard. It was during those visits that we had fostered our connection—weekends in Tarrytown and all those summers spent with Oma and Opa, playing in the woods surrounding their country home way up in the Catskills, far away from civilization and even farther away from my parents. We spent endless hours walking in the woods, Richard and I, building forts, making paths with old rakes, paths that curved in circles around trees so old, we could barely see their tops. I spent time in the kitchen with Oma, and Richard out in the woods with Opa, doing whatever it was they did out there.

When I realized during my drunken college haze that years, not just months and days, had passed since I had heard from my older brother, I was angry. Abandoned yet again. I wrote him off. He was dead to me, too.

Paddy discovered he had a brother-in-law when Savannah

was born. Classy, I know, but you have to understand, when starting a relationship, women are all like, Tell me about your family. What was it like for you? Reveal your inner pain to me. Blah, blah, blah. Paddy wasn't like that. I'm not, nor have I ever been, like that. Paddy never asked if I had any siblings, and I never told him—until I was forced into it.

Savannah was born on a Tuesday. On the first Saturday of her life, a bouquet of flowers arrived addressed to her. It was the craziest thing. She hadn't even lived in the house for a full week, and the kid was getting flowers and mail. That blew my mind. Anyway, the outside of the card read, For my niece, Savannah.

Paddy had flipped out. It was a total Lucy/Ricardo moment with me, the dumb one, doing all the 'splaining.

Why hadn't I told Paddy about Richard? I don't know. I guess I had wanted to keep that part of me to myself. Forever.

And now I was on a train, leaving one family for another. Why? Good fucking question.

Numb from the greenery rushing by my chalky window, I stared out at the suburban worlds of Mansfield, Sharon, and Canton as they tore past my swollen, tired face. Along with all the other travelers whose clothes clung to their sweaty backs, I was spewed out onto the sticky, foul-smelling platform in Back Bay. Richard's email had a signature at the bottom that included a phone number. Thanks to the wonders of Google, I'd been able to track down what I thought was a home address in Boston.

Pulling my wheeled carry-on behind me, I made my way up the obnoxiously long escalator and then out into city. The heat smacked me in the face. It was similar to being smothered with a wool blanket—so humid I couldn't breathe. Nothing smells worse than a city during a heat wave. Boston is especially bad. Being a harbor city, it has the added benefit of low tide. Things that are meant to be beneath the sea now lay exposed, allowed to decay in the summer sun and release their noxious gases into air otherwise perfumed with street garbage and car fumes.

Besides the smell, it's a scenic city. Old—I mean, really fucking old—shit—mingles with the new. Take, for example, the Hancock buildings. Yes, there are two. One small and squat, like a happy, old, fat teapot, and right next to it stands its young offspring. The brilliant blue monolith towers above its parent, dominating the Boston skyline. To me, that's Boston. The new attempting to dwarf the old, to outshine it, while we, the tourists, marvel at the resulting warring dichotomy that somehow works.

I navigated down the city streets, passing Asian women in their wide-brimmed hats, college students in their flimsy clothes, young mothers in Converse sneakers pushing retro-looking prams. I passed vendors hawking hot dogs, the foul smell of sauerkraut burning my nose hairs as I inhaled. Others offered t-shirts emblazoned with phrases like Green Monstah and Yankees Suck. Using the navigation on my phone—a left here, a right there—I moved slowly until I finally arrived at the brownstone row home matching the address I had found on the web.

My stomach squelched with acid, and although the heat had not subsided, my hands felt cold and clammy. This was it. The number matched. I walked up the marble stairs to the landing and looked at the names scrawled next to the buzzer buttons. Apt 1-Fisher, Apt 2-Atwood, Apt 3-Leary, and at the top, Apt 4-Musäus.

I steeled myself and pressed the button. Nothing happened. Now what? In my haste to get to my brother, it had not occurred to me to think past this very moment. I cursed under my breath at my stupidity. I should just go. I should reverse this whole asinine journey and get back to the people who mattered. I should ...

The door opened. A man held the door for me. Not my brother. Just a man I didn't know. He smiled and said, "Hot enough for ya?"

I nodded and walked into the lobby, mumbling my thanks as I stepped past him.

"Have a good one," he called over his shoulder and headed down the steps as the door clicked shut behind him.

I was in.

There was no elevator. Of course there wasn't. It was nine hundred degrees outside. I was, as always, grossly out of shape, and I was carrying luggage up four flights of stairs. Why would there be a goddamn elevator? As I huffed and puffed my way up the steps, I constructed a plan. I would wait outside his door until he got home. When he arrived, I would ambush him and make him understand that his new girlfriend had no intention of dating him, but instead planned to tear him apart, literally. And then she would do the same to me. If he had any sense at all, he would end the relationship, and, and ... I would figure out the rest when I saw him.

I turned and faced the last flight of stairs. Richard's apartment was at the top of the building on its own landing. The blood was pounding in my temples, and I could feel the burning heat in my flushed cheeks. God, I needed to sit down. Almost there.

I walked to the door and knocked. As my knuckles hit the wooden door, it swung open slightly.

Through the cracked door, I called, "Richard?" I was sure to use a soft voice, not wanting to startle him, or her. "Anyone home?"

I waited for a response, but none came. Taking a deep breath, I considered my options. I could wander in and see what I could see, or go home—just turn right around, close the door behind me, close the door on my past, and leave my older brother to his fate.

Guess which choice I made? If you went with option number one, you win an oversized t-shirt with Evie makes bad choices for my entertainment emblazoned across the front. Wear it with pride. It looks good on you.

The room temperature was a good ten degrees cooler than the stairwell. I relished the relief as a cool wave of air from the air conditioner made its way to face. I let out my breath in one long, relaxing groan. Then I entered Richard's apartment. A large leather sectional couch faced me, its back against an exposed brick wall. To my right three long windows lined up in a row. The windows did not have curtains, and I could see the neighboring building close by. The branches of trees that must have grown up from a courtyard, far below, obscured my view into the other apartments across the way.

I was in the living/dining room. To my left, I saw bar stools, indicating a breakfast bar. I stepped in farther and turned to close the door behind me. That's when I saw her. I gasped, somehow managing not to scream, and grabbed my chest.

In unison, the intruder grabbed her chest. There was a mirror behind the door.

"Goddamn it," I cursed under my breath. I looked at my own reflection and realized how rumpled and tired I looked, how exhausted and stressed I really was. Did I look like a woman about to confront a homicidal maniac? No. I looked like shit. As usual.

Glancing around the room again, I noted how sparsely decorated it was. It had the feel of a real estate showing. Everything looked staged, arranged just so, as if it had all been recently bought at a discount home store. There was even a fake potted amaryllis next to the leather couch, but it was covered in dust.

I took a few more steps, making my way towards the kitchen area on the left. That looked staged, too, with a bowl of plastic lemons on the counter. Something crunched as I stepped from the living area into the small passageway leading to the bedrooms, I assumed. Looking down, I saw broken glass everywhere.

I figured it was from smashed wineglasses. I could make out the stem of one glass and, possibly, part of the goblet of another. The floor was dark and sticky, and I was hoping it was red wine. Please let it be red wine. It smelled like red wine. But the hallway had two types of stains sprayed across the pale walls. One was a cranberry color; the other was brighter. Things were looking grim.

I peered down the hall and spotted bloody footprints retreating into the far bedroom. I tried not to step on them as I followed their trail. The bedroom was destroyed, and the window was an explosion of broken glass. It was everywhere, sparkling in the daylight, sending tiny prisms onto the walls. An elegant black-and-white photograph of a tree—the trunk enormous, thick, and imposing—hung at a disquieting angle, perilously close to crashing to the floor. The closet appeared to have blown up. Clothes were everywhere. Ties, shoes, men's underwear, and a few lacy lady things were scattered all around, the bulk of them in front of the walk-in closet. A bulb hung from the ceiling, swaying gently in the breeze from the open window, where hot air floated in, caressing my face as it passed.

Richard, what happened here? Where are you?

There was a bloody handprint next to the open window. The fingerprints were slender and long, not outlines of the thick, strong fingers of my brother. They had to belong to that bitch, Nomia. I would bet my life on it. Fury raced through my body, making me shudder at the memory of the upheaval she had created in my life. I hated her more now than ever.

Something in the closet shifted. I spun, ready to beat the living daylights out of anything that dared jump out at me. My foot landed with a loud crunch. Something made of glass crackled beneath my foot, but my focus was on the closet.

A sweater tumbled out. And I let out my breath in a long whoosh.

Just a stupid sweater. Relax, Evie.

It must have been knocked loose when the place was ransacked. I tried to shake it off, rotating my head in a circle and stretching my neck. That's when I saw the photo on the floor.

I leaned down and picked up the shattered picture frame, gently shaking off the broken glass. My brother stared up at me. His eyes more wrinkled, his skin more leathery from his years outdoors, doing whatever he does, but still him. My brother.

And her.

What the hell was she doing all snuggly with my brother in a goddamn photo?

Look. At. That. Bitch.

All of a sudden I felt like a squirrel was trying to gnaw its way out of my gut. I mean, I knew she was involved. But this. This. This photo. The proof of her existence on this continent. With my brother.

I felt the anger boil my face even hotter than it already was in the wretched, blistering heat. I shook my head, trying to create a breeze to cool me down. It didn't work. I was seething.

This is what I knew. Richard and Nomia were not here, but they were a thing. There had been a struggle. Nomia had been involved. And Nomia had been searching for something.

Why else would there be crap strewn all over the place? What was she looking for?

Well, if I knew anything, anything at all, and if my brother was trying to keep something hidden, I knew exactly where he would hide it. There's something to be said for growing up with another person. You know their dirty little secrets.

I went back down the hall into the bathroom and switched on the light. It was a standard small apartment bathroom in an old building. There was a clawfoot tub against the wall facing the door and a sink on the right, with a toilet sandwiched between the tub and sink. Everything was white. The tile, the shower curtain, the towels. And it was a mess. The bathroom had been equally ransacked. The contents of the medicine cabinet were now in the sink. Shaving gear, prescription bottles, toothpaste, Q-tips. It all swam in the white bowl. The door to the medicine cabinet above hung wide open, revealing emptiness. I wasn't interested in the medicine cabinet.

I stood in front of the toilet and lifted the lid off the tank.

Bingo.

Some things never change. My brother had always kept a stash of porn in a ziplock bag, safe inside the back of the toilet. And sure enough, peering at me from inside the back of the tank, I spied, not porn, but something else, something smaller.

I reached into the cool water and drew out the bag. It had been folded many times, concealing the contents within. Shaking off the water, I opened the bag and pulled out what looked like a skeleton key. An ordinary red tassel hung from the ornate hole on the end, but the other end was strange. There was something different about it. It didn't have the typical teeth-like appendages with which to turn lock tumblers. This looked like a computer chip. I held it up to the light as the realization dawned on me. It was a flash drive.

I heard a noise in the living room and quickly shoved the key into my back pocket. I looked around for a weapon, but all

I could find was a plunger. It would have to do.

I grabbed the wooden stick and held the ridiculous rubber bulb high in the air. Creeping back into the glass-filled hall, I moved as quietly as I could, listening for any additional sound from the living room. A new layer of sweat coated my already soaked body as fear filled my every cell.

I really was not built for this shit.

The shuffle of footsteps echoed in the mostly empty room as I drew closer. Almost there. There was no way I was going to drop out the window like Nomia had most likely done. She was way more agile than I was. It was fight. Flight was not an option.

I took a deep breath, let out my loudest battle cry, and flew— plunger held high—into the living room and ...

I scared the living shit out of a small, elderly woman in a classy red suit. She screamed back and clutched her heart.

"My dear God!" yelled the red-clad old lady.

"I am so sorry! Here, sit down. You are not who I thought you were," I wheezed, exhausted from my battle cry.

"Who on earth did you think I was?"

"Um," I stammered. "Would you like to sit down?"

"No," she said. "I would not. Where is Richard, and what are you doing here? Did you make this mess? Is that blood?"

"Whoa, too many questions. I am Evie McFagan, well Evie Musäus McFagan, actually. Richard is my brother. Pleased to meet you." Here is where I offered my hand, which was received with a curt look of disgust.

I withdrew my hand.

"Do you have any identification, before I call the police, Ms. McFagan? The neighbors had complained about loud noises, and I came to investigate. Richard is an excellent tenant. I find it hard to believe that you are his sister." There was a sniff and an upturned nose following this statement. I kid you not. The old bag turned up her nose at me. It was my childhood all over again.

With my own sigh of disgust, I pulled out my wallet and was about to hand her my license when I suddenly thought better of it. I dashed past her, grabbing my roller luggage on the way, and fled down the stairs.

I did not need to explain any of this shit to the police, and that was where the story was headed. She would need to call the police. Hell, I would call the police if I were her. The place was wrecked. There were bloody prints everywhere. It looked as if theft was involved, possibly murder. And a goddamn mermaid.

I was not about to explain a goddamn mermaid. I booked it down the stairs and out onto the street, regretting that I had given the landlady or super or whoever the hell she was my name.

I had found out as much as I could. Richard and Nomia were not in that apartment. Something had happened. Most likely, Nomia had killed my brother.

Oh my God. My brother was dead!

I stopped on the street, and a woman with a stroller slammed into me from behind. "Watch it, lady! What the hell are you doing?"

I didn't even answer. I just stood there, in the heat, with my stupid luggage. I was alone in the world now. Completely alone.

But wait a second.

Where was Richard's body? It's not like she could eat him all by herself. And that would have left an even bigger mess. What was the likelihood of her dragging him out on her own? I knew she had superhuman strength, but Richard is a pretty big guy. The neighbors had complained about the noises. Surely they would have also complained about a crazy woman dragging a six-foot man down the hall or past their windows in the courtyard. Right?

He couldn't be dead. Could he? Or was she dead?

I had come to Boston to warn my brother. I had failed. Something had already gone down, and I knew less than I did when I had arrived.

Now what?

I needed to get the hell out of Boston. So I headed back the way I had come as quickly as I could.

Once I arrived at the Back Bay station, I grabbed a Diet Coke and parked it on a stone bench next to a wino. I felt that I was in good company.

Pulling out my phone, I saw that I still did not have any messages. Damn you, Paddy.

I pulled up my favorites and pushed his fat face in my contact list. The phone rang. And rang. And rang. Finally, it went to his voice mail.

You have reached Patrick McFagan. I am unable to get your call right now, but do leave a message. Unless, of course, you are Evelyn. Then don't leave a message and do not come home. Thank you, and have a glorious day.

Cheeky bastard.

Where the hell was I supposed to go now? I sat there with my soda and stared up at the giant ceiling. Pigeons swirled around the glass dome, swooping down to pick up stray bits of bagel dropped by passing travelers.

I could hear the whir of the subway somewhere to my left, down below the escalator that flashed stair after stair.

Think, Evie. What should I do? Think!

Should I just go home? Should I call someone else? Who? I have no friends. Wait. There was one ... but, no. I couldn't call Rachael. She hated me. I scrolled through my contacts and found her name. But I didn't have the courage to hit send. I just sat there, staring at the phone, wondering what to do. Then it rang.

I pushed the accept call button and said, "Hello?"

"Hello. This. Is. Not a. Service call. Your. Home could. Be at. Risk for ..."

I started sobbing into the phone. The wino perked up and stared at me, then handed me a ratty napkin.

"Thank you," I blubbered and kept crying, loudly.

The robot voice kept yammering away in stunted sentences, and all I could do was cry. Then, out of anger, frustration, the need to vent, I started to talk to the robot.

"Yes," I sobbed. "Hi there. I think my brother's dead, and my husband, Paddy, just kicked me out, and they only had Diet Coke in the machine, and I think I just caught some disease from this nice man in rags!"

"If you. Act. Now. You can secure. Your home ..."

"But I'm in Boston," I wailed. Then sniffed loudly. The man next to me made a face of disgust. "You know what? I'm a grown woman. I can just take the train back to Providence and go home. Screw Paddy."

"This offer. Will not. Be around for …"

"Thank you, robot." I hit the end call button and immediately felt calmer. I needed time to process all that had just transpired. Plus, I had bought a round-trip ticket. Who was I to waste a round-trip ticket?

The wino was staring at me.

"You okay?" he asked.

I smiled at him. Here was a man without a pot to piss in, and he was asking me if I was okay. I almost started crying again because of the sheer kindness of his words.

"Are you hungry?" I asked.

"Starving."

"Come on. There's a Dunkin' over there calling our names. Let me get you a coffee and a donut."

"I would love an egg sandwich, and I take my coffee black."

"Done."

Two hours later, I was on my way back to Providence. During my wait for the train, I had passed the time with my new friend, Larry, the homeless guy. The distraction was just what I needed.

As the world south of Boston melted away, I thought about my situation.

How on earth do I always find myself in these predicaments?

I swear, I am Calamity Evie. If something is going to go wrong, it's going to happen to me. It had been happening my whole life. Maybe I cause it, maybe I don't, but it constantly feels like the universe is trying to set my toes on fire.

As things stood, my brother was missing. Nomia, the bitch from the watery depths of hell, was back in my life, and Paddy no longer wanted me in his. My husband had banned me from seeing my baby girl, and I'd just had coffee with a homeless guy named Larry. Wow. I could really fuck up my life in five easy steps.

I needed to find my brother. Once I found him and made him realize how dangerous things were … what was I thinking? Of course he knew how dangerous things were. He was missing, for Christ's sake. His house had broken glass and blood in it.

"Richard," I said to the milky window of the train. "Where are you?"

After a stinky cab ride back to my house, I found a note from Paddy taped to the liquor cabinet door. The irony of the placement was not lost on me. It read:

> *Dear Evelyn,*
>
> *If you are reading this, then you are home after I have asked you not to come home. Fortunately, we have not had any clients lined up, so I took the liberty of closing the funeral parlor for a few days.*

God, I could hear the snooty lilt in my head.

> *Savannah and I have gone elsewhere. That is all you need know. I suggest you get your*

things and do the same until I am ready to
speak with you about your priorities, i.e.,
this family.

Signed,
Your irate husband

I thought about setting the note on fire, but then thought better of it. Instead, I opened the liquor cabinet and found my friend Bourbon.

Bourbon doesn't judge me, unlike some people I know. I poured myself a tall glass and relished every sip as the nerves in my neck popped one by one, like strings breaking on a violin.

I kicked off my shoes and headed up the stairs, glass in hand. I found myself in my daughter's room.

We had painted it pink the previous summer. Aunt Catherine had a student whose mom did murals. We had hired her to paint flowers and butterflies on one wall of Savannah's room.

Her bed was neatly made, and I could see that her favorite stuffed hippo, Hippy (children are just so original when it comes to naming their stuffies), and his best friend, Zorky the rat, were missing. So was the quilt Aunt Catherine had made for her when she was born.

That meant Savannah and Paddy had vacated for the evening—if not longer. For real. There was no way Savannah would sleep without those three items.

I inhaled sharply through my nostrils and took a long swig, cherishing the smoky flavor. Then I shook my head.

I'm such a fuck-up.

I walked down the hall to the master bedroom and saw that Paddy had taken his overnight kit from the top of his wardrobe. Further proof that I was all alone.

I flopped down on the bed and nursed my drink. When I emptied the glass, I trudged downstairs and got the bottle.

Wash, rinse, repeat.

The world eventually faded away with the daylight.

I woke up around eight the next morning—surprisingly early for me—and cursed the lack of shades in our bedroom. Everything was too bright. My head, too heavy. My mouth, too fuzzy.

I padded down the stairs and considered my options. I could not stay here alone. I was too self-destructive. I was in desperate need of a friend. No, she was not a great friend. Most likely, she would enable me to drink more, but at the very least, I would be supervised. And that was better than my current situation.

Rachael Bass.

I scrolled through my contacts, found her name, and hit send.

"Evie," Her voice was smooth and confident. As always. "It's been a long time, you saucy hag."

"Hello, Rachael. I ..." I couldn't finish. For the second time in two days, I started sobbing into my phone.

"Evie! Evie? Are you there? What's wrong?" All the sugar and sultriness disappeared from her voice.

"Yes," I sobbed. "I'm here. I think my brother's dead, and Paddy sort of kicked me out, and I have a raging drinking problem, and I ... I ... I don't want to be alone! I need a place to stay!"

"Dear Lord. Where are you? Let me come and get you."

"I'm home," I mumbled.

"Stay there. I'll come and get you."

"Uh, okay. Are you sure it's okay for me to come to your house?"

There was a long pause. Then Rachael said, "It's been a long time, but when it comes to friends, I mate for life. Get your shit together. I'm coming, Evelyn."

She hung up. I took a deep breath and blew it out through puffed cheeks. The pain in my head snapped me into action. I gathered up my things, changed my clothes, and stepped into the bathroom. I grabbed an aspirin and a glass of water and headed out the door.

I sat in the driveway on my roller bag and waited for salvation.

Hunting the Merrow, the second book in *The Merrow Trilogy* is available for download at Amazon (amzn.com/B0178EN0BQ), Barnes & Noble, Kobo, and iTunes.

Paperbacks of both *Waking the Merrow* and *Hunting the Merrow* are available in these fine Rhode Island Independent Bookstores:

- TWICE TOLD TALES, Pawtuxet Village
- SYMPOSIUM BOOKS, East Greenwich, Providence
- WAKEFIELD BOOKS, Wakefield
- CURIOSITIES & MISCHIEF, Narragansett

QUESTIONS FOR DISCUSSION

1. At the novel's opening, Evie is a horrible mother and is unapologetic regarding her lackluster parenting. How do you view her decisions? What might have caused her to be such a terrible parent?

2. How does Evie evolve over the course of the novel? Can people really change? Or do they tend to stay the same?

3. A recurring theme in the novel is internal vs. external. Discuss the contrast between each main character's outward appearance and their personality and actions. How does each individual use his or her physical presence to move through this particular world?

4. Evie and Paddy have an unusual relationship. He tolerates her flaws, and he does what he needs to do to protect her. He also lies to her. Is lying to someone to protect them ever okay? When is it not?

5. Nomia's relationship with her pod is tumultuous. How has the way she has been treated by her aquatic family affected her? What do you think her motivation is for behaving the way she does?

6. Whenever Evie is near Nomia, she becomes physically ill. Why do you think Nomia has such a physical impact on Evie?

7. The novel juggles many plotlines, moving back and forth through time. Did this nonlinear method of storytelling detract from your enjoyment of the book's flow?

8. Do you believe in mermaids? There are many stories of half-human, half-fish creatures in the folklore of unconnected cultures across the globe. According to the National Oceanic and Atmospheric Administration (NOAA), ninety-five percent of our world's oceans remain unexplored, unseen by human eyes, leaving the possibility for many undiscovered species. Could an aquatic humanoid be one of them?

9. In chapter sixteen, Ronan witnesses the massacre of John Oldham and his crew. This was an actual event in history. Oldham was banished from the original Plymouth colony for differences of religious opinion. In spite of his expulsion, he became a successful merchant who traded with the Native Americans. In July of 1636, his ship was boarded and he was killed, along with five of his crew. It was presumed that Pequot Indians committed the murders, but this remains to be proven. The European colonists' retaliation for this attack sparked the Pequot War, which resulted in the annihilation of the Pequot people.

Historical records can be written to show a certain point of view. Is rewriting history to include merrow any different from writing history to show European colonists as justified in wiping out an entire population?

10. Some might say a fantasy life is all right for children, but not for adults. How do you feel about the genre of adult fantasy? Do you think there is a stigma associated with the term adult fantasy?

AUTHOR'S NOTE

Second draft was completed on Friday, January 10, 2014, at 2:29 p.m. New snow lay on the ground. My view was all white as I sat at my dining room table and mentally prepared myself to pick my daughter up from kindergarten.

Thank you for reading, dear reader.

There is more to come ...

ACKNOWLEDGEMENTS

This book would not be possible without the loving support of my family. Jeff, I know your job sucks—thank you for enduring it and allowing me to pursue my dream. Liv, someday you might read this. Know that being your mom was *always* my most important occupation. Mom and Dad, thank you for reading my work and telling me how amazing you think I am. I know it's your job to say that, but it's still appreciated.

A special thanks to the 2006 Aldrich JHS administration and English Department for sponsoring the Embedded Institute (EI), a cross-curricula reading and writing initiative. It was in the EI that I kindled my passion for writing. How many times did you lovely ladies say, *Heather, you should write a novel ... ?* Well, I did. Thank you for seeing something I had not.

To OUR Writer's Group—Chris, Joe, Oz. You inspire me! I would also like to thank my editor, Jo Fisher, for her grammatical wisdom, intense command of celestial timing, and Wonder Woman work ethic. You are amazing, Jo. A special thank you to Tony and Melanie at The Elephant Room in Pawtuxet Village, where a lot of this book was written. Penny Watson, you are a force of nature, and without your guidance, I would be lost in the Sea of Misguided Indie Writers. Thanks for throwing me a line. And to my friends, beta-readers, and family who have supported this crazy dream of mine, thank you.

Sushi and donuts for everyone.

BIOGRAPHY

Writer, artist, and underwater fire-breather Heather Rigney likes to make stuff. Stuff with words, stuff with paint, stuff that's pretty, and stuff that's not. Heather's stories reflect her dark, gothic childhood spent alone in the woods of northern Rhode Island.

Having discovered the works of both Stephen King and Clive Barker at the age of eleven, she started to wonder if she truly was alone in the woods, or perhaps not. The *perhaps* was what kept her up at night. Her imagination cranked out stories and dreams that she kept to herself. She was an strange child and didn't need one more reason for the neighbors to cluck, "That Rigney girl is so odd ... " But now that she's comfortable with her oddness, Heather loves sharing her stories with you, dear reader.

This novel was adapted from the short story, "Mermaids Are Not Nice," which can be found in the anthology *DIVE: A Quartet of Merfolk Tales.*

Look for "There's Something, Sort of, Definitely Wrong with Marvin," a YA short fiction story in *Stone Crown Magazine's* November 2013 issue at www.stonecrowns.com.

FOR MORE ON HEATHER RIGNEY

www.heatherrigney.com

www.facebook.com/heatherrigneyAuthor

Twitter: @yourFAVmermaid

www.goodreads.com/author/show/6542620.Heather_Rigney

Made in the USA
Middletown, DE
10 January 2018